F 816

D060684

Through the Dark and Hairy Wood

Through the Dark and Hairy Wood

Shaun Herron

Random House: New York

Copyright © 1972 by Shaun Herron

All rights reserved under International and Pan-American Copyright Conventions. Published in the United States by Random House, Inc., New York, and simultaneously in Canada by Random House of Canada Limited, Toronto.

Library of Congress Cataloging in Publication Data

Herron, Shaun.
Through the dark and hairy wood.

I. Title.
PZ4.H5668Th [PR6058.E68] 823′.9′14 72-2907
ISBN 0-394-47473-2

Manufactured in the United States of America by the Colonial Press Inc., Clinton, Mass.
98765432
First Edition

For
Thomas Herron
who set my feet in their way
when I was young

and for
Herself
who kept them in their way
thereafter

And I looked, and behold, a pale horse:
and his name that sat on him
was Death, and Hell followed after him.

One time Fergoman the Champion was walking in the morning mist by the shores of the lake when a litter of young wild pigs came storming about his shins.

He put his sword to them, thinking the way they would look, cured and hanging on hooks in his kitchen.

He was no more than done with that work when their mother the great wild sow came at him through the bulrushes with her terrible tusks.

The two of them fought in and out of the mist a long time, and more than once the bleeding sow reached Fergoman's strong legs with her tusks and teeth till he was weak from his own bleeding and began to cry for help.

His sister Finna heard him on the other side of the lake and dived into the water to swim to him. But when she got to the far bank his cries came out of the mist at the place she first came from and she swam the lake again, and his cries when she got where she started from were behind her, and she swam across another time.

In the middle of the lake, when her strength was gone, she heard her brother's dying shouts behind her, and exhaustion and grief weighed her down till she drowned, for she could not tell from what place he was crying out.

The people from that time called the lake the Lough of Finna, and the valley where it is they called Glenfin, the Valley of Finna.

And to this day in Ireland they will tell you that where the calling voices come from in the mist is a hard thing to know.

Part 1
Your Well-Bred Hunters . . .

One

For their worm shall not die, neither shall their fire be quenched, and they shall be an abhorring unto all flesh.

"The bloody Irish make me sick."

"They should tow the island into the Atlantic and sink it."

The din was deafening. Glasses clinking, glasses breaking, laughter, voices—hundreds of voices loud and shrill and drunk—and music from somewhere in the big room. It came from the far end. It was everywhere just the same. Who in God's name, Miro asked himself, thought of adding music to this noise? He was glad Eva had chosen to go back to their hotel after the film premiere.

"We can use the money," she said. "The people I can do without."

"I'll have to stay," he said. "I wrote the book."

Now he wondered why he had to stay. Nobody spoke to him. Nobody knew him. Nobody needed him. And this little lot standing at his elbow provided the only entertainment he'd had all evening.

The man now shouting was, Miro gathered, some sort of journalist. "I've just come back from Northern Ireland," he yelled above the music and the din, "and I want to ask you, Captain Strong, what the hell do the Irish *want?* I saw . . . *saw* . . ."—

he pointed to his eyes, perhaps to make it easier for them to understand—"with my own eyes, a policeman shot through the guts with an arrow from a crossbow . . . *a crossbow* . . . can you imagine . . . *a crossbow.*"

"My God!"

"But *darling . . . awful . . . primitive . . .*"

"I'm not sure I got the meaning of your question," the man who must be Captain Strong shouted. "Are you asking me about weaponry or political goals?"

"Jesus Christ!"

"I saw the police *beating* a fat woman in Belfast."

"All the women in Belfast are fat, darling. Cream cakes, I'm told."

An earnest young man said, "Please! Please! Captain, a serious question. You, sir, are an Ulster Protestant politician. You have an *enormous* following. You're making life hell for the Prime Minister of Northern Ireland. What is your goal, sir? Is it UDI?"

"What," said an elegantly naked-looking woman, "is UDI, darling?"

"That's what Rhodesia did—a unilateral declaration of independence. It means they just say to us English, 'Bugger off— we're going it alone.' Then you get the United Nations to pass a resolution against you and impose sanctions, and you have it made . . ."

"We do not," Captain Strong said, "wish to be forced into that position." He smiled like a cat in a basin of liver, and edged nearer to Miro, nodding recognition. Miro didn't know the man from Adam. But he knew his name. He was the man who kept the government of Northern Ireland tottering while he made speeches against it to thousands of cheering Orangemen—and in every speech declared his loyalty to the government.

"Are you Irish *savages,* Captain Strong?" a woman with large glasses and small, bare breasts asked. "Why are you burning one another alive, Captain?"

"Horrible! Horrible!"

"Aren't you *afraid* to go back to Belfast, Captain?"

"Will you kill one another to the last Protestant and Catholic?"

Donald Leary, the producer, pushed his way into the small circle and grabbed Miro's arm. "Miro, I want you to meet your leading lady—this is Caitlin Adams."

So this was the girl who played Eva in the film made from his book about his life as an agent. That's what this whole elegant and drunken scrum was about, tonight. "Ma'am," he said, and thought she was a poor thing beside his wife. Miss Adams gave him a gracious moment and withdrew. He had only written the book, not the screenplay. He was of no further use to her.

The book was a sensation. It made him rich. The film made him richer and would make him richer yet. He no longer thought about money. He could afford not to.

"This, my friends," Captain Strong said and took his arm, "is Miro."

"What do *you* do?" said the woman with steel-rimmed spectacles and no breasts.

"Among other things," Miro said, "I unbutton my shirt and open my tie in a bloody hot room with a noisy crowd." He did so.

"Well *darling*," the woman said.

The journalist said, "You're the man who wrote the book *The Geese Are Hissing Like Green Trees*?"

"No," he barked. "The book is called *The Trees Are Hissing Like Green Geese*."

"The book of the film we've been seeing? It was great."

"No. You've only seen the film of the book. The book was better."

"About your years with the CIA?"

"You could call it that."

"You must be very rich? They say it's sold millions."

"Yes."

"Miro lives in Ireland," Captain Strong announced. "On the Catholic side of the Border."

"Is it dangerous?" The breastless one smiled.

"Yes."

"Why?"

"I breed cows."

"That must be exhausting."

"My father-in-law, General Roberton, took to cows when he retired," the captain said.

"He took to cows?" the breastless one screamed. *"He must have been Irish!"*

Miro turned about and walked away. He was out of place here with these people: braying donkeys and horny bitches. He wanted to go back to Eva; he wandered towards the door.

Captain Strong took his arm from behind. "Are you leaving?"

"Who wouldn't?"

"I'll come with you, if I may."

"Captain Strong! Please, a moment." It was the journalist.

"I was leaving," Strong said coldly.

"Sir," said the journalist, "I *must* ask you this. I've just come back to London from Belfast and Derry. The things I've *seen!* Men burned alive, men tarred and feathered, men brutally beaten, gun battles in the streets, bands of *women* throwing fire-bombs at one another, churches burned . . . it's endless, Captain. It's *war*, Captain. You're a man of tremendous popular influence over there . . . what in God's name is the solution?"

"Strength, sir." The captain looked very military.

"You mean the mailed fist?"

"I mean strength, sir." The captain took Miro's arm and steered him through the door. "Share my taxi."

"I'll be glad to."

In the taxi the captain said, "You do come over from Donegal into Northern Ireland sometimes, Mr. Miro?"

"Often."

"Will you be coming soon?"

"In about a month."

The captain took out his little diary. "Your book, sir. I found it fascinating. Frightening, too. Unbreakable power is frightening. My wife enjoyed it too. She wants very much to meet you." His teeth click-clacked gently as if he were out of the stuff that makes them stick to the gums. Under the firm exterior, there was something funny about Captain Strong. Miro didn't try to analyze it; he wasn't interested enough to do that. But it was there: a faint suggestion of the ridiculous. He put it away. "Please come and stay with us. My wife would be *very* happy. Very *excited*." It was like an amendment upwards. "In about a month? How about . . . ?" He pondered dates and settled on one.

The man would forget about it, Miro was sure. He'd probably had too much to drink at the party. In the morning he'd wonder what the entry in his diary meant. Miro agreed.

The man didn't forget. He entertained Miro and Eva twice during the course of their stay in London, and his teeth click-clacked gently. Then he went home to the North of Ireland. When the Miros got home to Donegal, they found a letter from Strong, confirming his invitation. There was no escape.

"You'll have to pass through customs posts, and they're blowing up customs posts," she said. "You'll have to go to the bank, and they're blowing up banks. You'll have to pass through Derry, and they're fighting and burning in Derry . . ."

"Eva, Eva, Eva," Miro sang and took her by the shoulders and kissed her around the head of their two-year-old Michael. "Eva, they're only fighting in certain streets, and I'll not go near them. I'll be very, very careful."

"You're being very careful that we don't cross the Border with you. If it's too dangerous for us, why is it safe for you . . . ?"

"Come and wave to me." He closed his suitcase.

He hated to go anywhere without them. He hated sleeping alone. He missed them when they went west down the mountain to Glenties for an afternoon. He drove out of the driveway and turned east down the mountain towards Ballybofey. Beyond that was Lifford, and the Border and the customs post and Northern Ireland, where Catholics and Protestants were shooting one another and interested bystanders.

A way down the valley, where he could still see Summerfield and they couldn't see him, he stopped the car, stood on the bank of the road, and looked home.

That long narrow water shining between high green-blue walls was Lough Finn—the Lough of Finna. The white house up the hill from this end of it was Summerfield. They called it Summerfield because their summer-years together were long in coming, and they wanted them to stay. The valley that lay below him, running from the Lough to Ballybofey, was Glenfin—the Valley of Finna. His cattle grazed half of it. Fish were nourished in the quiet pools of its river, the Finn, which ran to the Border and joined the Foyle. His cattle watered in the Finn. Half a mountain and half a valley, by purchase and lease: he looked at it all and laughed and felt good.

"I'll be in and out of the North and back home like the hammers of hell," he said aloud, and drove on down the mountain, thinking of his good wife, his good son, his well-bred cows and his great good fortune.

He was content, and the Border was up the road a little way. He passed the Customs Post of the Republic and pulled in at the Northern Ireland Post.

He was not greeted by the officer in the road with his usual cheer.

"Get out and go in," the man said, unsmiling, and turned his head away with the look of a schoolboy caught up to something in the washroom.

Two

And the bramble said unto the trees: If in truth ye anoint me
King over you, then come and put your trust in my shadow . . .

That was Mr. Logan behind the counter: small, fat, genial Mr. Logan, looking awkward and evasive.

"Why're you . . ." he began, and began again with impatience, "What's your business in Northern Ireland?" He glared at a printed pad on the counter.

Miro leaned on his forearms and brought his head close to Mr. Logan's. "Bulls," he said softly. He had sat outside with Mr. Logan and smoked a pipe with him at least twenty times in the past two years.

"Jasus!" said Mr. Logan, as if the thought of bulls maddened him. "Where?"

"Downhill Farms today. Tomorrow, Mid-Antrim Stock Farms. The day after, Coleraine Producers."

"Have you any arms on your person?" Mr. Logan withdrew a little from the counter, his head down.

"Two," Miro said.

Mr. Logan looked up. "Firearms, for Jasus sake."

"That's an odd question, Mr. Logan."

"I *have* to ask you, for Jasus sake. They're blowin the bloody place apart . . . Every bloody day . . ." He glowered down again at something on the floor behind the counter. "Where will you be stayin?"

"With Captain Ronald Strong . . ."—Mr. Logan looked up sharply and Miro pressed the point—". . . Unionist member for Carrickfergus in the Northern Ireland Parliament at Stormont, whose address is Kilroot House, Kilroot, near Carrickfergus. A Protestant, without doubt."

Mr. Logan sighed miserably. "Aye," he said, "that's a big man. Look out the window."

The customs officer who had instructed Miro to get out and go in was searching his car. The hood was up, the lid of the trunk was up, the doors were open, the officer was kneeling on the back seat. He bounced, bent uncomfortably and pressed, bounced again, got awkwardly out into the warm green day, closed the trunk, the doors, the hood, and came inside.

"The same," he said gloomily. "Bloody nothin. There'll be holes in me knees afore this lot's done."

"What did you expect?" Miro asked him.

"Nothin. Bloody nothin. D'they think people's daft, bringin in one gun at a time at authorized border crossins when they can walk them over the fields in bloody dozens? Jasus, I wish the bloody polis had my knees."

"We're just doin what we're tole," Mr. Logan said. And as if in extenuation, "Durin the war they used to find packets of tea."

He stared unhappily through the window; between them they made a little silence, uncomfortable and heavy. "Goin through Derry?" Mr. Logan asked, still staring.

"Yes."

"The army'll stop you outside the city. Be very polite. Them bastards blew up an army truck early this mornin and killed five men. The soldiers," he said slowly, and turned to look with massive restraint into Miro's face, "are cross." Wearily he walked back from his counter and said, without looking round, "If I was a soldier I'd shoot the bloody lot . . . if I could find them." He stepped into the back room and closed the door.

Miro went back to his car. The other customs officer followed him out.

"Watch yerself," he said.

"I will." His own anger was rising. The fields were green and rich, the sun bright, the trees full and the streams clean. It was a place of gentle beauty and gentle men. Those two men back at the customs post were gentle men. They talked of pools, and fish and flies and the changing light, and the qualities of rain; and he remembered one damp day with plump Mr. Logan drawing on his pipe and asking suddenly out of a contented silence, "Tell me, sur, have you ever heard anythin to bate the birds singin in the early mornin?"

It was a long walk from the wonder of the birds singin in the early mornin to *If I was a soldier I'd shoot the bloody lot,* but Mr. Logan had walked it. And that was a long loss.

Leaving Strabane, Miro picked up an old couple laboring with their straw carrier baskets up a winding hill. In the summer heat, the old man and his wife wore heavy overcoats. He had one brown upper tooth in the middle of his gums; she had two teeth—one upper, one lower—an inch apart. Their faces ran with sweat. They grinned wickedly, like ill-intentioned trolls, and sat forward on the edge of the back seat, saying nothing.

He could smell them: fresh sweat, stale sweat, old clothes, and the odors of the farmyard. He had nothing to say to them. He tried, "It's a lovely day."

"Very sweaty," the old man said, and the old woman cackled.

"It's a right windey road," she said, and they grinned for several miles more before she said, "Here," and they took their baskets to the ditch and sat there, grinning still.

Miro rounded a bend, stopped, and opened all the windows to let their fragrance escape. It was still in his nostrils when the sign said *Derry 3.*

The soldiers outside Derry had Miro covered all the way to the roadblock. They were young, cold, stony, and wary. A young lieutenant stood back from the driver's door and said, "Open it, if you please."

Miro opened it wide.

"Step out, sir . . . Open the bonnet, please . . . Open the boot, please . . . If you don't mind, sir, sit in the back . . . Please kneel on the seat . . . Now press hard all the way across . . . harder . . . against the back too, sir, if you don't mind . . ." If

11

something blew up, Miro would be the first to go. Please, please, please . . . then they went at it themselves. "You came across the Border this morning?"

"Just a little while ago."

"Why?"

"To buy bulls and visit a friend. I raise cattle in Donegal."

"You are returning today?"

"No. Not for several days."

"Where will you stay?"

"With a Captain Strong of Kilroot. He's . . ."

"I know who *he* is. How do I know *you're* going there?"

Miro produced Strong's letter and the lieutenant read it carefully. "Miro?" he said. "*The Trees Are Hissing Like Green Geese*? That one?"

"The same."

"I read it. You might give Captain Strong a message, sir."

"Gladly."

"Tell him to get a move on." It was his first sign of feeling.

"Do I need to understand that?"

"No, but he needs to. You may go now."

Miro got back behind the wheel. "Lieutenant," he said, "merely as a point of interest, I'm sure you're ordered to stop and search, but are you also authorized to interrogate?"

"At my discretion. Obviously, in this situation."

"Of course. And whom shall I say your message is from?"

The lieutenant leaned down and said very distinctly, "Any soldier in this God-polluted midden." Impatiently he waved the car through the roadblock.

I wish I had listened to Eva, Miro thought. The cloudless summer day was heavy with shadows. He thought of turning back. She would listen to the radio all day every day he was away. Everything she heard would enlarge and encompass him about with threat. She wouldn't sleep at night.

But he was already in Derry, driving under the old city wall that kept out Catholic King James' besieging army three hundred years ago. Crooks' Drapery was across the street. Last summer they had taken a house in Portballintrae, a coastal village forty-five road miles ahead, and had bought bed linen they needed on sale in Crooks' Drapery. The plate-glass windows were intact that day. They were boarded up today, smashed to slivers in the rioting in Derry two nights ago.

"I'll have to tell Eva . . ." He had to tell Eva everything. New little things he saw were stored for retelling because she would like to have seen them with him; old little things they'd seen together made him wish she was seeing them with him again. She was with him like an inner skin and he loved his dependence. He'd look at the bulls at Downhill Farms and go home today. A red light stopped his progress.

He said to a man standing idly on the edge of the sidewalk, "You've had a few breakages here."

The man looked about at the boarded-up shop fronts and shrugged. "Ah wisht they'd break a wheen more," he said gravely. "It keeps the carpenters workin." Solemnly he squirted tobacco into the gutter.

He'd have to tell Eva that one; and about glimpses he got of the estuary of the Foyle and Lough Foyle as he took the road to Ballykelly, through Limavady, and north from that gray dreach town to Downhill. The river and the sea glittered in the sun, the trees were green, the hills round and full—the Irish, with their luxurious earthiness of eye and tongue, called them paps, for that is what they looked like, but the Calvinist Scots and English, who inherited the land after the Irish were driven off it, called them hills. The land had a vast stillness to it.

There were things about it that were hard to believe, and Miro found them harder to believe while he bought the Brown Swiss bull he wanted for his cows. The stockmen at Downhill were slow men with shy sidelong smiles; the farm manager a humorous man with a lively, good-natured wife. Over a drink on the sale he said, "Like a lot of good men I know, that bull can service twenty-five cows."

"Twenty-five cows?" His wife laughed. "Get away with you, man, what this country needs is more good men that can service twenty-five women—and give it all to one. Will you have another drink, sir?" she asked Miro quickly, and swept her broad buttocks out of reach of her husband's slapping hand. "If not, I'll say goodbye to you now." She walked from the room, calling back at the door, "He makes a brave try, the poor man, but he's gettin past it." They heard her laughing her way out into the yard.

They're a plain, good-natured people, a likable people, he thought, and honest to deal with. He enjoyed them. The shadows were hard to credit, and he found himself parking outside The Brown Trout, near Coleraine, before it crossed his mind again that the sight of the roadblock had made him want to go back home to Summerfield.

He ordered "big healthy salmon sandwiches and a pint of Harp lager," from a cheerful country girl, and got small squares without the crust. "I meant big—big," he said, "with the crust on."

"Och, them's a brave wee size," the girl protested, grinning happily.

"He wants *door-steps,*" the man at the next table explained to her, pronouncing *door* to rhyme with *poor,* as the Elizabethans did and Ulstermen do.

"Och, he can git his gub round them ones a damn sight easier," the girl said, and settled the matter by turning her back on them.

They were an amusing people. He finished his beer and decided to drive to Strong's around the Antrim Coast Road.

The high arches hanging above the road from Coleraine to Bushmills looked homemade: frail, unstable things with fretwork images of Protestant King William (known affectionately by Catholics and Protestants as Orange Billy) on his horse, eternally crossing the River Boyne to a victory over Catholic King James; and fretwork images of the prow of a ship of King William's navy, breaking the boom King James' men had slung across the Foyle at the siege of Derry. *Derry, Aughrim, and the Boyne,* the arches proclaimed in fretwork letters: the heroic trinity of the military victory of a Protestant Dutchman who was king of England over Irishmen loyal to a Catholic Scotsman who was king of England—happenings of three hundred years before, and still so fresh in the air it might have been yesterday. It was as if New England Tories and Patriots still fought the War of Independence in the streets of Boston.

And it was confusing. Miro remembered Shamus Kelly writing in *The Irish Times*, "Any man who isn't confused by Northern Ireland isn't well informed." But it was none of his business.

The roads were narrow, and he had never known till he came to Ireland how many and how subtle were the shades of green, or that trees could look so like soft, green cushions, or that over and on these gentle roads winding through hedges and woods and meadows of a hundred greens, and beside little rivers, such dark satanic violence could leap at the uninitiated, like the rites of some blood-boiling cult in a far and primitive place.

Above the road the Orange arches shouted

NO SURRENDER

and in white-paint letters three feet high, the road itself yelled up at the traveler

NO POPE HERE
TO HELL WITH THE POPE
REMEMBER DERRY

Remember? Miro remembered that last summer, on this same road running through Bushmills to Portballintrae and past the house they'd rented, they had watched the ritual celebration of the Battle of the Boyne on The Twelfth of July. (He remembered too that the battle was fought on the second of July; but this was "like the thing," as they said here, and now only historians remembered that all this passion of celebration was poured out on the wrong date, three hundred years after the event.)

The Twelfth was not just a day, as it might have been in Brooklyn or Birmingham—merely the 12th. It was THE TWELFTH, with the word spelled out, the meaning deep and clear, jubilant and ominous. Even the Catholics called it The Twelfth, with capital initials, and they stayed in their houses and watched it on television. On The Twelfth the Orange Order paraded.

Miro had brought Eva and one-year-old Michael to see one of the parades last year. Here in this part of the country it was only two miles long. In Belfast it was seven miles long. It came like an army, with banners, drunk with the drums.

Driving down this road now, he again could hear the drummers beating their big bass drums—bigger than the bass drums in any band—the Lambeg Drums. They were beaten with baked bulrushes with their heads bound in tape, beaten by sweating shirt-sleeved men who laid their wrists to the rims of the drums and whipped the bulrushes till their wrists bled—*Rum-tum, Rum-tum, Tiddley-um, Tiddley-um, Tiddley-iddley-um, Tiddley-iddley-um, Tiddley-um, Tiddley-um, Rum-tum, Rum-tum* and on and on and on and on and over again in blood and heart-attack purple-faced sweat . . . a savage sound, a threatening bullying sound, a manic sound, a warning . . .

"I don't want to hear them any more," Eva said. "Drive away, Miro."

But it was not easy to drive away. There were bands: fife and drum bands, accordion bands, melodeon bands, pipe bands, brass bands, marching men and boys with hot, set faces and drum-intoxicated eyes; there were thick-necked, red-faced marshals with long pikes, men and weapons chosen for their compatibility, and columns of men in blue suits and bowler hats and sashes and little aprons, marching under elaborate two-poled banners that jigged nervously and made the pictures on them dance—pictures of William of Orange on his white horse, still crossing the Boyne; or of renowned ranting Presbyterian ministers, who had in the past heaved strong words at the pope of Rome; or of the gates of Derry closed against papist James; or of the *Mountjoy*, the ship that rammed and broke the siege boom across the Foyle. They danced drunkenly in the strident hostile air.

"Are you tourists?" a man trapped beside them asked Miro.

"We are," he said and added, trying to sound like a visiting schoolmaster who was seeing new and amazing things that must be told to his class, "It's extremely *interesting*." For words out of place were apt to be regretted.

"Maybe to tourists. I was born here," the man said, "but I wouldn't live here. Look at them. They'd bring the whole province down in ruins on their heads before they'd make a concession to anybody about anything. My own brother's one of them," he said, "and he told me 'If they bring us down we'll take them all down with us!' And that's what they'll do."

A fife and drum band beat out,

> *"D'ye think that I would let*
> *A dirty Fenian get*
> *Destroy my loyal Orange lily-o,*
> *Orange lily-o, Orange lily-o,*
> *Destroy my loyal Orange lily-o?"*

"A dirty Fenian get," Miro explained to his French Catholic wife, "means a dirty Catholic bastard."

"Take us away, please, Miro."

But he could not. The year before, a doctor, driving to attend to a sick child, had been refused permission by the pike-bearing marshals to pass through the procession. The angry doctor had put his foot down and scattered the parade. He had also been fined by the courts.

Miro passed out of remembrance of last year, as he might have passed through a dark tunnel of trees into a summer day. He took the road out of Bushmills along the north coast, past the Giants' Causeway, through Ballycastle, and around Fair Head. He had time. Off there across the shining riffled water, thirteen miles away, was the Mull of Kintyre, the first sign of Scotland.

He turned south down the Antrim Coast Road. The sea was glorious in the sun, the cliffs were majestic, the villages were idyllic at the feet of the Glens of Antrim. It was a country for nature poets and landscape painters and tranquil farmers intoning *The Lord's my Shepherd* on Sunday mornings. There *was* no tunnel of trees. The darkness was *not* to be believed in; the darkness was only his acid daydream, provoked by the contradic-

17

tions of a summer day and salmon sandwiches without crusts.

He drove along the north shore of Belfast Lough in a state of induced tranquillity and turned into the Kilroot Road, at the end of which lived Captain Ronald Strong, M.P. He was ready for dinner.

Three

And behold, a basket of summer fruit

Captain Strong lived at the end of the Kilroot Road, over the railway crossing by the Kilroot Halt, behind a red brick wall in a deteriorating red brick house, on a knuckle of land that stuck out a little into Belfast Lough, but not out far enough to be impressive.

The brickwork of the house needed pointing. Captain Strong waited with his wife, the general's daughter, at the top of cracked concrete steps guarded by two ineffectual-looking lions. The nose of one of the lions was missing, the other had lost an ear; they were the deformities of decay, not accident. The captain's wife was handsome; perhaps she was once, and not long ago, impressively so. Miro had recently become acquainted with the word nubile. Marriageable, his dictionaries said; ripe, Miro translated it. Mrs. Strong was small with dark hair and large dark eyes and the round ripeness that comes to women of forty who are stirring to life again and briefly, with the vigorous greed of their twenties. (Wasn't Eva like that, and shouldn't he know what it was like? But Eva's eyes were gray and luminous and her hair was pale. Mrs. Strong's eyes were brown and appraising.) She examined him frankly, like an insurance appraiser examining a damaged car. The decay that was visible on her was slight and about her jaws. In a year or two she would have jowls. The look of strain was mainly about her eyes.

The captain was solid, soldierly and needlessly ceremonial. He need not have waited there at the top of his dilapidated steps like a head of state receiving a head of state. A servant could have answered the bell if there were a servant. If there weren't, housework in a house this size and in this condition could account for the slight dilapidation of a healthy woman's jaws. Miro looked at her again and found her still appraising, this time with a good-humored light in her brown eyes. Not work, he decided, time, and gave his mind to the captain.

"Miro, my dear fellow, how good to see you again." Strong came halfway down the cracked steps and made a politic pause for Miro to come halfway up. "My wife," he said with his back to her, and appeared to be aware of without being involved with her.

Mrs. Strong smiled as if that was what this occasion required of her, but her eyes speculated rather than welcomed. Now that he was here and they were there, Miro wondered why any of them had bothered. He didn't know these people, didn't want to know them, couldn't imagine why Strong had taken the trouble to ask him. He had accepted the invitation because he wanted to look at a bull not too far away and Kilroot was convenient, and he was a little curious about Strong, and at home, Eva did rhyme on about him not shutting himself up with his cows. "You have to meet people, Miro." He went stoically in among the worn furniture and the balding carpets.

"We'll dine much earlier than usual. I've been called out on rather important political business," Strong announced, as his father-in-law the general might have announced a change in the order of battle. "My apologies. I'll have to leave immediately after dinner." He was already in position before the empty grate.

Mrs. Strong glanced quickly at Miro, so quickly that he almost missed the little smile that came and went. She said to her husband, "But you'll be home tonight? Before breakfast, I mean." It was faintly undercoated with spite. It was Miro's first sound of her voice. She was English. It was a cool English voice that completed for him the picture he was building of the self-contained

Englishwoman's restraint, which never makes overtures but sometimes, by softening warmth, invites approaches.

Strong didn't look at her. "Perhaps," he said. He hadn't looked at her at all, Miro noted, and forgot to assure Strong that his emergency was understood.

"Political life, y'know," Strong said as if he had misinterpreted Miro's silence. "Things are extremely tense here at the moment. As you probably know. One's personal life isn't . . ."

". . . isn't anything, really," Mrs. Strong said vaguely, looking nowhere with indifference.

"Of course," Miro said. Strong's teeth aren't click-clacking, he thought; maybe in London he was out of the sticky stuff people with false teeth use? What does he want with me? he wondered, and half-listened to the captain's recital of his military history and half-watched Mrs. Strong on an old sofa, withdrawn defensively behind her collarbones against a flood of too-familiar talk . . . "My father-in-law, the late General Roberton . . ." Mrs. Strong closed her eyes and drew her lips a little tighter. Miro could almost hear her soundless shriek.

Yet there was a dignity about Strong that his wife's sly animus enlarged for Miro. The man was proud of his soldiering days. Maybe he'd liked the general. Maybe once upon a time he'd liked the general's daughter. Now, it seemed, he tried to ignore her. It might be his alternative to slapping her face in company. She had not been with him in London. Perhaps they had both been resting from each other.

Miro gave just enough of his mind to Strong to make sure he wasn't caught by a question. He gave the rest of it to his own questions: Why did this fellow ask me here? He's a big man; he can raise thousands at a political meeting. He kept the Northern government looking over its shoulder at him, yet he never made a precise political statement. ("Ian Paisley . . ." Miro heard, ". . . that political Billy Sunday . . . useful, but for use only, not for policy, or leadership or anything intelligent . . .") He's very busy. He hasn't said a thing that interests me and hasn't asked me a question. He has no interest in me or anything I am or have. Why bother with me? ("And Bernadette Devlin . . . read her book . . . her mother was a farming Devlin, her father a tinker Devlin, and never the twain shall meet, so she's taking it out on everybody. The fact is, sir, Ulster is a closed society that looks open and therefore invites people to make mistakes. The whole population of the province is a festering mess of small but deep social humiliations. Connections, not talents, lift you to the top . . .")

You too, Captain? Miro wondered. ("My schools were Methody and Queens in Belfast and Queen's Officers' Training Corps. The required school pedigree for Prime Ministers in Ulster is Eton and Balliol. My regiment was the Duke of Wellington's. The military pedigree requirement is Sandhurst and the Brigade of Guards.")

Ah. The captain was a festering mess of small but deep social humiliations. He married the general or his daughter, sighted in on the Prime Minister's job, and found himself with the wrong pedigree. Just like Bernadette. Just like Ian Paisley: his doctorate of divinity was not Edinburgh. It was Bob Jones University. That's like the thing, as they say in Ulster. In Ulster, everything casts a shadow, even ghosts. Miro gave his attention to Mrs. Strong, who was stirring. The captain looked at his watch.

"Ulster," Mrs. Strong said, "has two principal sins—social envy and masturbation." Now Strong closed his eyes. She said, her eyes on Miro's face, mocking her husband, "Young men leave their girls on the doorstep and nip round the corner to find a bush." She was almost smiling. Strong was staring desperately out the window to the sea. His lips were tight. "Louis Mac-Neice, a poet who came from Carrickfergus, said he was sick of 'your well-bred hunters, your dolled-up virgins and your ignorant dead.' There's nothing else in Ulster," she said, "as you probably know."

"There are bulls," Miro said, "very fine bulls," and wanted to laugh as his stomach told him to do; he kept a straight face, but his eyes gave him away.

"Bulls are for cows," Mrs. Strong said and smiled naughtily and stood up. "I'll see what's keeping Tomalty in the kitchen."

The air sparked. *Cohesion,* Strong said with a high note sounding under his baritone. "Ulster needs *cohesion,* and weak government is creating chaos." His eyes would not leave the sea, except to look at his watch.

Along the drive, in the turning circle where it ended, Miro could see Strong's elegant but antique limousine. It shone in the sun.

"What did you particularly want to see me about?" he said.

The door flew open and a large fat woman said, "Yer dinner's out." She banged the door behind her.

"Mrs. Tomalty," Strong said. "She and her husband are in service with us. I have Catholics on my staff."

Staff? Forty or two? They went in to dinner. Mrs. Strong was already in the dining room. These people had nothing to talk to him about—nothing of mutual interest anyway. Miro said, "You wanted to talk to me about my book, Mrs. Strong?"

"I did?" She looked at Miro, surprised; questioningly at her husband; and nodded her understanding. "I haven't read it," she said. "What made you think I had? Has everybody else?"

A small man served the soup. He wore highly polished black boots, highly polished black leggings, bottle-green breeches, and a white linen jacket. When he left, Mrs. Strong said, "He is Tomalty. Mrs. Tomalty's husband."

Captain Strong glanced at his watch. "News," he said and crossed the room to switch on a radio. He had not touched his soup, and did not return to the table. Two men in long waders came along the foreshore. The limousine was not in sight from this room, but the men came from that direction. They carried a bucket and long narrow spades, called Lurgan spades. They began to dig for worms in the wet sand. Strong watched them, standing close to the window. His intentness, Miro thought, showed in his back.

The BBC had news. They had withheld it until now, the announcer said, at the request of the Royal Ulster Constabulary.

At eleven o'clock this morning three men called at the home of the Reverend Dr. Wylie Corkey, the aged and revered moderator of the Presbyterian Church in Ireland. Mrs. Corkey answered the bell and took the men to her husband's study. She then went next door, as she did every morning, to have a cup of tea with Mrs. Ray Davey, an old friend.

When she returned, Dr. Corkey had gone, his car had also gone, the phone had been pulled from its roots, and an envelope addressed to Mrs. Corkey lay on the kitchen table. Inside the envelope was a communiqué from the outlawed Irish Republican Army, addressed to the Prime Minister. The government had directed the police to make public only two clauses from the communiqué:

These were, first, that Dr. Corkey would be well cared for and returned safely if all British troops were withdrawn from Northern Ireland before The Twelfth of July. If this was not done, Dr. Corkey would be executed;

And second, that there would be further abductions, meant to emphasize the seriousness of purpose behind the abduction of Dr. Corkey. These further abductions might be of members of the foreign consular service, or public figures—religious or political—or ordinary men and women on the city streets or the country roads of Northern Ireland. Or children. Children, they wanted it to be very clear, would not be exempt. The same conditions would apply in all cases, including the children . . . withdrawal or death . . .

The government appealed to parents everywhere to keep their children off the streets . . .

Miro shuddered out of his numb composure.

Strong stood by the window, still watching, it seemed to Miro, the worm-diggers, who had waded to the motorboat moored offshore and were now on their way down the lough. He said with startling equanimity, "They chose well. Everybody loves old Corkey. He's one of the harmless beloved, full of grace. Even the Catholic archbishop has praised his Christian grace. They chose with care. The people on the street, and the children. Very shrewd. Banks and churches are public, but people and their children are personal, frightening. This will send the balloon up." It was, Miro supposed, a cold, soldierly estimate of the reality of the situation. But cold. Very cold.

"They're savages," Mrs. Strong said. "Both sides. Their appetite for cruelty is . . ."

"Quiet," Strong said harshly. The BBC had more news.

At two o'clock this afternoon, while Father Brendan Kelly was preparing to leave the parish house of St. Malachai's Church, a man discharged both barrels of a sawed-off shotgun into the back of his legs and left a message on the floor beside him. The message declared that the shooting was a reprisal for the abduction of Dr. Corkey and unless the moderator was returned at once and unharmed, a Catholic priest would be shot every day for the duration of Dr. Corkey's detention.

"God damn them," Strong said viciously. "God damn them," he said again, still staring down the lough. The worm-diggers were almost out of sight.

"Savages," Mrs. Strong said, her fingers clutching her collarbones.

Miro said coldly, "How did they know Dr. Corkey had been abducted?"

"God damn them," the captain said, and without interest, "What did you say?"

"How did they know?"

"How did they know *what*?" The captain's mind was angrily elsewhere.

"That Corkey had been abducted. It's just been made public."

"God damn them." Strong looked at his watch. "Tell Tomalty," he snapped at his wife, watching, it seemed to Miro, the worm-diggers disappear from sight. "I must go," he said.

"Now? After this?" Miro shared Mrs. Strong's surprise.

"All the more," Strong said, and this time he looked at his wife. "Tell Tomalty," he said through his teeth.

She rang. "Tell Tomalty," she said to Mrs. Tomalty. "The captain is ready." The mockery was not amused now, but angry.

Chain of command, Miro thought and would have smiled on any other day.

Strong came back to the table and sat down. "My wife will be glad of your company," he said. "I'll probably not be back till morning. After this . . . God damn them . . . Watch for Tomalty," he said sharply to his wife. She went to the window.

"God damn whom?" Miro asked him.

"What?" Strong was puzzled, perhaps surprised; he was elsewhere, and angry. "God damn them," he muttered and did not answer the question.

Impatiently Miro went to the window and stood behind Mrs. Strong. The captain's car had been out of sight from the dining-room interior. He could see it now.

Tomalty came into view by the old limousine, his white coat now a bottle-green livery jacket; he had on a peaked cap. He stood with his hand on the car door, a stiff little figure, ridiculously to attention. "He's there," Mrs. Strong said.

"Call him."

Mrs. Strong beckoned to Tomalty through the big bow window. It was like a practiced and preposterous ritual.

"I'm off," Strong said. "Again my apologies. But you can see how things are. If we had a government . . ." But he lingered, checking his watch.

Miro was fascinated by Tomalty's performance. The little man opened the door wide with a flourish, as if for a potentate, got in himself behind the wheel, leaned forward, and turned the ignition key.

The car blew up with a tremendous explosion.

The dining-room window collapsed inwards, cutting Mrs. Strong's face and arms.

Mrs. Tomalty ran screaming through the front door towards the remains of her little husband in the burning, black-belching car.

The captain's wife held her bleeding arms towards her husband and cried, *"Ronnie, my blood, my blood!"*

The captain walked past her to the window; he did not seem to be aware of her. "That was meant for me," he said calmly, loudly. Proudly, Miro thought.

There was no point in hurrying to help Tomalty, who was beyond help at the instant of the explosion. Mrs. Tomalty was on her knees, screaming at the blazing car.

"It was meant for *me*," the captain said again, as if somebody had paid him a compliment. He walked to the phone. "Help her," he said. "There's a medicine chest in the ground-floor bathroom. First left . . ."

"Call a doctor!" Miro yelled at him and ran for the medicine chest, but when he came back Strong was talking to the police.

"Yes, and the army explosives men. Call them at once. They'll want to look at the car. Oh, he's dead. It was meant for me without doubt, but they got an innocent Catholic . . ." He rang off, looking around for the next orderly chore.

"*Call a bloody doctor!*" Miro yelled at him.

Mrs. Strong stood whimpering, her arms hanging, blood oozing down her neck and white dress and spreading its stain. "*Call a doctor, goddammit,*" Miro shouted again at Strong, and laid her on the sofa and bound her arms, and bathed and patched her face, and went out to look at his car. The windshield was a fringe of jagged glass—unbreakable, the manufacturer said—the upholstery cut to ribbons. He ran back into the house. Mrs. Strong was crying, huddled on the sofa. The captain was dialing another number. "Have you called a doctor?" Miro asked him and got no answer.

"*Northern Whig?*" Strong said. "This is Captain Ronald Strong. Get me Mr. Oliphant . . . Well, get him out of the editorial conference."

He was a politician. In the morning, after *The Northern Whig* came out, he would be victim and hero. And his dead driver was a Catholic; Strong would be an ecumenical victim and hero. A good player didn't miss that sort of trick. Miro wondered how useful his injured wife would be. Not much, it seemed. Or not yet. He picked her up and carried her upstairs. "Where's your room?"

"The second door," she said on the second asking.

"Can you stand?" He set her on her feet by her bed and threw back the covers. Her white dress was sodden with her blood. "You can't lie in that," he said and took it off. Her slip was bloodstained. He took it off. Her bra and panties were stained. "I'm not taking them off," he said. She didn't seem to hear. He put her to bed.

The police siren was whining down the Kilroot Road. "Will you be all right till I get a doctor for you?"

"Thank you," she said and closed her eyes.

Strong was still on the phone. Policemen and explosives men were scrambling from their cars. There was an ambulance and a doctor. Miro directed the doctor to Mrs. Strong's room and gave the police his version of what had happened. Then he walked to the foreshore, winding down his anger against Strong.

The paper caught his eye, flying like a flag from the stick in the wet sand. The end of the stick had been sharpened to pierce the empty edge of an envelope. It was addressed to Ronald Strong. Miro did not touch it. He stood to seawards of it and measured the angle of sight to the dining-room window. He had not seen this from the window, but he hadn't been looking for it. He went back to the dining-room window and tried to see the little flag. It was out of sight. He went back again to the stick and separated his footprints from the ribbed impressions of rubber waders. They came out of the grass opposite the smoking mass of Strong's car. He followed them to the bait-holes dug by the men he had seen on the foreshore, and from the holes to the water, opposite where the motorboat had been moored.

A young man was walking towards him. He had heavy dark hair, bristling eyebrows, and a wide black mustache.

"Police?" Miro asked him.

"No, sir. Army. You're Mr. Miro." It was not a question.

"So? You'd better tell the police about that." He pointed to the envelope.

"Another little message? My name's Mac Donnell. Not *Macdon*nell, sir. Mac Don*nell*. Colonel Bowen sent me to see you, sir. He'd like to see you."

"Bowen? Army Intelligence?"

"Yes, sir."

"I'd like to see him again but I haven't time. Thank him."

"It's important, sir."

"I'm sure it is. So are my cows."

"Cows?"

"Cows."

Mac Donnell stood in front of the stick in the sand, his back to the house. He drew the stick out, pulled the envelope carefully off and put it in an inside pocket. "We'd be obliged if you didn't mention this to the police, sir."

"You'd better convince me you're from Bowen," Miro said coldly.

The card he produced said he was Captain Alisdair Mac Donnell. The picture on the card was a good likeness.

"Why?" Miro asked him.

"That's what the colonel wants to see you about, sir. We want to see how Captain Strong behaves when there's no communiqué from the IRA."

"Why?"

"That's what the colonal wants to see you about, sir."

"Round we go again. Tell him I'm sorry. Some other time." He walked back to the house.

They were bringing Mrs. Strong down the steps on a stretcher. She had gathered herself and was composed again. Like an empress on a litter she signaled the ambulance men to stop.

"Thank you," she said and smiled on the good side of her face. "They're taking me to the cottage hospital. You were the only one who had time for me. Will you come to see me?"

"There were only two of us."

"Yes," she said. "Will you come to see me?"

"In the morning."

"Will you stay here?"

"No. I'm going to an hotel."

She signaled her bearers and they put her in the ambulance. I can understand why she cuts the bastard down, he thought.

Strong was coming out of the house with a police inspector carrying his RUC badge of office, the sturdy blackthorn stick. "The inspector's driving me to Belfast, Miro," he said. "I'll see you in the morning. You can fish for yourself in the kitchen, I imagine?"

He thinks I'll stay! Miro wanted to laugh. He said, "Your wife's in the ambulance."

"Yes." Strong got into the inspector's car. "The RUC will want you for the inquest," he said.

"He knows where I live," Miro said to the inspector and turned around.

Mac Donnell was at his elbow. The police car moved out. Mac Donnell said, "May I take you to Colonel Bowen, sir? This makes it rather urgent." He nodded towards the smoking car. Mrs. Tomalty had been taken inside.

"You can not. I have a bomb-blasted car of my own to think about."

"We'll look after that for you, sir. Where can I drop you?"

"The Royal Avenue Hotel in Belfast when I get my things."

On the way up the Kilroot Road, Mac Donnell began again, "The colonel . . ."

"The hotel, son. Forget the colonel."

He didn't speak again. The sun was bright, the land green. There was almost no traffic, only a great stillness.

There were no children at all.

Four

When will the new moon be gone, that we may sell corn?

The room was cool. It was eleven-thirty now and the long light of a northern evening gone. Miro put on his jacket and went to sit by the window.

The starlings on the Royal Avenue Hotel were rising and settling in their demented way, alternating their mass silence with hysterical flutterings and chitterings. They'd keep him awake, he knew; he could think of bed and was unable to face it. He could hear Eva's voice on the telephone just now after the struggle to get through. ("Is that the operator at Letterkenny now?" he heard a woman ask. "It is? Praise be to God. Can ye get me to Glenties? I'm havin the devil's own time . . . ye can? Praise be to God. Is that the operator at Glenties? It is? Praise be to God. Can ye get me . . . yer what? Yer *closed*? But it's himself that's tryin to speak to his wee wife and her out of her mind worryin. All right, darlin, God bless ye and may ye die in Ireland. What? Ye don't want . . . ? Well it's only a sayin. Is that Mrs. Miro? It is? Praise be to God. Himself's here wantin ye . . .")

"I heard the news, love," Eva said. "Come home. Where are you? Are you eating?"

He told her nothing except that he'd be home quickly. He thought the classic lines of the Provincial Bank across the street, in pale gray paint with white trim, looked like the Wedgwood ornament on their drawing-room mantelpiece at Summerfield; beside it, the dark, repelling bulk of the Ulster tourist office, with a gloomy cavern of an open porch closed in by a high stone railing. A small, very young prostitute sat on the railing, with a large, drunk client gripped between her thighs. Their laughter bounced along the empty street. The man put his hands under her thighs and lifted her off the railing. He staggered down the street, her legs wrapped around him, her arms dangling over his shoulders, their mouths together.

Somebody knocked on his door. Past twelve? He hadn't asked for room service. It was a gentle little knock. Reluctantly, he opened the door.

Stephen Riada was bigger than his brother Shamus, who wrote novels and kept the pub in Killyroe. Stephen had the same dark skin and big hooked nose and aggressive dark eyes. Shamus had chosen the pub and the pen, Stephen the army of the Irish Republic. He was now its chief of intelligence. He had one hand inside his jacket.

"I'm glad you're not in bed," he said. "I have a jar up my coat."

"Bring it in." Miro closed the door behind him. "What sort of bloody fool are you, Stephen? You're conspicuous swimming a mile offshore. They'll throw you in jail up here."

"I got Bushmills," Riada said. "I thought maybe if I brought John Jameson you'd suspect papist prejudice." He poured the whiskey.

Miro took it and sat on his narrow bed with his back against the wall. "How did you know I was here?"

"I suppose it would save a lot of ill temper if I told you straight out?" Riada took the chair by the window. "Bowen's man, Mac Donnell, told me. Shamus told me the other day you were coming up here, staying with Strong. I told Bowen. When they threw that clanker at Strong, Bowen sent Mac Donnell to fetch you. You wouldn't go to him, so I came to you."

Miro cupped his glass in both hands and felt an old wariness. "The Irish army and the British army have something on? That would sound strange in a Dublin pub."

"They're not likely to hear it in a Dublin pub." He brought his chair up beside Miro's bed.

"You're going to start whispering," Miro said. "Anything *you* have to whisper, *I* don't want to hear."

"Eva would." Riada said it casually and lifted his glass. "Here's to Eva and Michael and Summerfield. I hope they last." He was content to leave it there.

Miro pressed his back against the wall and thought it over. Strong had no obvious interest in him and said nothing to him that he hadn't said in all his speeches. But he wanted Miro in his house. Today. Had there been something to come that was postponed by the bomb? He didn't believe it. He didn't understand it. A man with a better opinion of himself would have assumed that he was worth knowing. Miro didn't assume it. What was worth anything in him was Eva's doing, he believed.

Bowen he had known and worked with in the past, and Bowen sent a man to fetch him when Strong was bombed.

Stephen Riada should be in Dublin and was here in the North, in his room, because he wouldn't go to Bowen. And Riada was talking in Irish riddles about Summerfield.

The uselessness of his years before Eva, the mountains and the peace of Summerfield had made Miro a silent man except among his few intimates. Uncertainty deepened his silence: then he thought, turning over stones. He thought now and said nothing. He did not look at Stephen Riada, but watched him. He felt intruded upon—not by Riada's presence, which he enjoyed when he came with Shamus to Summerfield to fish the lough, but by the hint of pressure. He sat like an Indian on his bed and waited.

Riada topped his glass. "Miro, did you hear me?"

"I heard you."

"The North is on the edge of chaos."

"Seems so."

"If the Unionists go to the gun and start a Catholic massacre, the Irish army will put men in here in civilian clothes. We can't stand over the Border and *watch* it. It'll be worse than 1920. It'll spill across the Border and up your valley, up your mountain.

They'll burn your barns, slaughter your cattle, burn your house . . ."

Miro stirred and said, "Stephen. Your branch took men down from the North to a camp at Dunree. You trained them as street fighters. They're up here now. Do you know they didn't kidnap Corkey? Or kill Tomalty—or bomb all the Protestant churches that have burned, or the banks . . . or threaten to kidnap and kill children? Did you help by training gunmen?"

"We made a mistake. It's done and regretted. But they didn't do these things. The IRA didn't do them . . ."

"The communiqués . . ."

"They're phony. That's what Bowen wants . . ."

"Fergoman and Finna on Lough Finn, is it? Whose voices do we hear, then? Where do they come from?"

"We don't know. That's what Bowen wants . . ."

"No." Miro got off the bed and put his glass on the dressing table. "Finish your drink. I'm going out to walk."

Riada finished his drink. "Why not let me drive you?"

"Why not? I won't sleep."

"We'll take my car. It's out front." Miro noticed that its plates were British and not those of the Irish Republic. Bowen looked after everybody's cars.

In the car Riada said, "Did you hear the news bulletin tonight?"

"No."

"They took a child. A girl of nine, the daughter of the Presbyterian minister of Ballyweaney, up Ballymena way."

Miro hunched his bulk down into itself to control the shiver that went through him. He made an angry noise in his throat and said nothing. His anger filled the car. His mind was on Michael.

They went west out of the city center into mean streets of back-to-back houses that sat together cheek to cheek. Here and there on a gable at the end of a street there were large paintings of William of Orange on his white horse, still crossing the Boyne.

"He's been at it a long time," Miro said.

"What Ireland needs," Riada said, "is a long attack of bloody amnesia." He pulled up to the curb and parked. "This is Protestant ground. We'll walk from here."

They walked for a mile through the same mean streets of tiny brick houses; as they crossed one narrow intersection and the sound of human outcry ahead of them increased, Riada said, "Cross the street and we're on Catholic ground."

"That noise?" Miro said. "You're taking me to a street fight."

"That's right."

"You've been here already tonight?"

"Just watching the preliminaries—the pubs are closed now. All hands are in shape and position."

Miro stopped him. "Let me get the picture," he said, pointing back the way they had come. "Down there to this intersection, they're Protestants?"

"Yes."

"Where are they? The streets are empty."

"And the houses are dark. They're in bed."

"And here where we are, up to the commotion ahead, they're Catholics?"

"That's right."

"And beyond the fighting they're what?"

"Protestants."

"Then why aren't these Protestants across the street pouring up this street to take the Catholics behind?"

"Because they're not street fighters. So far it's been largely a question of street rowdies in a few particular streets throwing rocks and petrol bombs at one another, with the professionals on both sides egging them on. The bombings and burnings and road minings and kidnappings—they're the professionals at work. It could be different tomorrow. Maybe those Protestants are not in bed. Maybe they're saying their prayers—or cleaning their guns. It takes a lot to make grocers and office clerks and shop stewards go to the gun. But there's a limit. Maybe *they* know about the child in Ballyweaney. What nobody knows is: Who has her?"

They walked in silence towards the clamor, the queer and increasing whirring shrill of young voices in riot that at a distance can be mistaken for children noisily at play in a park, till the

35

Shaun Herron

whoof of exploding firebombs becomes clearer, and the roaring of flames, and the increasing warmth of the air that turns to heat, and the sky that reflects the fires, and the malignant grumble of full-grown hystericals deepens. Somewhere close by to their left—it seemed just over the roof—there was the sound of accordion music. Around a bend in the street they came into the battle, and the heat met them.

The barricade across the end of the street was made of flaming oil barrels, iron bedsteads stacked high with anything that would burn, a double-decker bus, an army jeep, a police car, and an old truck.

They were burning like the Hadean pit.

Teams of young men ran awkwardly up to the fire, carrying articles of light furniture, swung them and heaved them into the flames, then threw their arms before their faces and ran back.

"What are they burning?"

"Their parents' furniture."

The houses that formed the flanks of the barricade and several houses behind them were also burning; the heat raged up the narrow street.

Young boys charged at the blast, shielding their faces behind asbestos boards, and lobbed firebombs over the barricade at the fire brigade, the police, and the soldiers, who stood well back on the other side, watching, frustrated and angry. Behind them a Protestant mob cheered and jeered, crying specific libels on the moral, spiritual, and genealogical legitimacy of the Pope.

A boy ran past Miro and Riada. He screamed, "Up the Queen wi' a red hot poker," bowled his firebomb like a cricketer, and ran back to safety. His hate and exultation in the leaping light patterned his face with grotesquely unstable shapes and shadows. He hopped up and down, clapping his hands as defectives do. "Up the Queen, up the Queen, up the Queen," he chanted jubilantly. He made Miro think of a lunatic clown who has set his own circus on fire and is dancing in the flames.

He took the boy's arm and pulled him out of the middle of the street. "Why won't you let the fire brigade in?" he shouted.

"They're not comin in, they're not comin in, they're not comin

36

in," the boy shrieked, a child in an hysterical tantrum. He turned to get another petrol bomb.

A middle-aged man stuck a bottle in the boy's hand. "Come on, Sammy boy. Back t'work." He shoved him towards the fire and went back up the street, shouting, organizing, inspiring the young. The boy lit the wick in the bottle and charged, yelling his battle cry.

Miro and Riada stood with their backs against a house, watching the human traffic rushing up and down the street to and from the fire. There was a malevolent joy about it, an ugly jubilation. Pairs of porters carried baskets and boxes of petrol bombs up the street to a safe distance from the flames. The adult organizer took an armful of bottles and roamed in search of idle hands and malingerers resting on duty; boys lined up at the baskets to receive their armaments and hurried back to the firing line.

Three men walked steadily into the midst of it all, two of them carrying a wooden ladder with a loosely rolled canvas stretcher lying on the rungs. The third carried a rifle that bore him down. He had been a tall man. He was wasted now, yellow-gray and sunken in the face, and his eyes were like empty sockets in a mask. A long red scar ran from his right temple down the caved-in cheek to the point of his chin. The man carrying the front end of the ladder could have been the same caved-in man when he was in full health. His face was the same face, but without the scar, without the yellow-gray color of death on his skin, and with his eyes still in their sockets. To Miro, they were brothers. He watched them and wondered if they might be figures in a nightmare.

The teeming crowd stopped to watch them lift the ladder against a house ten doors down from the fire. The whoofing of the firebombs stopped, the shouting stopped, the running stopped. The brother with life still large in him turned from the ladder and swept a commanding arm along the street towards the flames. He might have been a policeman on point duty. The traffic started again.

"Who is he?" Miro asked Riada.

"No idea. But maybe tonight's the night if he uses that gun."

The man with the death's head stacked his gun against the house. His healthy brother took him in his arms and held him. Then they shook hands, solemnly, with immense formality. The yellow man shook hands also with the third man and climbed the ladder, his brother close behind him, carrying the rifle. When he was firmly on the slates, he took the rifle and began to crawl slowly up the roof at an angle, towards the ridge. He stopped often, resting, but not looking back or looking down. Back on the ground, the hale brother opened the stretcher and laid it against the wall. It was at least four feet wide.

"A body in that," Miro said, "would almost touch the ground."

Colonel Riada did not answer. His eyes were on the man on the roof, now creeping with immense effort along the roof ridge, one leg on either side, the rifle slung over his shoulders.

Sammy came charging back from the bottle-baskets, a petrol bomb in his hand. He stopped in front of Miro and Riada to put a light to the wick, began his run, flung back his arm to lob his bomb, and it slipped from his hand and woofed around him.

"Get him," Miro yelled at Riada. "I'll get their stretcher."

He ran across the street and picked up the stretcher. But when he turned, the healthy brother stood in his way, silent, pointing the stretcher back to the wall.

"The boy," Miro shouted, "he'll burn to death. We'll roll him . . ." The man swung and caught Miro on the cheekbone, bouncing him against the wall. He came off it like a ball, the shafts of the stretcher digging viciously into the man's stomach. He went around him to the flaming child. Riada was beating on the boy with his jacket. Miro spread the stretcher and Riada rolled the child into it. They rolled him on the ground, beating him till smoke replaced flames. He rolled out of the stretcher onto the street, screaming like an animal in his throat, smoldering. Miro could smell his cooked flesh against the smell of burning oil and wood and mattresses and hot metal.

The organizer of boys-in-battle stuck a firebomb into a child's hands. *"Look what they done to us!"* he screeched. *"Give the bastards that for Sammy!"* But he stood well back from Sammy.

Miro shouted to Riada as other youths carried the howling boy up the street on part of a table top. "At the Dunree Camp you taught some of these people to light fires, Colonel. Why the bloody hell didn't you teach them to put them out?"

Riada said nothing. The man who hit Miro picked up his stretcher, examined it for damage, tested it for weakness, and put it back against the wall. He stepped back to watch his brother on the roof.

The rifleman was on his knees, laboring to find support for his weakness against a chimney stack. The rifle was too heavy for his wasted arms. It wavered in the air. He stood up to ease the strain on his sprawling thighs, laid the barrel of the gun across the open mouth of a chimney pot, and tried to sight it. It was a pointless endeavor. He was too weak to keep the barrel from sliding off the round rim of the pot. He shortened his grip, the walnut butt of the gun under his arm, and tried to steady it.

The direction had to be, Miro was sure, someone in the fire engine beyond the barricade. The rifleman jolted; the rifle fell, slid down the roof; the man came after it, legs and arms flinging in his fall, then settling as he rolled. The two men with him rushed to catch the body and were too late. It hit the pavement with a dead thud.

"Army sniper got him," Riada said. "They're watching the roofs from a block of flats across the road."

The dead man's friends lifted him grimly onto the spread stretcher, put the rifle beside him, picked up their burden and walked away slowly down the street.

"Ye forgot yer ladder, mister," a boy said to the man who hit Miro. He did not speak, and did not look at the people around him, but walked slowly through them.

"They'll be up from the South," somebody said, and the hanging canvas, not far off the ground, swung with their step. The man between the back shafts—the one Miro thought of as brother to the corpse—was biting his lower lip and his eyes were desperate with anger.

They were brothers, Miro thought, and they brought his stretcher with them. It's got to be a nightmare.

People leaned over the corpse as it passed, peered, crossed

themselves, and their lips moved. But the only sound was the roaring of the flames.

"That's what they do to us," the organizer yelled and shoved a bottle at a boy. *"Get at them, son."*

A large fat woman broke through the people and snatched the bottle from the boy's hands. "Git home wi ye afore I skelt yer face," she shouted.

"Let the wee lad fight," the organizer cried.

"Fight yerself, ye black bastard." She slashed the bottle against his head.

"I'm blinded, I'm blinded," he howled, trying to claw the petrol from his eyes. "Y'oul bitch, you've blinded me!"

"Git home t'yer bed, ye ignorant wee bugger," the mother shouted at her son and the boy shot out of her reach, streaking up the street past the slow movement of the corpse carriers.

"We'll go into Number 50 now," Riada said as if some ritual had come to an end.

Number 50 was like all the other houses in these streets. Step over the threshold into a little space at the foot of the narrow stairs; a door to the right led into the parlor—not more than nine feet by nine feet—and behind it a tiny cold-water kitchen and a water closet. The kitchen had no window. The stairs led up to and over a step straight into the front bedroom. There were three tiny rooms and no landing; one room let into the next and only the front room had a window.

The man who opened the door was small, perhaps thirty-five, with a white rodent face and a whispering voice. "Right y'are, right y'are," he said, rubbing his hands together and bobbing, "come on in. I'll give yis a drink."

"No, thanks." Riada was almost curt. He said to Miro, "This is Paddy Hagan," and left it there. It was of no importance.

"Yer welcome, yer welcome. Ye'll be the officer the colonel said was comin t'see."

The colonel, Miro thought, might have prepared him for his new status. But then, would he have come if Riada had told him? He thought not. Miro made a neutral sound.

Hagan rubbed his palms together and looked about him nervously. He jerked his head from side to side like a wary hen. He seemed to have planned the sequence of events in his mind while he waited for them, and with the fraternal drink cast aside no longer knew what to do. "Come on in the kitchen." He led them in. The floor was of large gray stone tiles. Hagan moved the kitchen table that was set against the wall under the sloping floor of the stairs. He took from the drawer of the table two fine steel rods with flat elbows on their ends. "They were made in the shipyard," he said, grinning slyly, and slid them through narrow slits in the floor on either side of a group of four tiles. The tiles came out together, bonded to a concrete block that sat in a wooden frame in the hole. "When we have somebody on the run he kin go down here. Go on," he said to Miro, "go on down. The colonel wanted us to show ye."

The shaft was wood-lined and had a rough ladder fastened to the lining. It was floored and ran into a well-shored and lined tunnel three feet square. The smell was dank, the air cold. They crawled forward through it by the light of a single naked bulb.

Miro asked Hagan, "How did you get rid of the earth?"

"I'm a carter."

"You're a what?"

"A carter. I have a wee lorry. I cart things, like loads of spuds, and furniture when people flit. If I was cartin bags of spuds we wud put bags of dirt in the cart, and wi furniture we put boxes of dirt, biscuit tins and things, ye see now?"

"I see."

The tunnel ended in an identical shaft. "Laverty's house is up the shaft," Hagan said. "Go on up."

"Hagan," Riada said, "what about the child?"

"What child was that, sur?" He lay on his side, his face against the wall of the tunnel. His voice was flat.

"The child taken today at Ballyweaney. I want the truth about it."

"Holy Jasus! A wee chile? They'll have us all massacreed." The dismay was in the words, not in their tone.

"Take us up," Riada said impatiently.

They came up into Laverty's kitchen, hauled out of the hole by their new host. "They'are, Colonel, they'are," Laverty said and shook hands enthusiastically with Riada and Miro. "That's not a bad wee hole, there now."

"It's well dug," Miro said. "Were you a miner?"

"Och no," Laverty said shyly and grinned with his head hanging. "I'm a gravedigger. They're in the front room, sur."

There were two men in the front room, and they were not like Hagan and Laverty. They were younger, harder, grimmer. They did not pretend to be friendly but sat side by side at a small table as if they were the presiding judges watching the presentation of the prisoners at a revolutionary court-martial. One of them said, "The two of you go on back through the hole and wait," and Laverty and Hagan went without a word and quickly. Laverty did not preside in his own house.

"What is it you want now, Riada?" the one who gave the orders said.

"I want answers, Mahood."

Mahood sat upright, his back very straight, his head high. He was enjoying the insolence of advantage, sitting with his comrade in the only two chairs in the room. The illegal IRA sat in judgment; the Irish army stood, its presence tolerated. Miro remembered now why the tiny kitchen looked so crowded. There were six chairs in it, the kitchen table, the stove and the sink and draining board and cupboards sticking out over the floor space . . .

"We'll hear the questions first. Answers we'll think about. First question?" Mahood said insolently.

Miro stood back against the doorframe. He folded his arms comfortably and let himself slump, studying their faces. Mahood was a big red man with a boyish freckled face. It was a reckless face, darkened at this moment by politic hostility. I wouldn't want him on my side, Miro thought; he thinks big thoughts and wants to do big deeds; he thinks with his bowels.

The other man was lean, tall, sharp-faced. There was no humor in his lines. His eyes moved constantly between Miro and Riada as if he expected some dramatic treachery and was ready. A compulsive conspirator, Miro decided. The roving eyes were peculiarly lifeless, the eyes of an executioner. Miro avoided them, looking past the man's face each time he tried to catch him in a direct stare. Miro smiled. He plays manly games, he thought, stare-me-down games; he's always proving something. They were ridiculous, he decided, in a sinister sort of way, like psychotic adolescents.

Riada walked to the table and leaned on it, his hands cupped under its edge. "Don't try that revolutionary tribunal bullshit on me, sonny," he said quietly. "I came to ask questions and you're going to answer them." He stepped back suddenly and the table came with him. He tossed it behind him.

Mahood and his comrade sat on their chairs, surprised and naked-looking. Mahood's trouser legs were drawn far up. He had pink, hairy calves. Miro saw them and smiled.

"Whod'ye think yer laughin at?" the executioner said.

Miro looked at him directly and said nothing for a while. His smile widened. Then he said, "When I laugh, you'll hear me."

"The child, Mahood," Riada demanded. "Who took the child?"

"What's the odds? It'll turn out the same."

"Who took the child?"

"We didn't. We didn't touch the banks, burn the churches, blow up the customs posts, take Corkey. They're doing it all for us . . ."

"Who is?"

"The Orangemen."

"Taking their own? Corkey? Burning their own churches?"

"Why wouldn't they? *They* want to fight. *We* haven't lifted a finger for weeks. They want a reason. What's the odds who does these things, Riada? They blame the IRA, put out false communiqués, build up a murderous head of steam in the Protestants. Fine. Let them do our work for us. The police don't catch anybody. Why? They don't want to. Fine. When it starts . . ." He stood up, spreading his arms in a big gesture of welcome.

"You want the blood to run, don't you, Mahood?"

"You can't finish something before it starts. When it does, you'll have to come in, and that we want, Colonel." He grinned cheerfully. "There'll be fighting over all the thirty-two counties of Ireland, and what comes out of it won't be your Ireland, it'll be ours." He pointed to the little table, lying on its side. "Now put the table back."

Riada picked up the table. "You're no Michael Collins, Mahood. Your trouble is that you think you are."

"When it comes, we'll see what I am, won't we?"

Riada set the table down in front of them. Mahood sat down and leaned his elbows on it. "If you've no more questions, the door's through there." The revolutionary tribunal was in session again.

Riada turned to the door into the kitchen.

"Riada," Mahood said.

"What?"

"You said you were bringing another officer."

"So."

"I know him." He poked his big red head at Miro. "He's no more one of yours than I am, but you sneaked him in here on a lie and we won't forget it. We've been up over his place. Three years ago it was thirteen Irish farms. Today, it's one American ranch and the Irish farmers are working in the factories across the water. When this is all over, there'll be no foreigners on Irish land. There'll be no foreign owners in the Irish fishing industry. There'll be no foreign owners of Irish stables or chicken farms . . . You're entitled to be told, Mr. Miro."

Miro turned to him. "Thank you, Mr. Mahood. When somebody tries to run me off my home place, come with them. The last chicken farm you people tried to burn down was run by a German. I remember it well. He chased you off his land with a shotgun."

Mahood boomed a laugh that rattled the room. "Take all the comfort you can from it," he said. "You haven't much time. The Orangemen are going to start on us on The Twelfth. Or did you know that, Colonel?"

Riada looked hard at him, then walked quickly to the front door, Miro at his heels.

They went back up the street, away from the fire. Riada said, "We could have gone upstairs and through a hole in the wall to the house behind Laverty's and out into the next street. We've been building these rat runs for a hundred years."

"You're telling me something."

"Yes. Mahood was telling the truth. We have so many informers among them, they're infested. The IRA is sitting on its hands. So who's got Corkey? Who blew the banks, took the child, land-mined those soldiers this morning, killed Tomalty? Bowen wants to talk to you."

"Cows, Stephen. Nothing but cows. I'll defend my own plot and give you a hundred to one against men like those two. Just drive me back to the Royal Avenue and thank you for the visual aid."

They heard the accordion music at the next intersection. "It's in the next street," Riada said.

"I want to see."

They turned right into the next street.

In his preoccupation with other things on their way here, Miro hadn't noticed that they had walked up a long hill from the car to the barricades. He could hear but not see over its lip, and the accordion music grew and with it the sounds of voices. Somewhere on the edge of this bad dream people were laughing and singing.

And dancing. They came slowly over the long lip of the hill and saw first the high light of the flames from the bonfire, then down at the foot of the slow decline, obscurant forms dancing square figures around the burning faggots.

"From dream to dream," Miro said. "In medieval Ireland, did they burn people at the stake?"

"Only in their houses," Riada said. "There's some sort of primitive mystique for us in burning houses." He touched Miro's arm. "Look."

The men with the corpse, which dangled almost to the ground and swung with their step in its canvas carrier, turned a corner into the street, from an intersection halfway down the hill, and walked towards the fire.

Their somber progress was like a pavane seen through the wrong end of a telescope. Their stride was long, with an inexorable slowness, as if their purpose was to transport a corpse in a particular way, by a particular route, to a particular place.

"Am I in bed, do you think? Having a nightmare?" Miro said.

"You'd think they'd be running."

"Why?"

"I don't know."

"They're like medicine men putting a hex on the village."

They found themselves walking well behind but in step with the corpse carriers, who passed between the little cheek-to-cheek houses, looking straight ahead, perhaps into the bonfire that grew larger with every stately stride. It was orange and black now, writhing and leaping tormentedly. The accordion music stopped. The dancing figures stopped. Their faces were distorted in the convulsing light.

The two men bore their burden through them. Shadows and changing shapes and silhouettes leaned towards the stretcher, and white hands fluttered to foreheads and breasts and dropped into the dark again.

Miro and Riada stood back from the edge of the crowd till the shadows and shapes closed behind the pallbearers, like a long swinging gate. Then they walked through the gate among the shapes.

They were young: boys and girls, young men and women with uneasy faces.

"Who's he?" a young girl said to Riada in a frightened voice.

"I don't know. They said at the barricade he was up from the South."

"You're from the South."

"Yes."

"Why aren't there more of ye before we're all dead?"

"Why aren't you at the barricade throwing bottles?"

"We were. We're goin back." Their faces were shifty in the firelight. They watched the men with the corpse, who were walking slowly away up the middle of the street; a frightened boy scratched his chest to cover a shiver. "Jasus," he said. They glanced nervously at one another and not directly at Miro and Riada when they spoke to them. "There'll be none of us left," the girl said again and stared after the corpse. Some of them might have been eighteen, a few were no more than twelve. But they were all children, Miro thought, for you can give a boy of eighteen the vote but you can't make him look on death unless you train him like a soldier; he is still a child. These boys left it to the girls to express their thoughts. They were far from the fury of the battle, the screaming frenzy of the charge into the heat, the hope of destruction across the safe shelter of the flames. But that thing on the stretcher was a corpse. A dead body. The young believe in death only when they meet it. There it was, passing up the street like a dirty plague. Some of them breathed carefully, just enough to do, as if death might infect them. There were no organizers here and no heros. Only children, no longer dancing.

And up the street, no more than a hundred feet from the fire, the two men with the stretcher stopped and stood still. They might have been resting, but their legs were straight and their backs stiff. The young people stared, not knowing what else to do, unstrung by the presence of a temple from which the Holy Ghost had so lately been evicted.

The man in the back of the shafts braced his shoulders and lifted his head. An immense voice roared out of him.

"*Ree-mem-ber,*" it cried, breaking like a shriek. It bounced against the walls of the houses on the narrow street, and the funnel of heat from the fire lifted it up, tortured and deformed like a badly blown bugle blast.

The girl beside Miro shuddered. "O, Mother o' God," she said. "I want to go home."

Riada put a hand on her arm to stop the shaking of her body. "O, Holy Jasus," she said. "Take me home. I want to go home."

"*Ree-memm-berrr,*" the man shrieked again.

"Psychos by the acre," Miro said and drew Riada away.

"Wait, wait," Riada insisted. "Where the hell are they taking that corpse? They're going up that street to the right."

"Take me home," the girl whimpered and stared around at the other children, huddling in their own fear.

They left them with it and went back to the intersection from which the corpse carriers had entered the street; they went left here, following a parallel course, running to the next cross street to wait for the stately progress of the carriers. But when they came, they were not stately; they were running, awkwardly, the corpse swinging and bouncing in its canvas sling. Miro and Riada ran again and waited. And once more. And here they stayed. Up this street, from which they drew back quickly, were two men in white coats, leaning against their ambulance, and in front of the ambulance, a parked car.

Miro said, "I think they carried him alive in that stretcher to within *his* walking distance of the roof. What in God's name for? To get him shot?"

Riada said, "This is it. I want to see it. We're on Protestant ground here."

There was nowhere to hide. The doors of the houses were flush with the street. They hugged the wall around the corner and listened.

The carriers were running down the street, more slowly than before by the sound of it. The voices were distinct: two with untaxed lungs, two gasping for breath.

"Get that rifle outa sight, Matt," an easy voice said.

"Barn . . . Barney . . . first . . . gently with him now . . . gently with him." The ambulance door opened and closed.

"Have ye got the pasteboard plates?" It was another unwinded voice.

"We'll only drop one plate. He said to drop no more than one." That was Matt, with more air in his chest. "He said you two report to the hospital and ask to get off the rest of your shift. Then go to the place and wait there."

"Right, Matt."

"Take it slow in Eglinton Street. We'll jump you just past Eglinton Presbyterian."

"I hope it goes right."

"What can go wrong? It's God's work you're doin. Have you got the letter safe?"

"Aye."

"Away on, then."

Car doors opened and closed. Engines started. The ambulance and the car moved across the intersection.

"I don't believe it," Miro said. "It's a nightmare."

"We can get two of them—if we find a phone and call the hospital."

They ran. But their car was now more than a mile away and they saw no call boxes in the streets they ran through. They were winded when they reached the car. When they got out to an arterial street and found a call box they had no coins. When they tried to get change from the only two people they saw on the street, a young man and his girl, the couple took to their heels and ran.

It was silly.

They drove to Miro's hotel and called the hospital from his room. The hospital was eerily cagey.

"How do you come to have this sort of information?"

"We heard them planning it." Miro felt silly.

"Would you give me an account of how you came to be in a position to overhear them?"

Miro put the phone down. "They're keeping me on till they trace the call. That was a policeman. I'm afraid it's done."

Riada stretched out on Miro's bed. "It makes you feel silly, doesn't it? If we'd gone to the hospital Bowen would have had to get us both out of jail and that would have buggered up a lot of things, including our faces. The police would have tried to beat something we don't know out of us. The RUC wouldn't buy my cooperation for any man's money."

Miro said, "I feel as if I'm in flight, like the mist rolling down Lough Finn in the morning; it makes you feel unreal. Go home, Stephen, wherever home is tonight."

"That's why Bowen wants to talk to you."

"What's why?"

"How can anybody blow this province to bits and nobody know who or where they are? That's unreal. Who were those men tonight and what the hell were they doing? Bowen's frightened. We're frightened. Strong frightens Bowen. He frightens us. It's his friends. It's his effect. It's everything about him. Talk to Bowen."

"No."

Riada got up. "Then bugger you, friend. When the thing starts, there'll have been nothing like it in Ireland since Cromwell put Drogheda to the sword. And if you think you can sit on your arse at Summerfield and watch it pass you by, you're a bigger bloody fool than I thought you were." He took his bottle and slammed the door savagely behind him.

The noise hurt Miro's head. He escaped into sleep.

Five

That which hath been is now; and that which is to be hath already been . . .

The dining room of the Royal Avenue Hotel was on three levels, but it had two moods. The first, its Spanish mood, derived, the management may have supposed, from its Spanish decor: a large white bull in relief on one wall, a large white-and-black bullfighter in relief on another wall, black grillwork, pink tablecloths, and waitresses in black dresses that were tight, short, and shiny. The second, its Ulster mood, derived from the waiters and waitresses. The waiters in their large, loose tailcoats—one of the coats had room in it for another thin waiter—might have been borrowed from the original illustrations in Carelton's *Irish Tales*. The waitresses . . .

Miro made his way up the steps to the third level where there was an unoccupied table.

"That table's durty," a short plump waitress in a short tight dress that exposed short thick legs shouted from the second level.

"Then clean it." Miro smiled down at her over the black iron grillwork of the rail. He might have been a Romeo indifferent to age, speaking downhill to a Juliet indifferent to calories. "I can see you all from here," he said.

Through the Dark and Hairy Wood

The waitress called on her colleagues on all three levels to bear witness. "Whit class o' people wants t'sit at a durty table?" she asked and turned every head on every level in Miro's direction.

Ulster's child is full of grace, he thought, and sat at the table of his choice. A copy of *The Northern Whig* lay on it with a corner in the marmalade. He tore the sticky corners away, ordered two soft-boiled eggs, toast and coffee, and asked his waitress to bring him some fresh marmalade.

"Whit for? Thir's plenty there."

He explained—gently, as he might talk down a half-broken horse—that he wanted marmalade without ink or newsprint.

"Jasus," she said, "what wint up yer nose this mornin?" and took it away. When she brought his eggs she brought back the same marmalade in the same condition. "Right y'are," she said, smiling a challenge at him. He let it pass and read the paper.

Strong was the lead story on the front page. This futile crime, he said, would not turn him from his public duty. Among those present had been Mrs. Strong (injured), Tomalty (dead) and Mrs. Tomalty (in shock), and Mr. John Miro (famous former spy and author). There was more from Captain Strong about cohesion, firm government, and his duty. There was no IRA communiqué. This puzzled the police and Captain Strong.

The word "body" in the headline below caught his eye. Two armed men had ridden an ambulance to the side of a Belfast street and removed the body of a man shot in last night's riots and believed by the police to have been a gunman imported from the South. "I think," a police spokesman said, "that he was somebody high up in the IRA and they felt it important that we shouldn't have a chance to identify him." The alert ambulance crew had recovered a pasteboard license plate that fell from the car when the body snatchers drove off. There was nothing about a "letter." There was nothing about the ambulance crew having gone missing after their shift.

"My eggs," Miro said to the waitress. "I said soft, not raw."

"God," she said, "who got outa the wrong side o' the bed this mornin?" and took them away, flailing the air with her hips. When she came back he had gone.

51

He phoned Eva. Their talk was the important inconsequential talk of those settled in their love for one another. Yes, he was fine; yes, everything was going according to plan; yes, he'd be home on time; yes, he missed them and loved them dearly and wished he were at home; yes, he'd had dinner at the Strongs. What kind of people? Odd. Well, sad in an Ulster sort of way. Hard to describe, exactly. Unimportant anyway. "I'll not be asking them to Summerfield." No, he hadn't seen anybody else they knew and had no plans to see anybody about anything but bulls.

"Why are you lying to me, Miro? I heard the news this morning. I want you home, love, please, now."

O God. "Just to save you worry, love. Look, I'll finish today, stay in Coleraine tonight, and come home in the morning. I'm safe—no danger . . ."

That was stupid of him. He should have known that if *The Whig* had it, the BBC and Radio Eireann had it. He felt stupid, but mainly he felt guilty.

He phoned the Mid-Antrim Stock Farms and explained that he couldn't get to them till the afternoon.

Then he called the desk to order a taxi.

"But your car's here, sir. At the door."

"My car?"

"Yes, sir. The young fellow brought it back. He left the keys at the desk and just said, 'Tell him Mac brought his car back and thanks very much.'"

The keys were in an envelope with a note. It said, "The number you're looking for is VMX613H. If you change your mind about seeing the Colonel, call 01-871-3408." He strolled to the corner at Castle Junction, turned and read the numbers on the parked cars as he sauntered back, took the right one and the road to Carrickfergus. The business annoyed him. Bowen had his car hauled off for repairs. Bowen provided him with another car. Bowen was trying to surround him. He'd see the bull at Coleraine tonight and be home first thing in the morning—in Bowen's car. Bowen could send a driver across the Border with his own car and take this one back. To hell with Bowen. He was resolute. Eva was frightened.

The nurse at the cottage hospital said, "It's out of visitin hours. Ye can't see Mrs. Strong."

Hospital rules are hospital rules, the doctor said. "Call her room," Miro insisted and watched the doctor's face light up with obsequious agreement. "Of course, Mrs. Strong," he smiled at the invisible lady, "I'll bring him along myself."

She was sitting up in bed, with strips of tape on both arms and a strip on her left cheek. She held out a hand for him to touch. "Don't move the chair. Come and sit on the bed—on my right. My left looks sinister when I smile." She smiled to prove it. Then she remembered. "It was good of you to come." The strain in her eyes was intense.

She was wearing a hospital shroud, almost up to her chin in front and tied loosely at the back. "They wouldn't let me have anything else," she said. "They're putting a policeman on the gate at the house. What good will that do? They disarm the police and then send them to guard M.P.'s and their families against bombers." Her nerves were strung. "I . . ." She folded her hands, composing herself. "Mrs. Tomalty's at her sister's. She refused to come back. She says that bomb wasn't meant for my husband. It was meant for hers, she says. The Protestants did it, she says, because they were Catholics working for Protestants . . ."

"Has she been here?"

"No. Her niece brought a note. I got it this morning. Here . . ." It was on her bedside cabinet.

"I won't read it," he said. His book was lying beside it on the cabinet.

"I've been reading your book," she said, "or trying to. The doctor brought me his copy . . . Mr. Miro . . . look . . . In your book, people . . . do people really always call you just Miro?"

"Most people."

"Why?"

"I don't know."

"May I?"

"Yes."

"I'm frightened."

"I can see that."

"I'm not badly hurt. Just cuts."

"I can see that too. I'm glad."

"I'm frightened. You know a lot about this sort of thing. Your book . . . I mean, these people . . . I'm not making sense . . . They're going to start killing one another like savages . . ." She breathed deeply, folded her hands again in her lap and said, "I must stop this." She sat quietly for a moment. "Your visit was horribly disrupted. But you'll come back now and finish it, won't you?"

"I'd like to. But my wife heard about this on the radio. She wants me to come straight home. I told her I'd be home in the morning. Your husband . . ."

"Yes." She smiled a twisted smile, not far from tears. "He'll not be home. He'll not be here, I expect. He hasn't been yet, anyway." She looked at him frankly. "He was too busy when that bomb went off to ask me if I'd mind not bleeding to death till he got top political mileage out of it . . . I shouldn't be saying this. Miro?"

"Yes?"

"Please come to the house. Your work . . . your book . . . I'd feel better with a man like you in the house. I know you have your own affairs . . ."

"Can't you stay here awhile?"

"Till my husband has time to think about me? They told me here I could go home tonight. It's not knowing who did it or why. They could kill me . . ."

He couldn't bring himself to say no, brutally. "Stay here tonight," he said. "You'll be safe here . . . They'll agree, won't they?"

"Oh, yes. I'm Mrs. Ronald Strong."

"I'll see what arrangements I can make and phone in the morning. How will that do just now?"

"You'll come. I know you'll come. In a few days I'll go to England. I don't care whether my husband likes it or not. He beats the government for not , . . but what *good* he's doing . . ." She let it drift away. "Your face is bruised," she said with an effort.

It was relief. He told her about it, but not about Riada. "I'd know them all again," he said. "The ambulance men too. And Barney. I'd know that face in its grave."

"These people are the awfullest damned people . . . Sometimes I can't abide any of them. You've told the police?"

"No." He smiled. "I was planning to bolt. It isn't my quarrel."

"It isn't mine. They're terrible people when this sort of thing breaks out." She lay back. "Some of them are very nice." She was tired. "What's your program today?"

He told her. Mid-Antrim Stock Farms at three. To buy a bull. "I'll have to go," he said.

"You'll phone in the morning?"

"I will."

"It's a big house. A policeman at the gate is nothing. You know. It's to have a man in the house. A man like you. You can do things. The way you bandaged me, put me to . . . put me to bed like a nurse. The doctor said your bandaging was very good . . . you were very kind and good. If you'd sleep in the room next to mine. The house is full of doors and windows. Would you? Am I being stupid?"

"No. I'll call. Stay here tonight. And you must relax." He took her hand to say goodbye, and she held on. "You'll be fine tomorrow," he said. "You had a severe shock."

She let him go. "I'll read more of your book." She was smiling unconvincingly when he closed the door.

"Goddammit," he said and walked slowly down the corridor. The doctor waylaid him. Miro said, "She's frightened. Why don't you keep her here?"

"Beds, you know. We need them."

"You can manage another night."

"Oh, yes. I was going to ask you about that book she has. One of my colleagues brought it to her. It's yours?"

"Yes. Good morning." Damn him too.

Captain Strong came in as Miro went out. "My dear fellow, this is good of you. I've just been to the house. I thought you'd be there."

"I went to a hotel."

"How is she?"

"Terrified."

"Yes. No need of course. The police . . ."

"She asked me to come back, since you're so busy. Couldn't something be arranged?"

"I really do regret all this, old man. But if you could possibly do it . . . finish your visit, I mean. She's probably a bit hysterical. Shock, you know. Women can't absorb this sort of experience the way we do. You can see what sort of bind we're in. The balloon's about ready to go up. I'm running every hour. Things are breaking . . . Do you think you possibly could?"

"I'll see." Why didn't he say it frankly? She's a damned nuisance to me just now—take her off my hands, old boy.

"Your face . . . ?" But Strong's mind wasn't on that either.

"Your wife asked me the same question. She'll tell you. It's a long answer. I'm running too."

"You'll not forget the Tomalty inquest . . ."

"They can call me." Strong always remembered the inquest, he noticed, whether his wife was bleeding in an ambulance or frightened in a hospital bed. Was his hospital visit public relations? "Captain," the doctor said. "Captain," the nurses said as they passed, and Strong raised his hand in response, lacking only a balcony. The doctor lurked. Miro said, "Goodbye," and walked out.

He slammed the car door. The woman was none of his business. She had a husband, even if he was a selfish bastard. He had Eva to worry about. But Mrs. Strong nibbled at him from somewhere, on the road to Belfast.

He checked out of the Royal Avenue Hotel, put his bag in the trunk like a man bringing something to an end. It was noon. With a feeling of liberation he went to look for somewhere to have lunch and left himself an hour to get to the stock farms. They were north of Belfast. It was the road home.

Charley Ballinger, the farm manager, was an easy, companionable man. Miro felt a long way from the turmoil of Northern politics and put them from his mind. He knew the animal he wanted, and within an hour the deal was complete.

"Teatime," Ballinger said, and when they had eaten their ritual buttered bread and fruit cake he said with pride, "Come and see my guns." They were fine guns: shotguns and rifles. Things to be proud of.

"I didn't think it was all that easy to own guns here. They're all registered?"

"All registered. All legal."

"Is it easy for anybody?"

"Well . . ." Ballinger turned the question away, smiling. "Pick one and come out and try it."

Miro would have preferred to take the road to Coleraine, but he was easy in his mind and spirit. Home was ahead. He followed Ballinger among his buildings, down a farm lane lined with great chestnut trees, and into a long hollow with, at the far end of it, twelve man-figure targets in front of a high dyke of sand, earth, and railroad sleepers.

"Pick your man and call your shots," Ballinger said and gave him a box of shells. "I put fresh cards on them this morning." The range was a hundred and fifty yards.

"In the head, on the first man," Miro said and laid his shot in. "Left chest . . . Right chest." They walked to the targets. The hits were where he called them. "Empty cans would be harder to hit and less expensive," he said.

Ballinger laughed. "It's not my range," he explained. "When the government disbanded the B Special police because the Catholics said they were an armed political police force, us old B Specials got permits to form private gun clubs. This is one of them." He winked in expectation of understanding. "We keep the eye in."

"For what?"

"For *what? The Whig* said you were at Strong's when they blew up his man."

"I was."

"Well, that's what for. It's coming, you know. Any day. We can't thole this much longer." Ballinger's broad red face was suddenly redder, darker. "The sooner it starts the sooner it's over. Once and for all, this time."

Miro didn't argue. "In Ulster, don't argue with Catholics or Protestants," Shamus Riada always told him. "All mental doors are closed and barred."

"I'd like to look through your big barn before I go," Miro said. "I could use one like it."

"You can't trust them," Ballinger said, heading towards the barn.

"Who?"

"The papishes. The Fenians. They want to bring us down. For fifty years they've been trying to destroy us. Every time you trust them they start at it again—bombing and burning." He stopped suddenly. "They're like bloody savages." His expression was black. "And kidnapping, by Christ. Corkey and that child! Holy Christ! It's got to end . . . the sooner it starts, the sooner it'll be done with. Once and for all." He plunged into the barn.

Miro heard one voice only. Mahood-Ballinger, he called it. "The sooner it starts, the sooner it's over." He couldn't keep his mind on the barn.

Ballinger was talking about the loading winches beside the three loading doors on the top floor when Miro heard the car. He looked out and saw it park by the stone gatepost at the end of the farm road. Three men got out, looked about them cautiously, and ran up the road to the yard. One of them was Matt. The other two were the men who dug bait on the shore at Strong's.

"Look, Ballinger. Do you know them?"

"No. What the hell . . ."

Miro caught his arm. "Stay here." Two of the men scouted the yard and disappeared from sight. The third man, carrying a black box under his arm, ran to Miro's car, put the black box on the ground, opened the hood, took from the box a light-colored canister with lead wires hanging from it, and leaned far into the engine.

"What the hell is he doing?" Ballinger said impatiently.

"Attaching an explosive charge to my ignition."

"Come on!"

Miro held him. "Stay put, will you! How do you know they aren't carrying those neat little gelignite bombs that are so popular in Belfast? Maybe you want one of them lobbed in here under us?"

"Oh." It was the sound a man makes when nothing at all has occurred to him. "What're you going to do? Just sit here?"

"That's all. Now shut up and wait."

"Wait for what?"

"Wait for the other two to show again. They're looking out for that character in my car. Will you sit tight, for God's sake?"

Ballinger settled. Miro checked the rifle in his hand and sighted it. He refilled the clip and shot it home again.

"Are you going to shoot him?" Ballinger whispered anxiously.

"Shut up." The man rose out of the engine, picked up his box from the ground, and waved his arm. Matt and the other lookout appeared, and the three of them ran for their car.

Miro sighted on the car. Its hood was hidden behind the stone gatepost. His sights were on the window above the back seat. He squeezed the trigger, and the three men leaped for the ditch of the farm road and rolled over. They were out of sight, covered by the bank. Slowly, Miro put six shots into the windows of the car, moving from back to front. Then he waited. The men were crawling towards their car under cover of the bank. He saw a head occasionally, as they rose to run, bending low. Then they bolted, weaving and bending, and flung themselves over the bank that covered the lower half of their car.

"I need luck," Miro said, "so keep still and quiet."

The gun was solid in his hands. He let the men crawl carefully into the car. It moved slowly. He had one shell in the chamber, three in the clip. The nose of the car moved out from behind the gatepost and he let go four fast shots. The car lurched and slumped, forward and right, and took off bumping and bobbing. He could see the driver wrestling the wheel. The front right tire was out.

"We can go now. To a phone." They scrambled for the house.

Miro called the number Mac Donnell had given him. "My name is Miro," he said and waited.

"My name is Bowen," a reedy little voice said and seemed to chuckle.

"I'm at the Mid-Antrim Stock Farms. Three men just planted an explosive in my car engine. Their car won't take them anywhere fast, but they're trying to drive it towards Belfast. I've seen all three of them before. Get off your arse and find them. And send a squad to get this thing off my car. *Then* I want to see *you.*"

"God is good," Bowen said. "We'll send a squad and one of them will lead you to me."

Miro put up the phone and sat in an armchair, his shoulders hunched, his chin on his chest. Mrs. Strong knew he was coming here. Nobody but Mrs. Strong and Ballinger knew, and at what time. He was silent for a long time, brooding on Mrs. Strong. And on Matt. And on the men on the foreshore. And on Strong.

Ballinger sat within the silence, brooding on Miro. "I thought you were going to kill that man," he said at last.

"Have you ever killed a man, Mr. Ballinger?"

"I've never killed anything but a hare."

"But you talk death as if you were talking about hares." He rolled out of his chair. " 'The sooner it starts, the sooner it's over,' " he quoted. "You think so, Mr. Ballinger?"

The shot-up car was four hundred yards down the road, empty; *of course* they had a back-up car and driver standing by. He paced till the squad came and a young man wearing tweeds and a wispy mustache said, "I'm to take you to Colonel Bowen, sir."

"Where?"

"The Deer's Cry Press."

"The what?" That was Bowen all right. "Go ahead," he said when they lifted the explosive from his engine.

A young soldier said, "They've got a ruddy practice range down there, sir. Wotd'they need that for 'ere?"

"Shooting hares," Miro said, "at the moment," and followed the young man with the wispy mustache.

Six

And I beheld, and lo, a black horse

Miro pulled out past the tweedy young man and waved him to the side of the road. "Will you," he said, "for the love of God be a lot less sedate and put your bloody foot down?" The young man put his foot down.

The house was the old Congregational Manse, up past the North Road Graveyard on the hill above Carrickfergus. The sign on the open gate said,

THE DEER'S CRY PRESS

That was Bowen, all right. Miro had always been sure certain aspects of intelligence attracted Bowen because he was a repressed prankster. In the glass porch of the house a card with Celtic symbols around its edges said,

> *I bind unto myself today*
> *The strong name of the Trinity,*
> *By invocation of the same*
> *The Three in One, and One in Three.*

It was a verse from St. Patrick's hymn, known to some as

"The Deer's Cry" and to some as "Patrick's Breastplate." Another day it would have made Miro smile. That was Bowen.

In the square hall a girl sat in a cane armchair beside a desk. Her skirt was high, her legs crossed, her hands flying at her knitting and her eyes flying over the pages of a book propped on the desk. She swept them all away and her skirt down in one experienced movement when he opened the door, but he saw the title of the book, *The Sensuous Woman*. The girl gave him a synthetic Christian smile.

"Where's Colonel Bowen?"

"Up here—watching you," a little voice said from the turn of the stairs.

The hair was long, luxurious back and sides, black, and in retreat from the forehead; the man had melancholy eyes and a vaguely semitic face with a Jesus-beard that cut a triangular wedge in his clerical collar. The body was slight and stooped a little, as if from too much meditation. "Good evening," he said, descending, and lowered himself down from the bottom step, searching the floor for hostility. "Come in here."

The room was laid out like a Christian Science reading room, but the shelves were stacked high with Bibles, tracts, gospel songbooks and scripture portions, daily readings and prayers for people.

That was Bowen, all right. It was like him to conscript Patrick in an Ireland to which the snakes he had driven out centuries ago had returned. One time, Miro remembered, Patrick was to be waylaid by men concealed on the road he was traveling; knowing this, Patrick made up a hymn and sang it as he passed their ambush. All the men saw was a red deer passing. Ever since that time, the hymn has been called "The Deer's Cry" or "The Breastplate of Patrick." That was Bowen. Miro's sense of unreality grew.

"We're colporteurs, Bible hawkers," Bowen said. "We hawk the good word door to door all over the province. The Bible in the North is like a high explosive—it opens doors . . ."

"And wrecks cars. You wanted to talk about Strong. Talk. I'm in a hurry to see him." He pressed Bowen into a chair and sat opposite him across a reading table.

"I'm glad to see you again, Miro."

"Agreed. So get to Strong."

Bowen turned a Bible in circles on the table. "I'd like to be in Yemen," he said. His melancholy eyes looked liquid.

"You're here. I have a personal interest in Strong. What's yours?"

Bowen said gloomily, "Did you know you can tell an Irish Catholic by his eyes? Dark gray eyes. Like slate roofs in the moonlight on a wet night. Did you know that?"

"I've heard it said. What about Strong?"

Bowen opened the Bible and appeared to read from it. "Other truths are vouchsafed to us here." He sounded like an Ulster Presbyterian minister in exposition. "Catholics aren't as clean as Protestants. Did you know *that?* Catholics are more criminal than Protestants. You can't trust Catholics. Their part of town is always dirtier than our part. If you put a bathroom in a Catholic's house, do you know what he'll do? He'll use the lavatory seat to frame his grandmother's picture. He'll keep coal in the bath. Did you know all this? Ask anybody."

"I've heard it all. Get to Strong."

"I'm talking about Strong." That was Bowen, all right. Miro let him talk. "Have you ever been to bed with a brown-eyed Irish Catholic?"

"Yes."

"So have I. But then we're not Ulster Protestants. If an Ulster Protestant goes to bed with a brown-eyed Irish Catholic he tells her he likes her dark gray eyes; and if she says 'Look at them, for God's sake—they're brown,' he says, 'Holy Jasus, wuman, ye don't know the color of yir own eyes!' "

"You've made the point."

"If I'm sitting in a nice Catholic house in a nice housing development in Derry, or Greenisland, or Springfield, or in a new apartment block in Catholic Bogside, they'll say to me, 'Ye kin see fur yerself—they keep us livin like pigs.' If I'm talking to the Catholic half of the eight-hundred-strong work force at Monsanto's works, they'll say to me, 'The American companies won't hire Catholics—the government tole them not to.' "

"You've made the point."

Bowen wagged his finger aggressively in Miro's face. "Ulster
is a great midden of that sort of farmyard shit, so ripe and rich
from centuries of shit-piling that the most amazing wild flowers
grow in it. The rain falls on it in abundance, and God's hus-
bandmen in their pulpits in churches and chapels turn it every
Sunday . . ."

"Shorten it, Bowen."

"And Strong and his friends water it till it's full of gas pockets
and explosions, scattering shit over everybody . . ."

"Very picturesque. Is that all you've got on him?"

"I haven't got anything on him except his ambition and the
ambitions of his friends. I can't put men on him because the
place is cross-hatched with connections till you don't know who
you're talking to. If I'm caught sniffing at Strong there'll be
bloody murder and I'll find myself posted to . . . what far out-
posts have we left now? But *he* asked *you* here. *You* were with
him when his man was killed. Don't leave, Miro. You're right in
on him. You're an outsider. You're his guest. Smell him out for
us. Dig around him. Put your tricks to work."

"Why? His ambition isn't good enough."

"Who benefits from chaos? This place is like a shriek now.
Who feeds the paranoia? Strong hammers away at the government. He wants to be Prime Minister . . ."

"Has he ever said so?"

"Not bloody likely. *He* never *makes* a precise statement. *He*
never *calls* for an Ulster unilateral declaration of independence
with the Queen as head of state, *but some of his friends do. He*
never *demands* more troops and an all-out bash at the IRA, *but
some of his friends do.* Does he ever deny them, contradict
them? Not bloody likely. He stands, Olympian . . ."—Bowen
held his arms and his head up dramatically and tried to make his
little voice boom—". . . on a thousand platforms in the middle
of a thousand fields in front of a thousand microphones and calls
for *strength* and *cohesion* . . . and he never mentions their
bloody ignorant bigotry, but he talks to it all the time. *He* never
calls for a provisional government of strength to deal with this
chaos—but his friends do." He picked up the Bible and threw it
at a wall. "I'll tell you this—when twelve men talk about a pro-

64

visional government, there's a good chance that only one of them knows where the chaos comes from that they're so anxious to cure."

"Strong, in your book?"

"Bloody right."

"And not a sausage?"

"Not a sausage."

"I have a sausage."

Bowen jumped. "What have you?"

"First things first, Bowen. Let me read your little mind. You're a conspirator by nature. You see plots everywhere. You see a coup d'état?"

"Bloody right."

"Done in what way?"

Bowen said, "Look. In some African or Arab republic, the army can take over. It has the guns. In our kind of society, armed takeovers are too complicated. So you create social and political chaos by planned violence—not by the exercise of power you haven't got, but by violence that makes people afraid, and then, when the source is identified, makes them angry enough to turn to violence themselves. Chaos! And all the time you're preparing the public to demand the alternative *you've* compelled them to look for *and at—you and your friends*. You don't *seize* power, you *inherit* it, to deal with the chaos *you* create. One man in a provisional government is always a political criminal."

"Strong?"

"In my book. He has the skill, he has the nerve and he has the motive."

"What's his motive?"

"His rating in the social system is only second class. I have a filing system on him and his friends. Gilbert Highet developed the system and he got it from the ancient Romans. Use it right and it'll tell you who's coming up in the scales and who's going down. I know their personal histories, some of their problems, their family histories, who their friends are, where their money's invested . . . Take Oliphant, editor of *The Whig*. He was born in Coleraine. Went to England. Became a key man on the *Daily*

Telegraph. Was offered the editorship of *The Whig* and came home. He had visions of importance, power, influence. He finds he's only the number-four editor in Belfast—frustrated ambition, not in the councils of power, bitter, a hero to a few university professors, but his circulation's falling—or was till he became the bigots' editorialist for 'strength and cohesion.' Now he wants a unilateral declaration of independence. He'd be minister of information in Strong's government. Take either of Strong's two trade-union friends. They can't get closed shops anywhere. With UDI and a free hand, every bloody housewife would be unionized. So it goes on. Strong? He married the daughter of the wrong general. He went to the wrong schools, joined the wrong regiment the wrong way. Second class all the way from birth. *And he hates it.* He's ruthless, full of humiliations and resentments, cold and cunning. What's your sausage?"

"Only Strong and his wife and Ballinger knew I was going to the Mid-Antrim Stock Farms at three today. Only you and Riada and Strong and his wife knew I saw Matt and Barney and the ambulance men last night . . ."

"God is good!"

"And the three men who planted that clanker in my car were —Matt and the two who were on the beach at Strong's when Tomalty was killed."

"Sweet Jesus. *We–are–cooking.*"

"Are we? You said the people get violent themselves when they identify the source of the violence. Riada says you haven't."

"Come upstairs. I've things to show you." He led the way, leaping the risers like a whippet.

The room upstairs looked out at the back on the golf course, and at the side, to the North Road graveyard behind a screen of trees. "You're between the quick and the dead," Miro said.

"All devout men are aware of this delicate balance," Bowen said piously. "Look at the stuff on my desk."

It consisted of printed materials and enlargements of it. Bowen handed Miro an IRA manifesto on the recovery from foreigners of Irish business and industry. It promised to burn out every foreign-owned business and restore it to Irish ownership.

Specifically, it named the fishing industry, horse breeding, chicken farming, silver mining, and cattle breeding. He examined enlargements of the type.

"This," Bowen explained, "was printed on an IRA hand press Riada and his branch knew all about. It operated in the back of a little sweet shop in Lifford, just across the Border." He took up the IRA communiqué left when Dr. Corkey was taken. "This was printed on the same press."

"You're telling me something."

"One day ten weeks ago, on early-closing day, the press, the type, and the stock of paper was lifted. It took a crew to do that, a lorry and somebody who knew how to run a lorry across the Border. Six weeks ago these incessant outrages began and the communiqués started—on the press we've been hunting for ever since. The IRA hasn't got it. It was this press that got Riada into the act. He knew it was missing. He asked us to let his branch see the communiqués. We thought he had a hell of a nerve, but we went along. His people and ours both proved it's the same press. That's when we began to get scared—on both sides of the Border. The IRA says the Irish and the British governments are working hand in glove—and in spite of the public disagreements on both sides, it's true. Who wants another civil war? The IRA does. Who else? Let's find out, old friend."

"Do I get cover?"

"Mac Donnell. That's all."

"I want some sort of identification that looks official in case the police nick me."

"We have some very nice forgeries. If you're caught and the police question them, we'll expose them as forgeries."

"If I risk my neck, I call the shots."

"Officially, I can't agree to that, and I can't send a wet nurse with you wherever you go."

"I want a gun."

"I can't agree to that either, but if you steal one here in the house when I'm out of the room, how am I to know?"

"Which phone gets me out?" There were three on Bowen's desk, green, red, and blue.

"Green."

Miro called Eva. It was a difficult conversation. She was worried. She was angry. She was adamant. "Look, love," he said, "I'm not sure about this bull. There's too much money involved to make a mistake. There's another animal I want to see. Just a couple of days, love, and I'll come leaping over the mountain . . ."

He said miserably, when he put down the phone, "That's the second time I've lied to her today. The first time was this morning and she caught me. There's something very childish about lying to your wife."

"Sit lightly to it, Miro, old boy. Everybody does it."

"Yesterday," he said, "everybody didn't. I didn't."

They ate. "What does your card index system tell you about Mrs. Strong?"

"Ah! We get to her at last, do we?"

"Is that something subtle? Sometimes I think you're a dirty little bastard, Bowen."

"Not dirty. Lecherous. And that feels great in a clerical collar. She's attractive. Her father was one of the unknown generals. They're from Durham. She's what we call a Geordie—the hottest women in England."

"You've checked?"

"From John O' Groats to Land's End. She's never quite fitted in Ulster. Never took them as seriously as they take themselves —nor the things they take seriously. Hasn't been a help to him in his political career—offended the right people at the wrong time. Nice woman, though, the cards say. Lonely. No relatives now. Odd thought that, isn't it? No parents, aunts, cousins, second cousins. Strong neglects her for politics. Stopped taking her anywhere. When he had a public debate a few years ago with Gerry Fitts, the Nationalist Member of Parliament, she was on the platform and laughed at all Fitts' jokes about her husband. That was the end of her public appearances . . ."

"Any scandal? Talk?"

"Not here. She goes to London occasionally. I've heard it said 'to have a man in comfort.' It isn't true."

"How do you know?"

Bowen grinned. "I had her tailed for a week. She hasn't had a man for at least a couple of years, I'd say. He sleeps at the back of the house, she sleeps at the front. Mrs. Tomalty had a niece living-in for a while. One of my men got a line on their comings and goings from the niece one morning about three, in a haystack. No sex. For Mrs. Strong, that is. The Tomalty girl was different. 'I don't know how she does without it,' she said."

Miro called the hospital. "I'll come and take you home later tomorrow," he told her, "unless your husband made some other arrangement?"

"None. He got an extra policeman. One at the gate, one on the grounds."

"Armed?"

"Unarmed."

"You'd better plan to spend some time in England soon. I can't stay more than a day or two . . ."

"Thank you," she said. "Thank you so much. I'm very grateful . . ." She was all cool cream English restraint. What are Englishwomen of her kind like in bed, he wondered. Do they preside over the event, like chairwomen of Women's Institutes? The Englishwomen he'd known in bed were all widowed landladies. They didn't belong to the Women's Institute.

"Work on her, Miro old boy," Bowen said. "She'll drop something. There's got to be something he does or doesn't do that isn't right, that doesn't fit. She'll know it even if she doesn't know she knows. She'll drop it. I want to see the news," he said. "The Cabinet's meeting. Our word is that there's going to be curfew, and a ban on all parades, and maybe martial law. That'll hit both sides equally. That'll provoke bloody murder."

He watched the news. The Prime Minister of Northern Ireland took advantage of the fact that almost everybody watched this edition of the news, and made a statement. The situation was grave. The situation was fraught with danger. He surveyed recent events and public anger. Because of the danger inherent in the situation, this evening the Cabinet had decided to ban all parades for an indefinite period. All forms of political assembly were banned as of now. A curfew was to be imposed from tomorrow night, lasting from 10 P.M. until 6 A.M. The gravity of the situation justified this drastic action. All sections of the community were asked to cooperate.

The tape had clearly been made earlier in the evening. The BBC had time to find and record reactions to this drastic action.

Captain Ronald Strong: He looked very well on television; it was the look of a solid, thoughtful, responsible man, deeply troubled. "We are threatened by chaos," he said, "and the people are forbidden to meet to discuss it." It was carefully calculated. He refused to say more. "This is not a moment for glib answers to glib questions." Why did he appear, when he was in his own house, to be something less than he appeared to be on the screen?

The editor of *The Whig*, Mr. Andrew Oliphant, a heavily jowled man, fat, immobile-looking, with a growling hoarseness in a deep voice: "The Cabinet has an immense talent for negative action. I notice that the Prime Minister did not announce the recovery of Dr. Corkey or the cruelly abducted child. Nor did I hear him mention any significant arrests. The search goes on, he said. So do the political crimes."

Mr. John Stevens, union leader: "Are union study sessions political assemblies? Because we're having plenty of them tomorrow. The telegrams are on their way. *No, it isn't a strike!* We're holding study sessions, I said. In the open air—football fields, mostly. Where else can we find the space for the crowds we'll get? We'll use ploughed fields if we have to. Speakers? Strong, myself, Oliphant, the Grand Master. People like that. Arrests? *I'd like to see them try it.*"

The Worshipful Grand Master of the Orange Order: "I will only say this: His announcement prevents the lodges marching to church on The Twelfth Sunday. *Does the Prime Minister think he will tell us when, where and how we will worship God?* It prevents our remembrance of The Twelfth the following day. *Does the Prime Minister think he can direct us to abandon our heritage?* We will hold our church parades on The Twelfth Sunday, and we will commemorate our heritage on The Twelfth, if we have to carry guns instead of banners, fifes, and drums. I am telling him that now. There will be no surrender, to him or any other compromiser.''

"That, I would say, was a call to do battle." Bowen put his feet up on a chair. "Interesting thing about television," he said. "When the man in power makes a statement, the telly can never find anybody who agrees with him. All those quacks are from the Strong gang." He switched off the television. "We have five days to arrest somebody or order out a burial detail. I'm going to bed."

Miro couldn't sleep. He went back to the room with the green and blue and red phones, and had to fight the pressure within him to call Eva and tell her he was coming home. He stood by the window and stared at the trees around the graveyard. The moon shone in. When he turned he saw the small flat gun on Bowen's desk, and a pile of shells. He took them back to his room and lay awake. His mind jumped nervously. He was making a mistake. Go home, his nerves told him. He was married, a father, substantial; no longer loose and paid for this sort of thing. He was being stupid.

He rebuked himself and shifted his mind. Strong was impressive on television; he seemed to diminish in his wife's presence. Why? Matt and Barney. Where do you put the corpse of a beloved brother? In a graveyard? No. But not just anywhere; he's your brother. He recalled how the two men embraced before Barney went up the ladder to the roof. They knew, by God, they both knew. What kind of people . . . ? Where do you put the corpse of your brother? Consumptive . . . ? Barney was rotten with consumption. Consumption is a notifiable disease. Barney didn't get that sick without leaving a trail. He drifted into sleep and was surprised when he awoke that he had been asleep at all.

Seven

God, who at sundry times and in divers manners spake in time past unto the fathers by the prophets . . .

He was a liar.

He cut himself shaving.

He had been a liar most of his life; for twenty-five years with The Firm it was his profession. His self-esteem rested in Eva's view of him, and twice yesterday he lied to her and once she knew he lied. It made him jumpy. Why didn't he tell her the truth and risk a quarrel? You can mend a quarrel; what do you do about deceit?

He packed again and put his things in the car. Bowen and Mac Donnell went out with him.

Bowen said, "The Strong woman's starved, Miro. Work on her. Women in bed'll tell you anything after a good round."

"You're a dirty little bastard, Bowen."

"It's depression that makes me that way. You'd better get us something. The RUC can't find those two ambulance men and all their employment records were dead men's . . ."

"Dead men from where?"

"Coleraine. We're checking backwards on them from the grave to the cradle. Maybe there'll be something. You're going over to Strong's?"

"I'm going to look for a corpse."

"I'd rather you went over to Strong's."

Miro said impatiently, "Do you want me to skin this cat?"

"You know damn well . . ."

"So it's my way or not at all, Bowen."

"Do what he says, Mac," Bowen said.

Mac Donnell said, "Where do you want me, sir?"

"Keep a way back from me. I want to know you're there. I don't want to see you there."

"Strong's speaking at their big rally in Larne just after lunch," Mac Donnell told him. "From there he's billed to go to Coleraine for an evening one. They've announced that it'll last till eleven—an hour after curfew. They're really putting the boot to the Prime Minister."

Miro took the road to Belfast and turned off to the sanatorium. He didn't watch for Mac Donnell.

He got past the hospital superintendent's secretary with difficulty and a little unpleasantness and his questionable identity card. No matter how immediate the crisis, he thought, there is always a bureaucrat whose status is more immediate. He stuck his credentials under the superintendent's nose.

"I see," the doctor said. "A kind of James Bond, with rank."

Miro sat down. "From the Prime Minister's statement last night you will appreciate the urgency of my questions. I need information about a patient of yours . . ."

"The connection escapes me. Information about our patients is confidential."

"Doctor," Miro said. "Did you *hear* the Prime Minister last night?"

"Didn't everybody?"

"In the situation he described, do you want me to record officially that all I got from you was bloody snoot? You're a government servant, man, and the government is in a very bad temper."

"Ask your questions," the doctor snapped, and his thin white nose quivered.

"He was six feet standing straight, and he weighed no more than ninety pounds, maybe a lot less. He had a scar down his cheek from the ear to the jaw. Left side. He was rotten with consumption."

The doctor's expression was peculiar. "We would say his illness was terminal. Where is he?"

"What does that mean?"

"You described a man who was here for three days. He walked up the drive . . . well, he was seen weaving up the drive by the doorman. I only know of this because of events. The doorman thought he was a drunk till he got close . . . What about this man?"

"What events?"

"He disappeared . . . night before last . . ."

"How?"

"Nobody knows how it happened. He was in isolation."

"His name was Barney what? From where?"

"Barney? That's his name? He had the health card of a man called Fred Davison. When he disappeared, the police had the medical bureaucracy hurry up their record processing. Fred Davison was killed in a car crash three months ago."

"Could this man Barney have come far under his own steam?"

"No. He was dying. Our assumption was that relatives who'd been hiding a man, rotten—as you say—with a terminal and notifiable illness, panicked and left him at the gate. That sort of thing happens. He hadn't the strength to come far on his own."

"Why would he come here, dying, and then run out?"

"That's really your problem, isn't it? I'd say medicine. Drugs. Maybe he felt a little better after medication that evening and believed in medical magic? Maybe he wanted back to his attic. These people are like that. He was an ignorant man, they tell me. A religious nu . . ." He caught himself.

"Nut?"

"Nut. They abound."

"I want everything you know about this Fred Davison."

The doctor asked the formidable woman outside to bring the information.

Miro put it in his pocket. "I want a picture of this man Barney"—and when he saw the doctor's face—"a word picture."

"Well, he was dying. All we could do was drug him. You'll get your best picture from the chaplain. He spent a lot of time with him. You'd waste your time with the medical staff. You'd also waste *their* time," he said maliciously.

"Let's take a walk, Padre," Miro suggested. He didn't like breathing in this place. He didn't like the smell. The disease frightened him.

They walked in the drive. The chaplain was tall, middle-aged, white-haired, and genial. He had very large eyes and seemed to like to touch people. Miro didn't like being touched.

"He wandered a lot in his mind," the chaplain said. "He wasn't long for this world, Captain. Where is he, by the way?"

"We're looking for him."

"I see. The police are too, of course. He's a walking plague, you see. I'm afraid he'll miss the Second Coming. Of course, you're not interested in his health?" It was a sly try, and Miro smiled at it.

"Tell me about the Second Coming," Miro said.

"He expected it quite soon. He was also looking forward to the whore of Babylon getting her lumps." The chaplain chuckled amiably. "That's the Roman church. And he talked to somebody called Matt. Do you happen to know who Matt is?"

"His brother."

"So. There was great love there. It came out in his ramblings. But Matt didn't come here." That distressed the chaplain. "Nobody came. No flowers. No messages."

"When did he expect the Second Coming?"

"Days. Yes, in days, I should say, from the way he talked to Matt. I wish I could have heard Matt's side of it." He looked deprived. "But of course I couldn't."

"No."

"Still, from the way the talk went, I'd say they were of one mind about it. Yes. One mind."

Miro looked about him with the appearance of unease. There was a small copse in the parkland behind the hospital. He pointed to it. "Padre," he said, "there's one aspect of this business I'd prefer to keep between us for the present. Nobody else here can help me with it. Can we walk over this way?"

"I want to help," the chaplain said eagerly, touching the larger world. They wandered over the grass.

"Now, tell me. From what you heard, you'd say Matt and Barney were, first, very devoted to one another . . ."

"Very. Very. Very."

". . . and religious . . . nuts?"

"Primitives." The chaplain smiled his correction gently and touched Miro's arm. "Religious enthusiasts. Very ignorant and very strong in their ignorance . . . anthropomorphic in the extreme."

"Yes. You know this kind well?"

"Very well. We have a lot of them. Extremely ignorant people and more superstitious than Romans. Ignorant. Very ignorant and full of the arrogance of ignorance."

"Well, then, I want you to help me to understand how they would act in certain circumstances. For example, imagine two brothers of this stamp . . ."

"Matt and Barney?" The chaplain's innocence shone.

"If you like. Now, suppose that an action of one of these brothers leads to the death of the other in circumstances the survivor can't explain to the authorities . . ."

"Barney's dead?" The chaplain spoke quite firmly.

"May we stick to our two hypothetical brothers?"

"Of course, of course. I see. I see. Yes. So the surviving brother cannot explain . . ."

"*Doesn't* explain . . . and can't. What would he do with the body? He's grief-stricken, of course."

"Of *course*, of *course*. I see *exactly*." His face had an eager look. "He'd bury him, of course."

"Himself?"

"He could. There's no legal obstacle. Anybody can conduct a burial. But this is where you need me, isn't it." The chaplain's mind was precise now, in his own field. His eyes were shrewd and his smile knowing, as if he wanted to say he knew what this was all about. "There's no theological obstacle either. There's a passage in Paul that makes us all pastors or evangelists or bishops or just about anything we decide we are. Very convenient. But the tradition is *there*. It's a matter of authority and *custom*, *tradition. Biblical* tradition. Ecclesiastical tradition. New Testament tradition. Hussite, Anabaptist, Congregational, Quaker . . . The centuries inhabit us, so to speak. Barney would do it himself, in just the same way and just the same words"—he looked up mockingly—"and probably just the same voice that I would use. *Authority* is indispensable, you see. Things have to be done *properly*—where eternal life is the issue, one covers all the angles . . . if I may speak so. You see? And this, of course, would be an unregistered death and burial?"

"Yes." So he pries while he informs; Miro smiled. "And tell me, Padre. Where would he do it? In a graveyard?"

"No. Not an unregistered death. But not far away from a graveyard. Not just in any field or backyard. Here is the force of custom, tradition, and authority again. And superstition, mind you. In their religion any hole in the ground will do—no consecrated ground or any of that rot. But death is very lonely and even if the soul has risen, the body has always had company. They're buried in graveyards like the rest of us—in normal circumstances, that is—and men like these, in the case of an unregistered death like this, would do it very close to a graveyard —for company, and custom, and superstition. Just over the hedge, I'd say."

"Just over the hedge?"

"Hedges unite fields. The roots feed on both sides. Walls divide. Look for graveyards with hedges." He smiled and nodded wisely.

"Not in the city. Somewhere in this district. It was a matter of time and distance, Padre. Tell me about graveyards . . ."

The chaplain's smile was angelic. "I have a morbid love for graveyards," he said and for five minutes talked with rapture of their mysteries and beauties. But he said at last, slyly, "Your interest is rather less poetic."

"On this side of the city. They seem to favor this side," Miro prompted, anxious not to disturb his absorption.

"Soil and situation," the chaplain said. He was thoughtful for a while, reviewing his estates. "I'm thinking of the necessities of the case. I have three places in mind. The first two improbable for reasons of situation. You see, there are graveyards that preserve bodies and coffins far too long. This means that quite often when a grave is opened, the last funeral is still there—at least in part, often substantial part—and since the new one must go down a prescribed depth, what can the gravediggers do? Get rid of the old coffin and the bones, of course. Sometimes they have to cart them away." It was not bizarre. Miro had seen it done. "But sometimes the situation provides a handy and concealed dumping ground, a . . . a boneyard, if you like." He took out a small diary, wrote in it and tore out the page. "Try these three."

"Thank you, Padre."

The chaplain laid a fondling pastoral hand on his arm. "You do interesting work. *Very* interesting. *Fascinating,* indeed." He squeezed confidentially. "And of course, *serious.* This *is* a serious matter?"

"In the extreme."

"Poor Barney," the chaplain said sadly. "We have a lot of primitives here, sir. I wish they'd all go to America." He let go and shrugged. "But they won't. They like it here." He grinned mischievously. "I suppose the climate suits them?" He nudged Miro. "Climate!"

"Both sorts."

"It will all rest quietly with me." The chaplain liked that. He was part of the darker side of the large world.

Miro watched him walk across the grass to the hospital, his head nodding wisely. Then he went looking at graveyards.

He walked the hedges, not expecting to find what he sought. A farmer working in his fields would see any unfamiliar mound and dig, or tell the police. The first two were too open. He left them and drove back to The Deer's Cry Press.

Bowen was in the room with the green, red, and blue telephones. He nodded at the phones. "Mac Donnell tells me you've been studying TB."

"Barney was there, nigh unto death. He skipped the night he was killed . . ."

"Anything to work on?"

"I don't know. I'm taking a walk. Will you still be here in fifteen minutes?"

"All day."

Miro went by the back door to the large walled garden behind the house. He let himself onto the fringes of the golf course by a wicket gate in the wall and walked up the hill onto the fairway. From there he could see the graveyard, and to the left of it, a pond, reed-ringed and with swans swimming; between the pond and the graveyard a grassed-over lane lined by large trees—oak, sycamore and elm—and thick hedges. It was not more than eighteen feet wide. He walked down into it.

The place was heavy and dark, the sun shut out by the hedges and overhanging trees. The grass was littered with human bones and pieces of half-rotted coffin. There were skulls, bits of rib cage, thigh bones, feet, whole hands and pieces of them, shin bones, vertebrae . . . coffin sides had had the brass handles removed. The gravediggers and their friends probably had a lot of fancy handles on their sideboards.

He walked slowly down the graveyard hedge—counting his paces, pushing aside human remains too large to step on—and forty paces into the lane he found it. A new mound, covered with dying cut grass, with a few dead flowers scattered on the grass. He groped through it and exposed the sod that had been sliced off and replaced over the naked clay. It wasn't quite covered. The grass was a supplement to the over-extended sod. Nearby he found where the grass had been cut, very likely by the look of it, with a bill-hook.

The flowers, he supposed, were stolen from a grave over the hedge. Oleander, ladanum, narcissus, white lily. That was odd. It made him smile. It was very Ulster. Oleander was Rose of the Brook; narcissus was Rose of Sharon; ladanum was myrrh; white lily—from the Song of Solomon. They were all flowers of the Bible. Some pious soul with a relative over the hedge and under the sod was probably wondering where the hell his flowers went. He went back to Bowen.

"Seen many corpses, Bowen?"

"Too many. Why?"

"Seen any after they've been buried and dug up?"

"None. What're you on about, Miro?"

"Barney. They buried him in your backyard—in that lane thing between the pond and the graveyard. Forty paces in on the graveyard side."

"Christ!" Bowen shot up. "You're sure?"

"No. We'll have to dig. Either it's Barney or some wife who's supposed to have left her husband. Three in the morning suit you?"

"Without a legal order?"

"If you go legal, I'm going home."

"We'll dig. I'll get a crew."

"Get a big manhole cover to hide the light. If it's Barney, photograph him front and sides." He grinned. "If he's not in a box you'll have to wash him."

"Christ!"

"Then put him back the way you found him—*exactly*. Sod, cut grass, dead flowers—everything. And give the pictures— three each, front and sides—to the news people with one question to go with the pictures: 'Do you know this man?' "

"If they do, who do they phone?"

"Don't tell them. Anybody who knows him will phone the papers, the BBC, the police. You'll hear. So will Matt. Maybe he'll try to reach his brother's grave, even if it's only to see if anybody's disturbed it. So put it back *exactly*, Bowen, and keep men in the graveyard and along the pond every night till he comes. If he comes."

He took the information about Fred Davison from his pocket. "Coleraine, you said the dead men came from—the ambulance men's cover, I mean?"

"Yes."

"Barney had a dead man's health insurance card. Fred Davison. The late Mr. Davison was from Cloyfin—two miles from Coleraine. You might track him back too, from grave to cradle." He gave the paper to Bowen.

"They always said you were great, Miro. I think you're bloody lucky."

"Damn right."

Miro was driving too fast when he passed the Kilroot Road.

He pressed his foot down, thinking of Strong. But he saw the little man at the end of the road, looking desperately at the passing car, his motorbike leaning against the ditch.

He saw him again when he roared past on his bike, waving triumphantly, but when he turned down the road to Whitehead to find something to eat, the little fellow was working on his bike again.

He saw him again while he sat in the café, eating fish and chips. The little man propped his bike against the curb, came in, and sat down beside him.

"Bloody motorbikes," he said and ordered fish and chips.

"If it's not in good shape why push it so hard?"

The little man laughed. "I like the feelin. Streakin along like a bullet," he said. "Ye can see the groun—ye'd think it was that close it wud take the skin off yer arse." He was high on something, probably just the sun and the sea air. "Yer goin round the Coast Road fer a wee run?"

"Just to Larne."

"Yer goin t'the big meetin?"

"I may while I'm there. If I have time."

"Jasus, that's somethin! There'll be thousands, bloody thousands and the guverment can stick its ban up its bloody . . ." He ate his fish and chips in vast mouthfuls and talked incessantly with his mouth stuffed. His face was flat, his ears enormous, and his vocabulary anchored firmly in the bathroom.

Miro passed him twice, and saw him working on his bike for the last time, on the outskirts of Larne. Each time the little man waved and shouted.

He was early for the rally. He found a place to park and went for a drink to kill the thirst of his fish and chips. The streets were crowded. A high proportion of the men wandering the streets in little groups were Orangemen, supporting the warning their Grand Master had given the government by wearing their Orange sashes. Twice he thought he saw the little motorbike man, but when he looked again he had gone, if he had been there at all. The town was electric with defiance. He heard it in snatches of talk: wild talk, angry talk, bloody-minded talk.

". . . drive the fuckin lota them into the Free State . . ."

". . . hang the fuckers in a Union Jack . . ."
". . . bury them in their own shit . . ."
Some of them were drunk, singing Orange songs. The pubs were full. He was content to stand outside one, his back to the wall, watching the people on the street. Three drunk men, their arms around one another, stopped opposite him, singing,

> *"O, Dolly's Braes, O Dolly's Braes,*
> *O, Dolly's Braes no more,*
> *We'll kick the Pope*
> *We'll kick the Pope*
> *Right over Dolly's Braes . . ."*

It appeared to be all they knew of it. They turned to stare at Miro, giggling, walking around him as far as the wall allowed, nodding at one another, laughing at their thoughts, smelling of porter.

"Slitter, slatter," one of them shouted and they laughed, threw their arms around one another again, and sang again . . .

> *"Slitter, slatter, holy water,*
> *Gimme no more o yer cheese,*
> *Fir the last I got it stuck in me throat*
> *An gimme the heart disease . . ."*

They turned again to Miro. "He's stannin fornenst the chapel," one of them said.

There was a Roman Catholic church across the street. Other men were stopping to watch, seeing the signs of sport, Miro supposed. He slowed his breathing and deepened it.

"Is ye loyal?" one of the men asked him, grinning.

"Very."

"Is yis goin t'chapel?"

"No."

"D'yis ever go t'church?"

"No."

"Is yis loyal?"

"Sing 'Dolly's Braes' wi us."

"Is yis loyal?"

They were all asking questions, not waiting for answers, not wanting answers. One of them pressed his hand against Miro's right shoulder, "Is yis loyal, mister?"

"Take down the hand, son." He saw the policeman's stately approach from the corner of his eye and could not afford to look.

"Take down the han, son," the man mimicked. "Spoke like a real papish," he shouted and withdrew his hand, closing it as it went back.

"Don't," Miro said and was misunderstood in the fumes. Some of the bystanders laughed. The supposed papish was afraid.

"Don't," the man mimicked. "Yis disn't want t'fight?"

"That's right."

"Sing 'God Save the Queen.'" The man turned for approval and support. "The Queen, aye? Kin he sing the Queen wi'out turnin his papish stummack?" He was back at Miro. "Sing the Queen, ye papish cunt."

Miro sang nothing and the arm drew back and swung. It was a slow, drunken, loping swing. Miro slammed his open hands against the man's exposed ears with all his strength. The man screamed and threw his hands to his head, staggering about in agony. Miro said to his astounded friends, "Take him away, you stupid bastards."

But they had forgotten their friend. They turned to Miro and found the policeman beside him. "Luk after yer frien," the policeman said to them. "Ye'd be better off if ye sobered up and stayed sober."

"Let him out from the fuckin wall," one of them said, leaning forward and holding back.

"From what I seen a minit ago, he'd ate the two of yis alive. Get away on outa the road or I'll blow the whistle."

Other hands moved them and they were pushed, protesting discreetly, off the sidewalk and along the street. Miro could hear their friend still howling.

"What'd'ye do to start them?" the policeman asked him.

"I stood here, as quiet as a virgin," Miro said.

Such odd talk startled the officer. "Ye didn't say nothin?"

"Nothing. They're in an ugly mood."

"They hiv good cause. Is yi a papish?" It wasn't an afterthought.

"No." Miro took his identity card from his pocket. "Read this, officer," he said.

The constable read the card. "Yes, sir," he said soberly. He touched his peak and started to move away.

"Constable."

"Yes, sir." He came back reluctantly.

"My wife is a papish." Miro moved away.

A great crowd pushed and shoved in the football field, and in the small grandstand bands took turns playing patriotic songs. The people closest to the stands, packed tight around the platform thrown up during the morning, sang the songs. A fat woman wrapped in a Union Jack climbed the steps and jigged to the music. The goal posts were rocked till they fell, and the crowds at either end of the field cheered these accomplishments. A solid column of bodies pushed slowly in against the crowd, which was already making movement difficult.

"There y'are," said Miro's little friend of the motorbike. "There," was about thirty feet from the platform and directly in front of the microphone.

"There y'are," Miro said and wondered why in this enormous press it had to be this particular creature.

"Ye come."

"I did."

The little man was carrying a brown paper bag. He took a sandwich from it. "D'ye want one?"

"No, thank you. You're hungry again?"

"Och, I just wanted a wee bite."

Talk was mercifully impossible with the bands, the singing, the talking, and the shouting. Even the feet shuffling in the grass made a straining sound. The gates were closed against all who would enter. The field was full.

"The Queen," a voice shouted over the speakers. The drums rolled, hats and caps were whipped off, the mass of bodies came solidly to attention, and the crowd sang *God Save the Queen.*

Miro had heard a great many national anthems sung. He had
never heard anything like this. In spite of his detachment from
all that it meant here in this field and in this place, it seized him.
Not slowly, growing in his mind as the voices—almost entirely
men's voices—rolled up out of the well of the field and filled the
sky. It seized him quickly, like a woman's cold fingers seizing
his belly; the voices *struck* the air, roaring cold fire or a lustful
passion. He shook; first in response to the dark intensity of the
roar

"God save our gracious Queen"

and his blood leaped. Drunk men stood solid on their feet, hands
down the seams of unpressed trousers, fingers closed into their
palms, eyes front, chests lifting, mouths roaring

"Send her victorious . . ."

for their victory was her victory, and sometime during dinner
two evenings ago Strong had straightened and stiffened and said
with terrible and pompous sincerity, *"Ulster is a redoubt of war-
riors . . ."* and Miro found himself fighting against the drawing
insistence of their fearful, passionate unity that he might know
and enjoy again such consuming unity with his fellow-men . . .
he was fighting a wish to be one with them, to be one with *something* that was more than the sum of those personal things that
now made up the substance of his life . . . What did he stand for
or fight for but home and family and cows . . . ?

Then it was over.

They were just men again, drunk men, nearly drunk men,
sober men, loyal men but only men—and again fragmented
men. "The Reverend Dr. Harrison," the loudspeakers said.

He was small, bald, bespectacled, and black-gowned, with
white banns on his chest that the sun shone on. "O Lord
God . . ." the unctuous voice droned, "we thank Thee for the
privilege vouchsafed to us this day, to come before Thee here
. . . Bless all our undertakings . . ." Heads were down, drunk
heads farthest down. "Bless our Sovereign Lady Elizabeth and

her family . . . Bless our leaders and lead them in the paths of righteousness . . . Restore Dr. Corkey and the child, so wantonly and cruelly seized by evil men . . ." Heads were up and looking about them; men changed feet like resting horses . . . "What a time t'need a pee," a voice said, and men with their heads up, staring around and waiting for the end, said *Shush,* indignantly. It ended in time . . . "Aaa-men," Dr. Harrison said fervently. "Aaa-*men.*"

"Captain Ronald Strong . . ." the loudspeakers cried.

This was a roaring crowd. It roared for him like thunder in a gorge. He stood straight and still before the microphone, doing nothing. *"Hip, Hip, Hip,"* the chairman yelled.

"Hooray!" The thunder cracked in the gorge.

He looked out over them, till the only sound was the faint far sound of traffic. He was an impressive figure, up there.

"It cannot go *on* . . ." he said quietly.

They cheered and clapped.

"It must *not* go on . . ." he said, louder by a well-calculated shade.

There was no clapping; clapping was inadequate. It was a football cheer.

"It–shall–not–go–on!" he shouted, and the yelling, screaming, roaring split the sky and went on and on and on and on . . .

Miro listened carefully. This was the place and the time for incitement. *Strength . . . cohesion . . . liberty . . . one purpose . . . one cause . . . one people . . .*

Cheer. Cheer. And cheer again and again. What he said was general, vague, but precise in every mind because their thoughts were already formed. He spoke in generalizations into their assumptions; he inflamed them . . . but there was no incitement. Captain Strong *said* nothing. The roaring crowd *heard* in what he did not say everything they wanted to hear.

In a silence, the little man said, "Will ye have a wee piece?" and offered him his paper bag.

"No, thank you."

"Then I'll go. I'll say goodbye t'ye." He offered his hand, formally. "I think ye'v seen the last of me." He bowed, grinning, laid the rest of his bag of sandwiches on the ground, and pushed his way backwards, through the press.

They were cheering the end of Strong's speech. There was nothing to stay for. If he couldn't get out at the gates he'd go over the fence. Miro turned and elbowed his way back. The little man was out of sight.

Five or six layers of bodies were between him and the paper bag when it exploded.

Above the screaming and moaning and cursing he heard a voice yelling, "Over there . . . over there," and felt the pressure of movement on his back. The mob began to move. "He went that way."

That way was his way, if he read correctly the pushing and shouting from behind. The hand on his elbow closed and Mac Donnell hauled him. "Go left," he shouted, "over the fence." He pointed in the direction of the gates. "There," he yelled. *"He's there,"* and the pressure swung.

The people ahead of the movement knew only that something had exploded. "Keep calm and quiet," the speakers shouted. "Don't panic."

It may have been the use of the word panic that started it; it may have been Mac Donnell pointing the avengers away from Miro. The small pressure from the people near the platform swelled and became the charging hysteria of a herd. Ahead of it men swung and pushed men who swung and pushed, and the high gates opened only inwards. "Keep calm. Keep calm. Please keep calm," the speaker said over and over . . . The men nearest the gates were jammed against them and the pressure increased behind; they were crushed, cut off in their screaming as the rolling volume of bodies collapsed the gates outwards, and the ranks behind the crushed men were driven forward, failed to mount the sloping falling gates, and were crushed in their turn as they bent and scrambled on hands and knees. They were trampled. Bodies piled. The carnage and the screaming grew . . .

Miro went over the high railing with hundreds of others. Men battered it down and escaped to the road beyond . . .

Then, in safety, their rage broke.

"*Waterfoot!*"

A young man stood on the roof of a car and screamed "*Water-foot!*" through his cupped hands. Others climbed onto other cars and screamed, "*Waterfoot! Waterfoot!*"

Men scattered, looking for transport. Cars were blocked, trucks caught in the pack, and dozens of raging men pulled their drivers out and piled in. Marshals appeared, opening the way at intersections for the commandeered transport.

Miro stood on a garden wall and watched it all. Mac Donnell motioned him over the wall. "Through the garden," he said and they ran. "Got to get to my car. They'll burn Waterfoot. It's a Catholic village up the coast road." They found his car six streets away and Mac Donnell radioed his message. "I'll take you to yours," he said to Miro. "I saw you park it."

Miro said nothing on the way to his car. He sat hunched in the seat, his eyes fixed on the dashboard, his hands woven together between his knees. The bone shone through the flesh over his knuckles.

"What did you think of that?" Mac Donnell asked him.

Miro did not hear him. His forehead was tight and sore, his mind straining over the details of the day. He first saw the little assassin and his bike at the head of the Kilroot Road. He was waiting there, expecting me. To come to Strong's? To come to Larne to see this meeting? It didn't matter. He knew where to pick me up—at the Kilroot Road. He passed me, I passed him; I thought I saw him twice on the streets; he was on me in the field. It was me he was after.

His anger was a high-pitched note in his head, a shrill strain in his throat. He was trying to swallow.

Mac Donnell could hear his breathing. Christ, he thought, I'd rather have a wild animal after me than that one. He stopped the car. "Here you are."

Miro was not listening. Twice. Twice. Twice. It beat in his head. Twice. Twice. Twice. He did not know about the crushed and trampled bodies. It would have made no difference.

"*Twice,*" he said aloud. "*Twice,*" and shook his locked hands.

"Twice." He opened the door. "Tell Bowen I'll deliver the bastard," he said. *"Twice,"* he said. "He tried *twice.*"

Mac Donnell watched him walk to his car. "He's like an animal, Colonel," he phoned Bowen. "He's in such a rage he can hardly breathe."

"God is good," Bowen said.

His head was bursting.

His chest was bursting.

His heart was bursting in his chest. His foot was flat to the boards and he could scarcely see.

He lifted his foot and let the car run to a stop. *"Jesus Christ,"* he said, exhausted by rage. *"He tried it in a crowd."*

"Psychos!" he yelled. "They're all psychos!" and started the car and drove slowly. He stopped again at a horse trough at the foot of a hill, doused his face in cold water, went over the ditch, and lay on his back in the grass, breathing slowly, waiting for sanity.

Then he drove to the hospital. His anger was cold and malignant; his mind was full of blind men, green men, orange men, creeping over tumps of heather towards one another in the night, with Summerfield between them.

Eight

And I looked, and behold, a pale horse.

The policeman at the gate saluted. No, ma'am. He had seen nobody near the place. Yes, ma'am; he was keeping a sharp lookout.

The policeman inside was sitting on the steps between the decaying lions. Oh, no, ma'am, he said with a very red face, he wasn't in a daze. He was alert, watching everything that happened. *What* had happened? Nothing, ma'am.

"We'd better lock your car in the garage, Miro. My husband's using my little sports car. We'd better search the buildings around the courtyard, Miro. We'd better search the house, Miro . . ."

Miro dropped her bags in her room. "You'd better calm down," he said and took his bag through the communicating door to his room. The rooms were identical, with their own bathrooms, the same beds, the same French windows, the same balconies, the same uncomfortable everything. He opened the windows in both rooms to let in the smell of the sea.

He saw her through the glare in his head, like a plaster figure in a window display behind plate glass. She'd let something drop. Bowen was right; there'd be a pattern to Strong's life, and something that didn't fit in. Stir her about a bit.

"Do you sleep with your husband?" he said abruptly.

"Sleep? Which . . . ? You go to the point, don't you? What do you mean by 'sleep'?"

"Both." Funny. You expected cold-cream English shock and got small talk.

"Neither."

"Show me the place."

"You've finished with that subject?"

"For the moment."

"How long can you stay?"

"I'm not in a hurry now," he said.

"I'll show you the place." She was amused by something, or pleased by something. They went through the house. As Bowen said, Strong's room was at the back. From its windows Miro could see over the wall to the Kilroot Halt, beyond it to the bungalows built on the site of Dean Swift's first rectory, and beyond that the length of the Kilroot Road.

"Show me the grounds."

"The grounds" were half a mile long behind the red-brick wall, and from one hundred to a hundred and fifty yards deep, according to the erosion line of the shore. They ended, she said, at the mouth of the Kilroot River. Tomalty's cottage was at the end of the neglected vegetable garden. It was painted washroom brown, inside and out. It had a kitchen, a parlor, a bedroom, and a bathroom.

The door was unlocked. When she opened it, he said, "I don't know your name."

"Names," she said. "Amelia Jane. I've never liked them."

"Which does Strong use?"

"Neither. He used to use Amelia. Now he sometimes calls me 'you.' I don't like talking like this. I shouldn't really."

"I'll call you Jane."

She took his arm on the way to the river. "Thank you for coming," she said.

They came on the mouth of the river around a broad rock and a grassy hummock. The river mouth was no more than two hundred feet wide. There were trees on the far bank and a dinghy hauled up among them. In the middle of the channel an old motorboat was moored. It was, he was certain, the boat in which the bait-diggers had gone down the lough.

"Your boat?" he said.

"No. The schoolmaster's."

"Why don't you sleep with Strong?"

"Which?"

"Both."

"He cut me off. He gives all his time, energy, and thought to his political passions. And he doesn't like me."

"Tell me about the schoolmaster."

"You do skip about, don't you?"

"All right. Whom do you sleep with?"

"Nobody, so far."

"If you were mine the question wouldn't arise."

"I believe you. Your book said a lot about . . ."

"It said too much."

"Did it?"

"I've always been afraid of Englishwomen like you. Cold, restrained, haughty."

"You could be mistaken."

"Tell me about the schoolmaster. Is he a friend of Strong's?"

"Of course not. Wrong caste. He's only a local schoolmaster. He's nonpolitical. He's weird. He won't talk to adults, only to children. And his eyebrows are the bushiest in Ireland. Wild white hair, a long knotty face that's deep red, summer and winter. Walks like a giraffe, with big long gangling strides, and his head moves backwards and forwards like a giraffe's. Oh yes, his left arm moves with his left leg and his right . . . you know, the opposite of normal people. Have you ever tried to walk that way?" She tried it, to show him.

"Does he ever use his boat?"

"I've never seen him in it. It just floats there."

"What's his name?"

"Dubois. Around here they pronounce it Dew-Boys."

Miro sat down on the grass, took off his shoes and socks, and rolled up his trouser legs. "Come here," he said and carried her to a rock a few yards out in the water. He took off her shoes and tossed them ashore. "Bathe your feet in salt water. It's good for the nerves. How deep is it out where the boat is? Can I wade?"

"No. I think it's about five feet deep. You'll have to swim."

"Hell."

"If you can quiz me about my sex life you can swim in your shorts." She was companionable.

He swam in his shorts and hauled himself into the motorboat. He went over it, inch by inch, looking for anything, and found only some wood chips on the stern sheets, under the tiller. Somebody had whittled a stick here. A stick with dark green skin on it. A stick about the thickness of the stick Mac Donnell had taken, with the communiqué, from the sand on Strong's foreshore. Then he heard the movement of the dinghy on the far bank. He didn't look. He was watching the signals Mrs. Strong was sending. She picked up her skirt around her hips and waded ashore.

Miro waited in the boat, not looking. The dinghy drew alongside. The man with immense bushy eyebrows, wild white hair, a long, knotty, deep red face and a thin, high neck rested his oars and picked up the shotgun from the seat.

"You're in my boat, where you have no right to be. Get out of it." The shotgun lay in the crook of his arm, pointing just past Miro's chest.

He sat tight. "Pointing an offensive weapon is a crime," he said quietly.

"Do you want your head blown off your shoulders?" The dinghy drifted in on Miro. The barrel of the shotgun was only a foot from his chest.

"Put the gun down if you want me to go." He held the wood chips in the palm of his left hand where Dew-Boys could see them.

"If you found them in my boat, leave them and get to hell out of it. I'm not telling you another time."

"You're Dew-Boys, the schoolmaster," Miro said, watching the wood chips in his hand. "Tell me, Dew-Boys, who used your boat the day Tomalty was blown up?"

"Nobody uses my boat—not you, not anybody else. Get out of it and go and do your lechering with that woman in her own house."

Miro's right arm whipped forward and his hand closed on the gun barrel. He pulled it across his chest as it blasted. Dew-Boys might have pulled the trigger. Miro might have dragged the trigger against the schoolmaster's poised finger. It didn't matter. He hauled on the gun and Dew-Boys lurched forward, off-balance, as the boats pulled apart. Miro tossed the gun towards the far bank, reached over for Dew-Boy's long hair, and dragged him, cursing obscenely, out of his dinghy. He dropped him between the boats, dived overboard, and swam ashore, the chips still in his left fist.

Mrs. Strong was fixed where she stood, her skirts still held around her hips. Miro waded out of the water. Dew-Boys was scrambling about near the far bank, searching for his shotgun, cursing insanely. His dinghy drifted gently away into the lough.

The inside policeman came charging round the hummock. He saw Mrs. Strong first, exposed from the hips, then Miro dripping in his shorts, then Dew-Boys flailing the water, dipping under it with his arms and head like a massive water hen, his long white hair veiling his face. He bobbed up, tore his hair from his face, and screamed, *"Fuck you!"* at Miro, saw the policeman, and dipped out of sight again.

Miro whispered to Mrs. Strong and she dropped her skirts about her wet legs, laughing.

The policeman said, "What the . . . what the . . ."

"Dew-Boys discharged his gun by accident, and the kick threw him out of his punt," Miro explained. "Leave him to it."

"Yis, sur. He's harmless."

"You got here very promptly."

"I was just keepin close, sur."

"Don't."

"Yis, sur." The constable hurried away, disappointed. As he came round the hummock the hope had stirred in him that if he did his work faithfully and well, he might have a privileged insight into something he had never seen before—the quality with her skirts pulled up to her knickers, with a man stripped down to his shorts. It was hard for the Ulster working castes to believe that the women of the quality really liked it. If they liked it, why did most of them have only two wains apiece and why did their men nobble so many servant girls? He had lost a chance to find out.

While he bathed and got into his pajamas and dressing gown, Miro's mind roved over Dew-Boys, over Strong, and over Mrs. Strong; over the boat, the worm-diggers, the teaching-loon, and the possibility of connection. Its roving over Mrs. Strong was more personal and more particular. She was companionable. Walking back to the house, she had laughed about Dew-Boys. "He was like a feeding crane," she said; and, "You're like a holiday, Miro," she said. The strain was going from her eyes.

He sat by the open window of his room and waited for her to come out of her bathroom. He could hear her singing. She was waspish with Strong. What did they quarrel about? He turned her over and over in his mind, like a man choosing stones for a slingshot: What could he tell her that would throw Strong off-stride if she came out with it? What *did* they fight about? What sort of *situation* provoked their quarrels? What did he know that a woman who wanted to hack at her husband's image could use on him?

She came out in her bathrobe, singing, walked straight to his room with her hairbrushes and combs, ruffled his hair as she passed, and brushed her hair at his dressing table. She was certainly in a companionable mood. She wanted to be close to him. She was using him like a hairbrush, stroking herself for comfort.

"Do you and Strong quarrel?" he said.

"We used to. Not much, now. Now we don't talk much."

"When you do quarrel, what's it about?"

"His politics. Or my going to England for a break."

"What about his politics?"

"They're inhuman. They're a projection of himself. They're obsessional. I've never seen anything like it in anybody else. He doesn't speak to me for days . . . thinking, thinking, thinking. He goes out for long walks at night . . . thinking . . ."

"Why do you stay together?"

"I think they call it negative attraction. He can't afford a marriage failure in this Holy Land, and I have no relatives, nowhere to go, nobody to go to, no money—no anything. He doesn't beat me and nobody else has asked me to run away and marry him. The best offer I've had was just to run away and sleep with a man. Too insecure."

"You'll have to go to England for a break. You know that."

"I know."

Miro waited for the silence to surprise her. "A bomb went off at his meeting at Larne . . ."

She stopped brushing and her mouth tightened. "Were you down there? Was anybody hurt?"

"Yes. I didn't want to distress you, but I listened to the news while you were in the bath. You'll hear it anyway. Two men killed by the bomb. Nine men were crushed in the rush to get out of the football field . . ." He waited and watched her. "The gates opened inwards. They were trampled to death."

"Don't . . ." She stared at herself in the mirror, then brushed again, roughly. "This is a fearful place . . . they'll never change," she said.

"When he comes home you'll simply have to insist that you can't stand it. Get out of it for a month . . ."

"I'm going to. There'll be a row, but I'm going to. I'm going to. He'll say I have no right to go and give people a chance to say *his* wife can run away for a while and thousands of his little supporters' wives can't."

"It's eerie," Miro said, looking at the sea, casting in her discontent, "but the most vicious things happen and they don't act on Strong as you'd expect tragedies to act on a public leader who cares about the people he leads. All these things are like assets to him . . . like contributions to his campaign funds. Doesn't he ever express public sorrow . . . ?"

"No." She put down her brush. "I don't think he feels it. Am I disloyal talking this way? Maybe—I *feel* disloyal. In everything . . ."

"What does that mean?"

"It means everything." She pressed the bristles of two brushes together. "Everything," she said again. "Six months ago I'd have felt guilty thinking that . . . I thought it and did feel guilty. Today? No. Today I feel *entitled* . . . He left you to look after me when that explosion cut me." She turned to him. "Did you realize that with Tomalty dead and burning in that car he left here without even *speaking* to the man's wife?"

She gathered up her brushes and combs. "I always have hot chocolate before I go to bed," she said. "Shall I make some for us?"

"Why not?"

"Five minutes."

Miro stepped out onto the balcony. He filled his mind with Eva to push out Mrs. Strong. The moon was high. The tide was out and the shore silent. The policeman on duty inside the grounds was walking through the salt grass above the sand. In the stillness he could hear the man's boots swistling in the stiff grass. In the stillness he heard the roaring of a sports car along the road from the village of Eden. How did the driver keep out of police or army hands, making that noise so long after the curfew hour? He heard the gear-change. The car had turned into the Kilroot Road.

Miro ran to the back of the house. It was Mrs. Strong's sports car. It was Strong. It stopped near the head of the road, then turned into a field and was tucked in tightly behind the hedge. The driver got out and started across the fields towards the Kilroot River. He was not running, not hurrying; he was striding steadily.

Miro ran back to his room and got into bed. What brought the man back? In one hell of a hurry, if his meeting ran an hour after curfew? He was going to the river to skirt his own wall, use its shadow for cover, and come into the house by the courtyard. Why? Me? Suspicion of a starved wife? If that was it, maybe there'd be a quarrel . . . Miro said to Mrs. Strong as she came back with the tray, "Where does Dew-Boys live?"

"Up the river and across the Larne road—opposite Castle Dobbs." She was making room for the tray on his bedside table.

"The two men who were digging bait on your foreshore just before Tomalty was blown up—they planted the bomb."

"I suppose so." She handed Miro his mug of hot chocolate and sat on the bed. She didn't want disturbing talk.

"The boat they went down the lough in was Dew-Boys' boat."

"Oh."

"The wood chips I picked up in Dew-Boys' boat were whittled from a stick they stuck in the sand. They stuck a communiqué on the stick . . ."

"But there wasn't one . . ."

"There was. I had a look at it while the doctor was attending to you. One of the officials took it away and asked me not to mention it."

"Why? Why in the world?"

"I don't know. Strong would have known Dew-Boys' boat."

"Oh, yes."

"He was watching it."

"Oh." Her mind was not on it. "Tell me in the morning. Not now. I like saying that to you. 'Tell me in the morning.'" She grinned at him. "It sounds domestic. Are you comfortable? I want you to talk to me."

"I am talking to you."

"But not about me. You're like a holiday. Did I say that before?"

"Yes." He didn't like hot chocolate, but he drank it slowly and looked at his watch. Strong would need a quarter of an hour. He'd had ten minutes of it. Mrs. Strong, he decided, had the long night in mind and was working on her nervous disloyalty. She wasn't sure what to do, or how to do it.

She drank quickly and put her mug on the tray. "If you're lying down I'm not sitting up. Move over." She said it quickly, as if saying it slowly was too specific. "Let's have a good long natter. We don't have to get up early." That sounded domestic too.

He moved over and she lay down on the covers beside him and stretched, wiggling her bare feet. One thigh showed where her bathrobe parted a little. Perhaps she was unaware of it. Miro wore Eva about him like a charm against witches, and felt unjustified resentment. He had collaborated with Mrs. Strong in their passage to this point. What the hell would I have done if Strong hadn't shown up? he asked himself. Spent the night making love to her? Yes, he said and resented her encroachment on Eva. He felt self-righteous, or priggish, or foolish. All three. And Strong was certainly taking his bloody time.

"What was that?" he said.

"The policeman at the front. Don't think about him." She stretched hard, her hands against the headboard, her feet reaching. "Oh-h-h, I feel *good*." The robe opened a little more. She must feel the air from the windows on her bare flesh. If she did, she was enjoying it. "I wish we were in a bungalow on a bay in the West Indies," she said. "Far away from the Ulster papishes and prods and their politicians." It was a step in her direction.

He heard the creak and set her bolt upright on the bed. "That wasn't the policeman unless he's coming up the back stairs," he said.

This time she heard it. "I didn't hear the car," she said, "but he often comes up that way after one of his walks."

"He . . ." he almost told her and decided not to. Strong's sneaking approach would cause more trouble if he threw it in later.

"What a contemptible . . ." She looked at the tray and the two mugs. "What a disgusting Ulster vulgarian he is." She ran to her room, pushed a chair by the window and grabbed a book. "*Blast him*," she hissed across the distance and sat down, pretending to read. Englishwomen of her sort, he thought, always kept something of their boarding-school days.

Miro put on his dressing gown and slippers, switched off the bedside light, and went out onto the balcony. Below, the policeman struck a match and lit his pipe. Before long, if all went well, he might be listening too hard to remember to draw on it. Miro gave his ears to the rooms inside. Both French windows were open, the policeman was at rest below; Miro propped himself on the end of his balcony rail and waited.

He heard the door of Mrs. Strong's room thrown back against the wall; and the following silence.

"Oh," Strong said. It was a question. He had not found what he expected to find. Then, "You're not in bed?"

"You're back," she said. It didn't sound as if she had turned her head.

The main light went on in Miro's room. He heard the hot chocolate mugs knock together on the tray.

"Where's Miro?" It came out clearly into the air—his teeth clacked.

"He was there last time I saw him."

"Where?"

"In there. In bed."

"Why?"

"To sleep, I suppose." Her voice was vague; her tone inattentive.

"And where were you when you saw him in bed?"

"In there."

"Doing what?"

"Drinking hot chocolate and talking."

"Why is he in this room?"

"Because I put him there. It's closer."

"The door was open."

"I wanted that, too."

"Hot chocolate!" he said. "Hot chocolate for two. You bloody little scullery maid!"

Miro heard her book fall flat on the floor. Her voice came from the connecting doorway. "The general would not have liked that," she said. "And neither do I." It was her Yardley's cold-cream voice; a chairman-of-the-Women's-Institute voice; in a rural district, a voice from The Hall.

"I can see what you like," he shouted. "I can see on the pillows. A head on each of them."

"Two heads," she said. "One on each pillow? Is that how it's done? I don't remember." Then she said, "By the way, I'm leaving tomorrow. I'm going across the water for a month—for a rest."

"For a rest? God, the nerve of you! After this I suppose you need one! You cheap little bitch."

"You don't *know* that, do you, Ronald? And I'm not going to tell you."

Strong made little angry noises and his teeth clacked as if he were opening and closing his mouth.

She shouted, "Don't dare touch me."

Miro moved to the open window. Strong's hands were working, his shoulders hunched. He was close to her.

"What have you got on under that robe?" he shouted and clutched his mouth.

"Go to your room and fix your teeth," she said coldly. "You're anything but impressive holding them in."

Miro heard a foot on gravel below. He looked down and saw the policeman peering up. The constable saw Miro and skipped back under cover of the house.

"What's under it?" Strong shouted and grabbed. He pulled the robe open. "Nothing! *You cheap whore!*" He grabbed his mouth, settled his teeth, and lunged at her shoulders. *"Did you? Did you?"* he yelled. *"Say it! Did you?"* It was high-pitched, squealing, frantic. He wasn't the commanding political leader or the impressive platform performer. He was a husband, screaming his pain over damage to pride and property. *"Did you?"* he yelled and let go to rescue his teeth.

His pain was greater than hers. "You don't know, do you?" she said. "If I did, you couldn't use it in the newspapers, could you? It's no use to your career, Ronald. Not like Corkey and the child and those men at your meeting at Larne today. You don't really *need* to know, do you, Ronald? Your supporters don't know, so it doesn't affect your political future." She was spitting at him, bitter, vengeful, and hacking at a pound of flesh she had wanted to hack at for months.

"No, no, no," he said plaintively. "You didn't. You wouldn't . . ." The captain had tucked his wife conveniently away in a compartment he might or might not open again, and somebody had opened it for him. It was unbelievable. It was humiliating. It was not convenient.

"If Dew-Boys had shot me today when Miro was in his boat you could have used *that* in the papers, Ronald . . ."

Strong's arms went straight down, his fists closed. "Shot," he said oddly and accepted the change of subject. It seemed to be equally important.

"Dew-Boys took a shotgun to us today . . ."

"What were you doing at his boat?" It was another change of subject. It sounded important.

"Why didn't you tell me those men got away in Dew-Boys' boat?"

"What men?" One hand was at his mouth, guarding his teeth.

"The men who killed Tomalty. You saw them in Dew-Boys' boat . . . You watched them. Miro found things in it . . ."

"Where is that bastard?"

"I'm here, Captain. Let's talk."

Strong spun round, his face contorted. "Peeping! Listening! Get out of my house," he yelled.

"When we've talked. And we're going to talk . . ."

"I'll call the police . . ." Strong turned to the door.

"Call the one who heard you call your wife a cheap whore." Miro nodded to the window. "Down there, Captain," he said and closed the window. "Close the other one, please," he said to Mrs. Strong. "I want to talk to your husband about murder."

Strong ran at him. Miro stepped aside and tripped him. Strong sprawled across the bed and rose slowly, holding in his teeth.

"No, please," Mrs. Strong cried. She didn't hate the man. She didn't feel much of anything. But she had lived with him, happily, for some of their fifteen years. She didn't want to see his humiliation.

Miro said, "You parked your car up the road and sneaked around the wall . . ."

"Did you do that, Ronald?" Mrs. Strong said pathetically. "Did you?"

"What did you expect me to do? With this bastard in the house alone with you. I had a right to find out . . ."

"Is that why you came home? To see if I was . . . ?"

"Who called you, Strong?" Miro said.

"I was not called."

"Ronald, did you really believe I would . . . ?" She astonished Miro.

He said, "We'll talk about Barney and Matt, Strong, and the man who tried to blow me up in Larne and caused eleven deaths—and Tomalty. I know why you got me here, Captain. You wanted an outsider, an independent witness in your house, not some Ulster Protestant, not your wife, but a name people would know, somebody who knew about this sort of thing . . . You wanted me to tell an inquest that I saw an attempt on your life go wrong and kill your poor Catholic driver. Wasn't that it?"

Strong got up, striving for dignity. "Now I don't believe a

word I read in your book, sir. *Fiction!* Like *that* vicious statement." He pushed his teeth back and stood erect, trying to look contemptuous, like an outraged Victorian.

"Nobody but you and Mrs. Strong knew I was going to the Farms. But Matt and the two men who got away in Dew-Boys' boat put a bomb in my car there. They knew I was going to be there. You knew, Captain. Your wife told you, Strong. Didn't you, Mrs. Strong?"

"Ronald?" she said.

"Why, Strong? Because I saw Matt and Barney? Because I could identify them and the ambulance men? I told your wife I could. They're yours, aren't they, Captain?"

Strong looked at his wife, his shoulders down and back. "How can I reply to this sort of thing?" he asked her. "Names I never heard, lunatic charges . . ." He was white, stiff with dignity. "This man violates my bed . . ."

"No, Ronald. No."

"He abuses my house and now he abuses me."

"Ronald," she said, "Dew-Boys told him to take me to my own house to do his lechery, and you came sneaking back . . . Did that man call you, Ronald?"

"I don't know that man. He wouldn't dare call me. You know I don't know the man." Miro ignored the words and listened to the voice.

"I don't know what you're saying about him, Miro," Mrs. Strong said and sat down. "I don't understand your talk." She was drained and sick-looking and confused.

"I know you don't," he said. "He knows you don't. I'm sorry you had to go through this. But the truth is that every disaster contributes to his campaign and he *makes* these things happen. *These men are his.* The man who picked me up at the head of the Kilroot Road and followed me on his motorbike to Larne and laid a bomb at my feet and killed those people was *his man.*"

"No," she said. "No. No. That couldn't be. No. No. That's not possible. It's a terrible thing to say. No. He couldn't do that. No . . . no . . . no . . ."

Strong walked slowly to the door. "I shall deal with this," he said. "I shall deal with you, sir." He stood in the doorway. "I shall deal with you," he repeated. And again, "I shall deal with you." He walked away.

"Why don't you want to call the police, Strong?" Miro shouted after him.

He heard him go noisily and, it seemed, uncertainly down the creaking back stairs.

"Why did you do that to my husband?" Mrs. Strong said, her head shaking.

"You couldn't believe it of him, could you?" he asked her gently, hunkering down beside her chair.

"Not that," she said. "No. Not that."

"Then you'd better go across the water," he said, "for it's true, and he hasn't long to go. Go and stay with some friend. Don't be here when they get him. They're going to get him."

"No. Not that."

"Get into bed," he said.

She was crying. "Yes," she said and got into his bed because it was there. He covered her and put out the light, took his clothes to her room, took her door key from her purse, and dressed.

He went downstairs and called the policeman into the hall. "Get your partner and the two of you come inside. I'm going out and I don't want Mrs. Strong to wake up alone in an empty house."

"But the captain's in, sur."

"He isn't."

"But I heard him, sur."

"I know you heard him, and I don't want to hear from anybody else what you heard. But he's not in now."

"Is there somethin wrong, sur?"

"Get your partner and see that nothing goes wrong. Stay in the house till Captain Strong comes back and throws you out, or I come back."

"There's a curfew, sur."

"I have a pass."

He didn't want to use his car, make explanations, or show passes to the army or the police. He wanted time to think. He'd muffed it, he knew. He knew nothing about women. He'd slept with them by the hundred and still didn't know what they thought, how they thought, how they felt. All he knew was that he had exhausted and distressed this one, and he hadn't known how to use her to break her husband. So he walked to Bowen's, through Eden village and up the road past the salt mine, then west over the fields, and across the golf course.

They had reached the rough wooden box when he arrived in the green lane between the pond and the North Road graveyard. Bowen didn't have to wash Barney's face to get his pictures. When it was done, Barney went back into his box, into his hole, under the earth, and sod and grass and dead flowers. The soldiers tidied the ground like a platoon of spinsters.

"When that picture appears," Miro told Bowen, "have somebody here to wait for Matt. Maybe he'll come. But as soon as Barney's identified, dig him up and get to his family. When they see him, they'll talk—he's got to have parents or cousins or uncles."

He reported to Bowen on events at Strong's house. "I'm going back to get my car and make sure she's all right. Then I'll be back here. There's a man called Dew-Boys . . ."

"Dubois? The schoolmaster?"

Miro gave him the details, about the boat, the wood chips, the shotgun. "That bastard *knows* Strong. I'm sure of it. Check his phone. See if he made a call today to Coleraine or anywhere near it. Somebody called Strong back. He didn't suddenly begin to think, in the middle of this mess, that his wife's a tart."

"You're wasting your time on Dew-Boys. He's just an Irish eccentric."

"Call him anything you like—but check his phone calls."

"I don't think he's ever long enough in the real world to make a phone call."

"Make up your mind *after* you check his phone, dammit."

"I'll drive you as far as the Kilroot Road," Bowen said. "At least I'll know where I'm going . . . I still don't know with Strong. All we've got are accusations—and four days to their D-Day. We've got less than four days to lift them, Miro."

"Strong knew that boat was Dew-Boys—and he watched men get away in it. You've got that . . ."

"He can plead shock and confusion. It's nothing."

"Try Dew-Boys' phone. Don't forget to do that. Somebody called Strong and it wasn't the police. It was that freak. And Strong'll give you something soon. He said he'd deal with me. He'll try again. He was climbing the wall tonight."

At the Kilroot Road he followed Strong's example and went across the fields and around the wall. Strong didn't do his own dirty work; there was no point in making it easier to do.

The light was out in the hall. He had left it on. He groped for the light switch and found it. The two policemen were trussed like chickens and propped against the wall.

The man with the gun was small and hooded. "Upstairs," he said.

"You again," Miro said.

The big man he hadn't seen pushed him forward. "Hurry up," he said. "We want the woman, too."

"Are you taking us on your bike, or on your stretcher, Matt?" Miro said.

The little man laughed. "Yir full of nice wee jokes," he said. "Upstairs."

Part 2
And Your Ignorant Dead

One

Dead flies cause the ointment of the apothecary to send forth a stinking savor

The Ninth of July: "What's your name?" Miro asked the little man on their way upstairs.

"Call me Henry," he said and pulled off his hood. "Take it off, Matt. Yil smother."

"We keep meeting, Matt," Miro said. "Why?"

Matt pushed him into his room. Henry shook Mrs. Strong awake.

She was befogged and frightened, and unable to speak. She looked at Miro helplessly.

"Get up and put yir clos on, missus," Henry said. "Yir comin wi us."

"What? Who are you? Why are you in my house? Miro?"

"For the present, do as they say," Miro said.

She was on her elbow, holding her bathrobe over her breasts, gathering her wits. "Why?" she said firmly. "Who are they? *Get out of my house*," she ordered. She was gathering her anger. "Are you taking no action?" she asked Miro.

"What would you advise just now?"

She sat up in bed and surveyed them angrily. "Get out of my house," she shouted.

"Get outa bed, missus, and put yir clos on."

She glared at Miro. "My husband was right," she said. "Your book is fiction. You're not man enough to have done the things you wrote."

Henry dragged her out of bed. Keeping herself covered made resistance impossible. Miro did nothing to help her.

"Have you any further revelations about my husband?" she said to him. "Did he send these two thugs?"

"Git yir clos on," Henry said. She moved towards her door. "Where the hell ir ye goin?"

"To my room to put my clothes on. That's what you ordered, isn't it?"

"Yir room? Whose room's this?"

"Mind your own damned business," she said.

"Watch her, Matt," Henry said.

"Like hell he will," Mrs. Strong said. But Matt went with her.

"In yir bed, aye?" Henry looked covetously towards her door. "I've heard tell one man's not enough fir wee wimen."

"In case you make a serious mistake, Henry—she quarreled with her husband in this room and got into bed in serious distress. I went out—as you know. Don't make that mistake."

"Aye." Henry wiped his mouth.

"Wear slacks," Miro called.

"Go to hell," she called back, and did what he told her.

They put their hoods on again and took their prisoners downstairs. "Give this to yir bosses," Henry said and left a communiqué at the policemen's feet. Outside, out of sight of the police, they removed their hoods. "The river," Henry directed. "Wade," he said at the bank.

Miro carried Mrs. Strong on his back when the water got too deep for her. There were no boats in sight. In the middle of the river mouth, the water was up to his eyes. He went forward in slow, difficult leaps against the pressure of the water, gulping mouthfuls of air. He scrambled up the far bank breathing hard. Matt was carrying Henry on his back. He let him down.

The shore was stony. "Stay on my back," Miro told Mrs. Strong.

She tightened her grip and whispered, "Where are they taking us?"

He said, "Wait."

Two hundred yards along the shore they turned left and climbed to the road and a parked car. Matt drove, Miro beside him. Henry was in the back with Mrs. Strong and his gun. "No smart doins," he said, "an no talk."

They went north, on back roads, chilled; they changed cars twice and the pace got faster, the chill deeper. The rain came down. They left the back roads and climbed onto high moorland and roads that felt like sand on a rock bed, with the rocks sticking through the sand. No doubt the car wasn't theirs; they ran it over the rocks as if they had borrowed it without permission.

Then over a wooden bridge, up a steep track, around a sprawling house, and into a garage at the back. From it they were taken along hardwood corridors and into a room with one small light. Mrs. Strong shook constantly. Miro folded his arms for comfort and found none.

"This woman will die of pneumonia unless you get her warm dry clothes and something hot to drink. So will I," he said.

"We don't want that, do we?" Henry said, and closed and locked the door.

There was a single bed in the corner of the room, with blankets piled on it. "Get your clothes off," he told her. "I'll wrap you in these blankets."

She tried to undress, with desperate and futile attempts at haste. Her own shaking made it impossible, and she stood, trembling, and let Miro undress her. He wrapped her in blankets. "Walk about—don't lie down." She stumbled about the room while he stripped and wrapped himself in blankets. Then he made her lie face down, pulled the blankets from her back, and breathed into her between the shoulder blades. Slowly the shivering diminished as the heat spread in her, and presently the trembling stopped. "Whether you like it or not," he said, "I'm going to rub you till your skin hurts."

When it was done she lay under the blankets, curled in a ball,

111

and watched him do push-ups, skip, lash about, and bounce on his toes.

"How old are you, Miro?"

"Why?"

"Nothing."

He wrapped himself again and sat on the edge of the bed. There was nowhere else to sit.

The room was large, and near its back wall, surmounted by a tank, was an ancient and enormous bathtub. "Ever slept in a bathroom before?" he asked her.

"Yes. Do you know where we are?"

"No idea. But they don't intend to keep us here very long. All they have on that window is a drawn blind. The door isn't straight. I could shift it out of its lock in no time if we were left alone for a while. So they don't intend to leave us alone."

"If you'll look out the window, I'll describe what you're looking at," she said.

"You will?"

"Go on."

He let up the blind on the window. "It's early light," he said. "But I see mist and rain."

"How far can you see?"

"Straight down a hill, and up another hill—two hundred yards in that direction. Less to the left and right."

"A hundred yards down a track, a river?"

"Yes. But you felt the track under you in the car and you heard the wooden bridge. It's a good game, though. Keeps the mind from clogging up with fear."

"That's the Bush River," she said.

He came back to the bed. "You're guessing."

"Forgive me for what I said to you, Miro. I've bathed in that tub and slept in this bed," she said. "This is Oliphant's house. It's a shooting lodge. What in the name of God is happening?"

Miro patted her consolingly and went back to the window and looked out into the mist and rain. The rain was fine and drifting; the mist was rolling like a wet cloud. He pulled down the blind. "We needn't tell them we're curious."

"You paid no attention to what I said," she complained. "This is Oliphant's lodge. *The Whig*. The editor of *The Whig*. *My husband's friend*."

"I heard you. Pretend you're sleeping." He was sitting on the edge of the bath when the key turned.

There were three of them this time—Henry, Matt and a young man in his twenties with a pale, thin face and bright, restless eyes. All of them carried guns; Matt had an armful of clothes. "We'll dry your clothes as well as we can, missus," he said. "You can wear these."

Mrs. Strong was curled in her blankets, her face hidden. She did not stir. "She's exhausted," Miro said. "Let her sleep."

"There's some for you, too," Matt said and dumped them all on the bed. He put a pair of large slippers and a pair of laced bush boots on the floor and turned to leave. He had no plans, it was clear, to dry Miro's clothes.

"Matt," Miro said. "I want to talk to you."

"No talk," Henry said and gestured them out of the room.

"There's not much room in that bed for the two of you," the young man laughed as they crowded through the door.

"*About Barney*, Matt," Miro said emphatically.

Matt stopped. Henry pushed him, but the big man did not move. He looked over Henry's head at Miro.

"I saw him last night. Just before you took us."

Matt pressed Henry and the young man out of his way and came back into the room. "Barney is with the Lord Jesus Christ," he said quietly, but the pain in his eyes showed like bright little spears.

Miro said, "The Gospel according to St. John, Matt. Chapter eleven, verse forty-three. 'And when he thus had spoken, he cried with a loud voice: Lazarus, come forth.

" 'And he that was dead came forth, bound hand and foot with grave clothes; and his face was bound about with a napkin. Jesus saith unto them: Loose him and let him go.' " Miro stood up, his blankets wrapped around him like an Indian. "The Lord Jesus Christ said to Barney, 'No, I am not in this wicked thing. Tell your brother Matt,' the Lord Jesus said. 'Send a messenger with my word that the Lord is not in this thing . . .' "

"Holy Christ!" the young man at the door said and started

to laugh. "Why didn't the Lord Jesus deliver his own messages?"

"No more talk," Henry shouted. "Come on, Matt. Out."

The young man laughed again. " 'And he that was dead came . . .' Oh, Jesus Christ! Oh, Holy God . . . !"

Matt spun with astonishing speed. "Keep him quiet," he screeched, and the young man's mouth dropped open. Henry nodded dumbly.

"All right, Matt, all right," the young man whispered. "I'm sorry, Matt."

"I saw him last night, Matt. These men are not believers. They don't know what we're talking about. *They* don't *know,* Matt."

Matt turned slowly, looking at Mrs. Strong on the bed as he turned. "She's your whore," he said. "You're no believer." He swallowed and his huge Adam's apple rose and fell.

Miro watched it move and hooked the blanket with his thumb, opening and hardening his hand. I'll kill him if I have to, he thought, and said, "She's no whore. She quarreled with Captain Strong last night and was frightened. She's a good woman, Matt. You see to it that none of them harm her. I pushed her into my bed because she and her husband were in my room quarreling and he ran out of the house and she was frightened and I had to go out . . . I wasn't in bed with her . . ." He said softly, "I'm a believer, Matt. I went out to see Barney." The Adam's apple leaped again. Miro almost whispered in the stillness, "Why did you do it, Matt? The Lord Jesus told Barney he didn't want it. He doesn't want you with this gang, Matt. They're not believers."

"Come out, Matt," Henry said intensely.

"Where did you see Barney?" Matt asked. The gun hung by his side. He was holding it by the barrel. It was useless. If I slash him now in the throat I can get the gun and use his body as cover, Miro thought. But they'd shoot Mrs. Strong before I could kill either of them.

"At the TB hospital," Miro said. "That's where I was last night."

"You walked all that way?"

God damn all rational lunatics, Miro thought. "The doctor

drove me there and back. He left me at the head of the Kilroot Road. Why did you do it, Matt?"

"You're an evil, lying man," Matt said.

"You're denying the Lord, Matt. 'And when he thus had spoken, he cried with a loud voice: Lazarus, come forth . . . Then many Jews which came to Mary, and had seen the things which Jesus did, believed on him.' You don't believe on him, Matt. You think he no longer has power, Matt. You're not a believer, Matt."

"*I believe!*" the man shouted. "I believe."

"Why did you do it, Matt?"

Henry moved quietly. He touched Matt's arm. "Come down, Matt," he said, "come down," and pulled him slowly back. The big man moved step by step backwards towards the door, his eyes screwed small, fixed on Miro's face.

Miro said, "He's at the hospital, Matt. Where he was for three days, before you took him to the roof . . ." Both men were pulling Matt now and he stood against the pressure, his eyes fixed wildly on Miro's face. "He was holding flowers, Matt. Myrrh, and white lily, and Rose of Sharon, and they weren't dead either . . . They were fresh . . ." They pulled on Matt's arms and he backed into the doorway and out to the landing. "Henry," Miro said, "we need food and something warm to drink." He said it softly, still looking into Matt's face. He was certain Matt didn't hear him.

Henry did. He came in and picked up Mrs. Strong's wet clothes from the floor and backed away again. "I'll give you a bullet in the gut," he said and closed and locked the door.

"What were you trying to do? Get us killed?" Mrs. Strong asked impatiently from the bed.

"Get up and put on whatever they brought you. Matt'll be back." He sorted their clothes and tossed hers to her.

"That's an old suit of Oliphant's," she said. "What has he to do with this?"

"The same as Strong. I told you. These are his men. Strong creates the chaos, then he fights it. Campaign contributions. What sort of a fighter are you?"

She sat up on the bed, clutching a blanket to her. "Will they hurt us, Miro?"

He dropped his blankets and stood naked. "Get out of the bloody bed, woman, and put something on. You still don't believe me about your husband and his political friends."

"No. How could I believe it? He couldn't do it. I couldn't believe it. It's insane."

"Isn't Ulster? Get up, for Christ's sake." He put his legs into a pair of long woolen drawers and pulled them up. They were the right length and twice his width at the waist. The shirt was like a tent, the suit a Norfolk jacket, and a pair of shooting knickers. Nothing stayed up securely, so he stood with one hand in his pocket, the knickers unfastened below the knee. "Get up," he snapped and pulled the blankets away from her.

She was in no better shape. "I've seen Mrs. Oliphant wearing this stuff," she said. "I need string or pins to keep the pants and skirt up."

"You'll get neither from them. What sort of a fighter are you?"

"I want to go home," she said simply.

"Then you'd better be willing to go all the way, for you're not meant to go home."

"Don't frighten me, Miro."

"I'm trying to make you want to do anything that has to be done."

"What has to be done?"

"I'll think of it." He went to the window and put up the blind. The rain was heavier, the mist thicker. It drifted around the house.

"The hill you saw across the river," she said, "it's called Corkey."

It entered his head like the sound of an explosion. "Maybe we're nearer the old man and the child than we know. Does Oliphant have big parties here?"

"He used to, in August. We haven't been here for three years."

"How many can he sleep in this place?" But she didn't answer. They were on the stairs again, all three of them. They stood about the doorway, staring. "The best people in their huntin togs," the young man said, grinning.

"What's this boy's name, Henry?" Miro asked.

"Kane."

"K-a-n-e or C-a-i-n?"

"Don't call me a boy," Kane warned Miro.

"Son, I don't think you're big enough to be called a boy."

"Git down the bloody stairs," Henry said impatiently.

They went down holding their clothes, Henry ahead of them, Matt and Kane behind, to a large lounge with a great stone fireplace. Mrs. Strong's clothes were steaming on a string before burning logs.

"Eat," Henry said and pointed them to a table.

Bowls of porridge. Spoons. No knives or forks. Nothing that could serve as a weapon. Miro looked for the fire irons. They had been removed. Porridge didn't sustain a man for long. "Is this all?" he asked.

"All yis'll need," Henry snapped.

Kane sat on the floor by the door, his back to the wall, watching Miro and Mrs. Strong, his gun across his thighs. Matt paced the room, looking from his unquiet spirit at Miro, looking nervously out at the mist and rain, shifting his gun from one big hand to the other. His pace quickened. He circled the large room, dragging his gun by the barrel, unable to keep his head from turning to Miro; and again up and down before the windows, his head swinging from the mist to Miro, from Miro to the mist. He wiped his mouth with the palm of his hand and went halfway round the room and back to the window.

"Sit down, Matt," Henry said, and Kane grinned.

"How did Barney get the scar on his face, Matt?" Miro said, his mouth full of porridge.

Henry crossed the floor and hit him with his gun. "Yir gonna stop it," he said. "Tell him t'stop it, missus, or I'll shoot the legs off him."

"You're going to shoot us anyway," Mrs. Strong said. "That's why you don't hide your faces . . ."

Matt said, "Papishes. Papishes did it. They cut Barney." His back was to the wall. He slid gently down to the floor, his big red peasant face gleaming with sweat in the cool room. He made deep sobbing noises in his throat, and rocked from side to side. "Papishes," he said, and his head sank down.

Kane grinned. "The blessins of religion," he said.

Miro thought Matt was moaning in his throat, but the sound took form and he sang in a deep strong voice:

> *"Up from the dead he arose*
> *With a might triumph o'er his foes*
> *He arose a victor o'er the dark domain . . ."*

He jumped to his feet and started for the door.

"Matt! Houl on a minit . . ." Henry rushed to obstruct him, and Matt pushed him aside and ran out into the rain and around the house. Henry ran after him.

Miro got up from the table.

"Sit down, mister." Kane got quickly to his feet and pressed his back to the wall. "If yi make me shoot ye, Henry's gonna say I wanted his job."

Miro sat down again. "It's Henry's job, is it?"

"An he likes it." That amused Kane.

"You don't like it?"

Kane shrugged. "I kin do it."

"We're to be shot?"

"Aye." His grin was an invitation to conversation.

"Why? We're hardly in a position to repeat what you say. Why are you going to shoot us?"

"Yir there. Yir a frien of Strong's. She's his wife." Mrs. Strong laid her head on her forearms on the table.

"And that's all? That's enough for you?"

"Yir a stupid man."

"Make me wise."

"Strong runs round the country shoutin fer a new guverment. But he's one of them. He's a boss. Dis he think the workers are stupid? He doesn't give a shit fer the workin people. He'd give them more of the same if he shifts the bloody lot that's in. Well, it's too late in the day. Luk anywhere in the world. The people are armin. Thir takin thir freedom. Thir throwin down the capitalist exploiters . . ." His face took on the fixed expression of autospeak. Kane seemed to be recollecting something learned.

"Oh, Christ . . ." Miro moaned.

" 'Oh, Christ' . . . my arse," Kane shouted. "I was born on a stupid durty wee farm. My stupid mother was a stupid durty wee farmer's wife and they made a stupid durty wee livin an all we iver heard was the sort of shit that big lug Matt talks—Jasus and Orange Billy and the bad papishes"—he spat the word "stupid" with venomous relish as if it brought a special relief—"and when there was a strike in the linen mills fer more money to buy dacent clos, some big fat stupid bastard come along an shouted 'Home Rule is Rome Rule' and all the stupid shits went back t'work fer the fat bugger that shouted it." He was warming to his subject, waving his gun to emphasize his argument. "They're shoutin thir big fat stupid faces off about bringin work here—more factories, more jobs, more trade. Whose factories? Fat Germans, fat Frenchmen, fat Yanks, fat Englishmen. Who's gonta make them fatter? Us! Exploiters! Bloody stupid fat exploiters. They'll take ir sweat an turn it into cash and send it back t'Germany an France an America . . ."

"You sound like the IRA. That's what they say . . ."

"Yir gittin smarter. They make the papishes mad at the prods. We make the prods mad at the papishes . . ."

"And they all get killed and you take over?"

"Och, fir Jasus sake, yir still stupid—nothin's the same after a thing like this. When it starts, the workers turn on their exploiters an take over and there's no more prods and papishes an no more bosses and the people . . ."

"No more," Miro said. "I've heard it all. They mouth it in Quebec, in Brazil, in Paris, in Berlin. They yatter it on every campus. It's in the pamphlets. Now tell me about you. Matt's sick. Everybody's stupid—including these smart workers who'll rise up just because *you* start a bloodletting. So tell me, you bright boy —how well are you?"

Kane's grin was malignant. "I wisht I had Henry's job," he said.

"Well, ye haven't," Henry said, storming into the room, "an that big godforsaken bastard's gonta see Barney an"—he reached Miro and slashed at him with his gun and missed—"yi

done it an yi done it on purpose, yi rotten bastard . . ." He
slashed and Miro dodged, picking up a chair with one hand to
parry Henry's attack and keeping his drooping trousers secure
with the other hand. "I'm gonta shoot yi in the guts when yir
time comes . . ."

"Henry!" Mrs. Strong said it like a command, and Henry hesitated, then turned to her.

"What?"

"You're not my husband's men?"

"Jasus, wuman! Strong? Us?" He leaned over the table towards her. "Maybe we'll do him next, missus. All he has fir us is
a big mouth an the right upbringin."

"This is Mr. Oliphant's house," she persisted with great composure. "Are you Oliphant's men?"

"I don't know an I don't give a damn whose house this is, missus."

"You just do what Dew-Boys tells you?" Miro said quietly.

"Dew-Boys? Who's Dew-Boys, fir Jasus sake?" He looked
mystified. He looked too mystified. He said to Kane, "Dew-
Boys? Who's Dew-Boys, Kane?"

"Jew boys is what sells furniture an goes bankrupt ivery six
months." He slapped his knee in appreciation. "Tell us more,
mister."

"Well, let me try this one. Just how do you know you won't be
disturbed in Oliphant's shooting lodge?"

"How d'yi know Barney come up from the grave? If yi don't
shut yir bloody mouth, I'm gonta shoot yir gut afore yir time."
Henry was disturbed. He fingered his gun nervously and looked
from Kane to Miro, from Miro back to Kane. "Jist shut yir
bloody gub."

"Who exploited you, Henry? Did you always want a motorbike when you were young, and the frustration turned you into a
gunman? It's always frustration, isn't it?" He was shouting
back. "What does that big word mean, Henry? Kane knows. It
means you didn't always get your own way when you were
young. Or you always got it and getting it drove you round the
bend. Either way, you don't have to admit to yourself that you're

just a common bloody criminal—this sort of bullshit allows you to think you're a superior bloody criminal. You commit political crimes. Bullshit. You're just a bunch of goddamned thugs who can read pamphlets . . ."

Henry came at him . . .

A car roared around the house and down towards the bridge. Henry changed course to the window. "I shuda shot the big bastard," he said and turned again to Miro. "But when it's time I'll shoot yi in the gut t'make up fir it."

He sat down on the fire curb. "Turn on the wireless, Kane. Let thim hear the news about themselves."

"You don't want to hear about yourselves, of course? You're not in this because you're sick, Henry. You're in this because you're a liberator."

Henry squeezed the trigger and shattered a window. "Did I make that clear enough?" he asked.

With his relentless grin, Kane said, "Yi missed him, Henry," and the news came on.

"Yes. Yes," Captain Strong was explaining. "I came back from a great meeting at Coleraine. My friend John Miro had very generously . . . very generously agreed to stay with my wife . . . He brought her home from the hospital in my absence, and after the meeting I drove home. They waited up for me and we talked for a while about things . . . I forget what, but about the meeting . . . That was one thing . . . We had a drink . . . my wife made some hot chocolate for us, and we talked for quite some time about the Coleraine meeting . . ."

Eva will hear it, Miro thought numbly.

Mrs. Strong looked at Henry and then, with a puzzled expression, at Miro. It hadn't been quite like that. But a man has to save face.

". . . and since I had a great deal on my mind I decided to take a walk. I do a lot of my thinking walking at night. My wife and Miro went to their rooms and when I looked in before I left the house, they both appeared to be asleep . . . I didn't disturb them." Mrs. Strong shook her head.

"He's a liar," Henry said scornfully. "Whit was *he* doin?"

". . . when I came back the two policemen were tied up and Miro and my wife had gone. There was the usual communiqué from the IRA . . ."

"Was there any sign of a struggle, Captain?" the interviewer asked.

"None. Miro must have been restless. Apparently, he got up and went out. According to the police the two men who jumped them waited for him to come in and got him too. I suppose," he said and hesitated, "I suppose these evil men think that by this means they can compel me to abandon my efforts to win order and peace for this province. We in Ulster . . ." he said firmly, ". . . are not that kind of people . . ."

Kane switched off. "You told us Strong an his missus were fightin, Henry," he said.

"He told us that, not me," Henry said, impatiently thumbing at Miro. "They're all bloody liars."

"We are *not* bloody liars," Mrs. Strong said. "God help us, I don't know what we are."

"What's the difference?" Kane said. "Yir done anyway. So's all yir stupid kind."

A car was coming through the mist, over the wooden bridge. Henry pulled Mrs. Strong's damp clothes from the line and threw them to her. "Up the stairs," he said. "Put them on. Keep him, Kane. I'm goin wi her."

"*I'm* going with her," Miro said quietly.

"Keep him, Kane," Henry said.

Miro walked round the table and took Mrs. Strong by the arm.

"My clothes aren't dry," she said faintly, and Miro held her as she swayed.

"Yel not be needin thim long," Henry said. "That's them come fir us," and Kane hit Miro from behind across the side of the neck.

The sound of the child crying was the first thing he heard: the long, raking sobs of childish anguish. Then Kane shouting, and a firm old voice remonstrating. Then no more voices. The rain was lashing the house; the wind whined across the hills. Mrs. Strong was not in the room.

He got off the bedroom floor where they had dumped him and went shakily to the window. His head was howling. He let up the blind. The clouds were down around the high ground; the rain was driving from the north, from the ocean.

He tried the door; it was locked. It was time to go, he decided, but not without Mrs. Strong. He had to get her back here. He tried the window. It was stiff, but it opened. He closed it again and hammered on the door. Something Henry said about Mrs. Strong wouldn't come to mind.

Kane came.

"Where's Mrs. Strong?"

"Go an lie down on yir bed."

"Where is she?"

"Did yi hear me?"

Miro went to the bed and lay down. "Well?"

"They come fir her."

"Who came for her?"

Kane was nervous. His gun was firmly set for Miro's stomach. "They come fir her. She's near Glendun by now."

"Tell Henry I want to talk to him."

"Henry went wi thim."

Miro sat up slowly.

"Down. On yir back or I'll do it . . ."

He lay down. "Henry went to do his job," he said. "Is that it?"

"That's right."

"To kill that woman?"

"That's right."

"For your lunatic bloody schemes?"

"Fir the revolution."

Miro lay still. His stomach convulsed. "You're not fit to live," he said. "If I hadn't heard and read so goddamn much of it, I wouldn't believe it. You people . . . retarded infants . . . mental defectives . . . God! *Liberators!*"

"Yir next," Kane said pleasantly.

"And then the old man and the child I heard you yelling at."

"That's right."

"Why don't they use you, Kane? Are you all mouth and no nerve?"

"I'd do yi wi pleasure."

"Bugger off."

"They'll be back fir yi in two hours. I'll offer to do yi." He was grinning again, but he had to retrieve the grin. It kept fading.

"Go away, you putrid little psycho."

When the key turned Miro went to the old bathtub and bathed his face in cold water. The tank above the tub rumbled. It sat on a heavy wooden platform supported by four steel columns set in steel plates on the floor. The columns were laced together with crossed spars. He heaved on one of the supports. The structure trembled but it was firm. He tried each column and got no more encouraging results. The window, he found, was about forty feet from the ground, with nothing on the wall that would give him a toe hold. He could break his back out there.

He tried the columns again. They were firm, but they trembled. Anything that trembles, he decided, man or water tank, can be brought down. He went to the door and stood with his back to it. If I came charging in here, he thought, I'd be right in line with the front left column. He stood with his back to the front left column and checked the line of approach from the door. His shooting knickers were a problem. Their waistband was around his hips, and only lightly. He took them off.

Patiently, he started. Strongly at first, with his shoulder against the column, he heaved. The structure trembled. His heaves were powerful. He waited for movement, putting all his strength into the pressure. Movement came slowly, and slightly; but when it came, he established a rhythm and maintained it, rocking steadily, watching the platform. Chips and dust poured down on his head. He breathed the dust, rubbed it from his eyes. It was three-quarters of an hour before the column shifted enough with his rhythmic pressure to satisfy him. The tank was moving. The platform tilted forward slightly and was down a few inches at the left-hand corner. He risked some extra pressure with his aching shoulder and leaped away as the tank broke from the outlet pipe. But it stayed on the platform, pouring water into the bath. He put the rubber plug in.

There were three pipes up to the platform, an intake, an outlet, and one that appeared to have no purpose and was probably an abandoned outlet. He tested them cannily. They were loosened by the movement of the tank, but whether they were loosened enough to serve his purposes he didn't know and couldn't find out without running the risk of bringing the whole thing down. They would come away at the top—they were free there already. Whether they would come free at the bottom he would know when his life was on the line.

He took the blankets from the bed and stacked them in small loose cocks between the door and the tub. The door listed. There was a gap almost an inch deep between the frame and the door, above the lock. He tried to lift it and couldn't move it far enough to release the lock. But the door was light and old. He stood back and slammed his foot against it. It cracked. He jarred himself to the shoulders with his second dig, and the edge of the door split. He put his foot through the panel as Kane, yelling, reached the stairs. The door was slightly open. Miro ran for the window, kicked it out, and was back under the tank, shouting insanely when Kane reached the door and rammed it open, his gun level. He saw only Miro standing behind the left front column in his shooting jacket, long woolen drawers, and laced-up field boots, his hair wild and gray with dust.

"I'm going to wreck this bloody house, Kane. Room by room I'm going to tear it down . . ." He gripped the outlet pipe with both hands. "Come and stop me, you stinking psycho," he screamed and heaved forward on the pipe. It gave forward at the top and turned in the elbow at the bottom, pointing towards Kane chest-high, like a thin bazooka. The tub was full and flowing over.

"Stop it, yi stupid bastard," Kane yelled.

"Come and stop me!" Miro closed his hands around the loose support.

Kane squeezed the trigger and fired into the wall a foot from Miro.

"Come and stop me!"

Kane charged; his feet caught in the blankets and he lurched forward into the extended pipe. Miro heaved back on the supporting column and leaped away as the tank rolled and fell on Kane. It hit his back and rammed the pipe into his chest, rolled on down his back and legs, and blocked the door. Miro hauled Kane savagely off the pipe, put on his shooting knickers, and fastened them up securely with the dead man's braces.

He raced through the house, shouting Corkey's name, and found the old man and the child in a back room downstairs. The door was locked and padlocked. The keys were in Kane's pocket. The windows of the room were boarded up. The old man and the little girl came out, shielding their eyes from the gray, wet light.

"Have you been in the dark all this time, Doctor?"

"Except when they took us to the bathroom. What have you to do with this?" The old man was fearful. He was tall, erect for his age, and his hair and face were gray. The child held his hand and shrank from Miro. "Are you one of their bosses? They talk a lot about the bosses . . ." The old clergyman was vague. He talked nervously and stroked the child's hand.

"I'm in your category and I haven't any time to talk. Can you walk? Over hills, in heavy rain? Can the child?"

"For a bit," Dr. Corkey said.

"Start by walking up and down while I go over this place, then we'll go, as fast as you can travel. Did you ever hear a phone ring here?"

"No."

Miro went through drawers and cupboards. He found a linen-backed ordnance map and stuffed it inside his shirt; one black oilskin in a closet and a rubber ground sheet, but no handgun and nothing that would shield him from the rain. Henry would probably kill Mrs. Strong with his little gun. He found no money. Henry would have that too.

"Put this on." He gave Dr. Corkey the oilskin and tried to wrap the ground sheet about the child like a shawl. But Dr. Corkey had to do it. The child wouldn't let Miro touch her. "We go," Miro said and led them down the track towards the river.

They moved slowly. "Can you move any faster, Doctor?" Miro asked him.

"A little, I think." But he moved no faster.

The wind and the rain pushed them from behind. "I don't think the child can go far," Corkey said.

"I can handle that if you can keep going. Up. Up. Higher up," Miro said, as the old man turned left into the road. He stopped them and said to the child, "I'm your friend, dear. I came to help you. You'll have to stop being afraid of me. I'm going to carry you. If you cry, I'm going to beat you. If you go on crying, I'm going to leave you behind. Do you understand?"

The child stared and said nothing. But she did not withdraw when he picked her up. Her little body was hard with strain and terror. He swung her to his back and said, "Let's get you home to your daddy and mummy."

"I heard a woman's voice this morning," Dr. Corkey said.

"Mrs. Strong. Captain Ronald Strong's wife. I was their houseguest when they took us."

"Are we leaving her?"

"Don't frighten the child any more, Doctor. Captain Strong is a widower this morning."

"Dear God."

"Keep your wind for climbing."

The doctor's wind was already failing him. The hill was long and rough, with tumped grass. Miro put his arm about the old man's waist and helped him forward.

"I can't go far. Why don't you hurry on with her?"

"Listen." The car was coming back from its mission to Glendun. Strong had been a widower for some time. It was Miro's turn. Where, he wondered, did they intend to leave me to be found? To the east over these bare, wild hills lay the Glens of Antrim and the Coast Road, and to the west the fertile farmlands of Mid-Antrim. While the cloud was down and the rain driving, they were safer in this upland desolation—so long as they could keep moving; so long as he could find a place to leave these two helpless people while he got to a house with a phone. It would take Henry and his funeral party only minutes to go over the house and read the sign. Then what would they do?

He put the child down. "Open your oilskin, Doctor, and cover this map," he said. He found the shooting lodge on the ordnance map. The road to Glendun went past the lodge northwest and southeast, then swept in a loop around Glenbush Forest and northeast to the Glendun River and east to the glen that reached down to the coast. Almost a mile from the lodge in the direction they were taking, a road went southwest to Drumrankin and Corkey. There was a school marked at Drumrankin and a post office at Corkey. That's where they would look first—they would assume that he headed for the nearest phone. The Corkey post office was two miles from the shooting lodge, on the edge of the fertile land. The next post office was south-southwest of them at Newtown Crommelin—five miles on the map; more up and down and around the wet, naked hills. But it was the safest way to go. Henry and his undertakers would drive to Corkey to wait for them. They would wait a long time for an old man and a child. Miro could make Newtown Crommelin before them, if he could find a place to hide Corkey and the child.

A house was marked on the northern slope of Slievenahanaghan, straight ahead. If he could find it in this cloud, he could leave them there. If the doctor could survive.

"They'll be poor Catholics in that house up there," Dr. Corkey said cautiously.

"I don't care if they run a whorehouse," Miro said. "Your friends down there weren't Catholics and one of them was an ardent Protestant. God damn you people."

"Yes, indeed," the doctor said mildly. "I think He's done that already."

They crossed the dirt road to Corkey in half a mile. Miro had to drag the doctor up the ditch. The old man's legs were going. They were less than a hundred yards up the hill on the other side when the car went past. Miro and Eva had driven for days over this wild land last summer, and in all their time up here had seen three cars. The one that passed behind them was Henry. Nobody would come up here in this storm without an urgent purpose, and Henry had one.

The hills were quiet, except for the wind and the rain, and the rustling sound of the enveloping clouds. Twice he lifted his charges over drystone walls rather than waste time searching for breaks. And he underestimated Henry.

From behind, the first voice cried, "Ho-o-o," and the second to the right—he thought it was to the right, but bouncing off the cloud the way it did, he couldn't be sure—"Ho-o-o," and the third still farther to the right, "Ho-o-o." Maybe one or more of them had driven to Corkey. Three of them were beating the mountain, keeping in touch and in line.

"Slide down, child," he said. "Get on my back, Doctor, and hang on hard." He pulled the child up in front of him, hoisted her legs over Dr. Corkey's, and lodged his arms under them all. "Hold one another on. The little girl's legs will stop the circulation in yours, Doctor. It'll hurt. Let it, or we're all dead." He started to climb.

His back was breaking, his arms were stretching, his legs were trembling, and his heart bursting. "Ho-o-o," said one; "Ho-o-o," two answered; "Ho-o-o," three called; "Ho-o-o," four put in for the first time, or the first time Miro had heard him. He pushed harder, stumbled, stopped. "You're choking me, Doctor. Lower your hands a bit." But the old man's hands were slipping, and they ran back up to Miro's throat and leaped to his chin. Now his neck was breaking.

He couldn't do it. He knew he couldn't do it. It would be better to measure the gap between the voices, lie down, and hope they would pass in the cloud. Then what would they do? Go back down the hill? To where? He attacked the hill. The little house with the overgrown thatch stepped out of the cloud to meet him. Both halves of its door were closed against the day. He put the child down and knocked hard. His arms trembled. Dr. Corkey slid from his back and sank to the wet, dirty yard. Miro let him lie. The little girl cried quietly, leaning against the wall.

The half-door opened. "Aye?" The face it came from was red and lined, and dirt lodged in all its cracks.

Miro picked Corkey off the ground and drew the child to him. "This is the Reverend Dr. Corkey that was kidnapped, and this is the child from Ballyweaney."

"Aye? Pleased t'meet ye," the face said, peering.

"The men who took them are coming up the mountain behind us. Hide them for me. Please."

A black-and-red hand with black broken nails pulled at the black-and-red face. The eyes grew smaller. "Och. Ah wudn't want t'git mixed up in any o that," the face said.

"I'll pay you. Anything you want, I'll do it. Just help us."

"Och."

"For God's sake man—the child. Corkey's an old man . . ."

"Och. Ah hiv nuthin t'do wi them sort o things . . ." He closed the half-door and barred it.

"The common people will all rise up with you, Kane, if they can get off their cowardly bloody arses," Miro muttered bitterly, "like Barney." He dragged his burdens across the yard, looking for cover, and found it in a small, whitewashed building stacked six feet high with hay. He threw the child up and boosted Corkey after her. "Get right to the back and stay there. Stay as long as you have to. Don't move for hunger or thirst till the army gets here. They'll be here today, sometime. Stay back and stay quiet and don't get down to close the door. Leave it open. I've got to get to a phone. *Stay there*." He left them without waiting to hear them. They probably said nothing.

"Ho-o-o." They weren't far from the cabin but far enough to be out of sight of it. They'd be in the yard before they saw it in this weather. He ran to his right, across their line of advance, waiting to hear their call again. "Not far enough yet," he said when it came, and kept going.

When it came again he was on their left.

"Ho-o-o."

"Ho-o-o."

"Ho-o-o."

"Ho-o-o."

"Ho-o-o," Miro called.

Five now. They called again. Still five, the fifth farther to the left. They tried again. Still five. Still farther to the left. They were testing. They knew. They kept trying, closing together from the sound of it. He kept calling. Then they stopped. They had his direction. They were speading again. He turned south, running blind. "Ho-o-o," he heard. Four times. And again, fading. They were beating east. He kept running, downhill now, until he could run no more. When he went forward again it was into the bank of a river. The map said it was the Aghanageerah. He waded it, knee-high, and climbed again. South-southeast now, up hill and down, two miles to the road through Skerry West. He went round the village. No post office, no phone; and

more than a mile to Newton Crommelin, going downhill. He
kept close to the road and dropped into the ditch when he heard
the cart coming towards him. The man with the reins sat
hunched on the seat over the horse's rump, his head and shoulders covered with sacking against the rain; behind him in the
cart were three large milk containers. Miro let him pass and
took the road behind him, the sounds of his feet covered by the
rattle of the wheels. He was on the cart and had a wrist around
the man's neck before the heaving of the cart made him turn.

"I'll break your neck if you try to look," Miro said. "I want the
change in your pockets. Get it and lay it on the seat beside you."
He pulled the man's head back. The money was laid on the seat.
The victim couldn't see the tweed sleeve above the hand that
picked up the money. His head was too high for him to see the
sleeve above the wrist that pressed his Adam's apple. Miro
pulled one of the sacks off the man's shoulders and put it over
his head. "On your way," he said and was back into the ob-
scuring cloud before the sack could be hauled off. He heard the
cart pick up speed.

The cloud was thinning. He could see the crossroads with The
Skerries Pub on one corner and opposite it, the post office—a little shop with the post office sign above the door. He came out of
the field and crossed to it.

The man behind the counter stared: shooting jacket, knickers
gaping at the waist, unbuttoned below the knee; laced field
boots and long drawers; with the wet running from him to the
floor.

"I want to make a phone call."

"Aye." The postmaster nodded to the shelf against the wall.
His look said he had seen much, but nothing like this. A car
stopped outside. It was driven by a girl, who helped the old
woman in the back to get out, adjust her balance on her walking
stick, and stump stubbornly into the shop, shaking off any further help. The shop bell rang as Miro got through.

"Bowen?" Miro said and watched the street.

"Miro? Where in God's name are you?"

The postmaster reached under his counter, brought out a
newspaper, stared at it, handed it to the old woman, who waved

it away. She was intent on Miro's clothes. "Good God!" she said and took the paper, gaped, and handed it to the girl, who gaped. "Good God!" the old woman said again, and limped to Miro's side to listen.

"I'm in the post office at Newtown Crommelin," Miro said. "They killed Mrs. Strong . . ."

"I know. They phoned and told the police she was under the bridge at Glendun. How did you . . . ?"

"Just listen, Colonel! They've been using Oliphant's shooting lodge."

"Good God!" the old woman said.

". . . They were to kill me next, then Corkey and the child on the tenth and eleventh. I've got Corkey and the little girl." He gave Bowen directions. "Get somebody there fast, Bowen, before they both die of pneumonia. Matt left the lodge to see Barney at the TB hospital . . ."

"What the hell . . . ?"

"Just listen, damn you. He's probably been there and is on his way back looking for me. And Bowen . . . they don't know Strong's in it. Dew-Boys is the ringmaster. He's probably the only link Strong has with them. Lift the whole lot of them—Dew-Boys, Strong . . ."

"Miro! I can't touch Strong till I have proof. If he's touched, it has to be the Prime Minister who says so."

"All right. Get Dew-Boys and get up after this lot."

"I can lift Dew-Boys. He's nobody . . ."

"Bowen, they're right behind me up on the hills and I have to move before they get here. I have no money, no gun, no transport, and I've got to get some. I only have minutes to move . . . And Bowen, what about my wife? She'll have heard the radio . . ."

"Riada's on to that, Miro. She'll be fine."

"Fine, my arse—she'll be out of her mind. If I don't get moving, she'll be a widow . . ." He put down the phone.

"*You,* sir?" The old lady stuck the paper before Miro's face. There on the front page were Captain and Mrs. Strong and Miro and the dead face of Barney, with the caption, "Who is this

132

man?" Matt could have seen it by now. Matt would be murderous by now.

"Yes, ma'am. I can't wait, ma'am . . ."

"Give him a couple of fivers, Janet," the old lady said, "and take my car. I know Jane Strong . . ."

"You knew her, ma'am. She's dead. Thank you, I'll take anything you give me."

"The keys are in the car," the girl said.

"You were calling the army?"

"Yes, ma'am. Goodbye, ma'am . . ."

"Good God," he heard her say again as he left, "the riffraff have taken us over in Ulster."

Miro started the car and glanced in the rear-view mirror. Henry was sitting beside the driver of the car that turned the corner at The Skerries. Miro put his foot down and whipped around the tight bend at the foot of the hill as the car behind shot forward. He went through the empty streets of the main part of the village with nothing in the mirror and put the car into a lane on his left. The car was old; it didn't have the power; he would be caught out on the road by the one behind, which shot past the end of the lane going fast. He ran back behind the houses to the post office. That old lady was his way out. She'd reach Bowen for him with a destination. The destination he had in mind made him shudder, but it was the best he could think of in a hurry. She was still there.

He gave the girl the keys. "It's not fast enough, ma'am. They'd have run me off the road." He wrote Bowen's number on a telegraph form and put it in the girl's purse. "His name's Bowen," he said, "Colonel Bowen. Get through to him and tell him to send Mac Donnell or somebody to pick me up at the convent inshore from Port Vinegar . . ."

"God! That's ten miles!"

"Yes, ma'am. Tell him to wait. Your car's in that lane beyond the village . . ."

The back door opened. Henry came through the back shop, Miro's gun in his hand. "Out the front," he said and turned his face from the lame old woman.

Her stick swept up under Henry's wrist and Miro felled him. He took back his gun and the shells from Henry's pocket.

"How was that, young man?"

"That was ducky, and thanks for the 'young,' " Miro said, smiling. "Now you'll have to face his friends. They've just pulled up in front."

"I'm Mrs. Ogilvie of Glenray House. Can you get there?" she said. "Port Vinegar's too far."

He went out the back door. The men in front were getting out of their car. The rain was slackening. The cloud was lifting. Glenray House was a mile west, on the main road to Glenariff. It was a lot closer than Port Vinegar. It might be harder to reach for all that.

He wasn't going to make it to Port Vinegar or to Glenray House. He was sure of it.

In front of the post office the road dropped down briefly to a hairpin turn that went east, dropping again sharply into the main part of the village. Behind the post office a field too steep for anything but goats fell down to the houses.

And they were down there too. He was looking down into the rest of the village, and over it to the lane beyond, and one of them was leaning against Mrs. Ogilvie's car. That was less of a problem than the fact that he was leaning and looking up at Miro. There were three others who stood out like warts. They were on the three streetcorners he could see, waiting. The man by the car put two fingers in his mouth and shrilled and came running at the village. The men on the corners turned sharply in circles, looking up and down their little streets; but they kept station. Miro threw himself down and rolled; the map of the little streets was photographed on his mind. He picked the house he wanted and rolled to the back door and lifted the latch. There was a woman in the three-roomed house, sitting in the middle of the kitchen floor in a long zinc tub, smothered in suds and nothing else. Her mouth and eyes were wide open, her tongue half out of her mouth. She was unable to speak. She was unable to move. The soap, in a hand arrested on its way to her shoulder, was bright in the gloom. But the hand tightened on the slippery bar and it squirted across the floor.

"A-g-g-g . . ." she said, trying to scream, and nothing else came. Her eyes moved from Miro's face to the gun in his hand. "A-g-g-g," she said again.

"Don't," he said. "Don't make a sound. Will you listen to what I want to say?"

She might have agreed. She might have screamed. She could do neither.

He saw the paper on the table. "The paper this morning," he said. "I had my picture in it, and Captain Strong's and Mrs. Strong's. I'm the one called Miro. The men who kidnapped us are all through the village." He was speaking slowly, articulating clearly, his gun pointing at the woman's head. It might keep her quiet. "They killed Mrs. Strong this morning. They're going to kill me if they catch me. Do you understand?"

He got no response. "Dr. Corkey was kidnapped, and the little girl," he began again, slower than before, speaking softly, persuading terror away. "I got them free and hid them up in the hills. The army is coming to get them." He waited for a sign from her and got none. "These men are looking for me. *They– will–kill–me*. Do you understand?"

This time she nodded. He thought she nodded. The movement might have been a nerve spasm in her neck. He searched for things to say to ease her fear. "I have a wife, a little boy . . . I wouldn't hurt you. I just need your help. Will–you–help–me?"

"Ca . . . ca . . . can't . . ." she said, choking.

"I know you're afraid," he said. "I'm not asking you not to be. I'm afraid too. Those men are going to kill me. Who are you?"

"Tea . . . tea . . . teacher."

"Schoolteacher?" (How old was she? Twenty-five?)

"Yes."

"I won't hurt you. Is this your house?"

"Yes."

"There are at least seven men out there, waiting to kill me. Do you know Mrs. Ogilvie of Glenray House?"

"Yes."

135

"She helped me in the post office. I'm trying to get to her house. Will you help me?"

"I can't." She lowered her arm slowly and covered her already lather-hidden breasts with her hands.

"Where's your towel?" When she nodded towards the room on the right, he said, "If I get it for you, you won't shout out? I won't hurt you."

"No."

He brought her large towel and held it high while she got out of the tub and wrapped herself. "Get dressed and let's see what's to be done," he said and waited, watching the street from behind her curtains. One of them was on the corner across the street, his head swiveling. Twice their car passed up and down the street. Henry was in it, beside the driver again, patrolling the village. There were three men in the car and four on the streets; or three on the streets and one back at Mrs. Ogilvie's car. By any count, in a village of this size—compact, with short streets, and covering very little ground—there were four too many—or five, or six too many. If the army came through here, all they had to do was stand still and look dull, and the soldiers would pass them by. The girl came from the bedroom in slacks and a heavy sweater.

"Are you afraid of me?" he asked her.

"Not now. You're the man in the paper. I'm just afraid. I mean, one minute I'm sitting in the tub and the next I'm in the middle of this. I mean, the way people are killing . . . There were three young soldiers . . . They were only eighteen, in civies, drinking in a pub. They took them out and shot them and piled their bodies in the ditch . . . They were only wee boys . . ."

"When was this?"

"Near Belfast last night, just before the curfew . . . it was the first thing on the news this morning, and then the bit about Mrs. Strong and you came on, and the captain was talking. They really shot the poor woman?"

"Yes."

"If they find you they'll shoot me, won't they?"

"They might. Yes. You can't be grateful to me for choosing your door."

"That's right. I'm not." She was looking over his shoulder at her back window. "There's a man in the back field."

The man was halfway down the slope, moving carefully, one hand in his jacket pocket. He moved across their line of vision, standing against the sides of backhouses, slipping his arm around to try the latches.

A woman's voice said impatiently, "Yil have t'wait. I'm in here," and he moved quickly away.

A man at a back door yelled, "Whit the hell d'yi think yir doing there?"

"I'm lukin fir a friend," the man on the slope called.

"In my shit house? Git t'bloody hell outa there or I'll shift yi."

The searcher went up and over the hill.

"He was easy put off," she said.

"They don't want a disturbance," Miro said encouragingly. "They just want one clean shot at me. They'll not hurt you." He wished he believed it. "When they get me, they'll go. You saw how easily they're put off."

"Aye," she said without conviction.

"I don't know your name."

"Mary Robinson."

"Protestant?"

"People always ask you that in this country. My father's a Covenanting Presbyterian."

"What's that?"

"People always ask you that too. It's hard to explain."

"So is everything else in this country. You could get out now. They don't know I'm in your house. You could walk up the field to the post office and go to somebody's house."

"Aye." She looked at him sideways.

"Put on your raincoat and go ahead."

"Aye." She put it on and searched the steep field. "Well, I'm away. Good luck." Her hand was on the latch. "I feel bad, doing this."

"Go ahead. And thank you for not screaming."

137

"Aye. I could hardly do less. I hope you get away." She was gone. He watched her up the field into the back door of the post office. He put the wooden bar into its slot and went back to the front window. Henry's car went past again on patrol. The man on the corner was still there. There was no sign of recognition between him and the men in the car.

Miro barred the front door and sat down to think. He thought of Eva, and Mrs. Strong, and Tomalty, and the men in the football field at Larne, and the three young soldiers, and an old rage boiled. He was *sitting* here. Just bloody well *sitting*. Waiting. If Mac Donnell or anybody else got here it wouldn't be for an hour. These creatures didn't know he'd had time to get in a call for help, but they knew he'd been in the post office and might have made a call. They wouldn't wait around long, patrolling and watching. They knew he had to be in one of this short row of houses. He hadn't had time to get farther. Soon they'd start going from house to house, with men back and front to cut him down if he tried to bolt. There'd be neither conscience nor compassion in anything they did. He checked his gun and counted his shells. The clip had been full and there had been twenty shells in his pocket. There were five bullets in his gun. The missing one killed Mrs. Strong. Henry had used Miro's gun. Rage closed his eyes.

He checked the back again. Mary Robinson was coming down the slope, carrying a long paper parcel. He slid the bar out and waited for her.

The parcel was a shotgun. "Campbell's like a raging bull," she said. "He sent me back with this."

"Who's Campbell?"

"The one that runs the post office. They pulled the phone out by the roots and hit Mrs. Ogilvie. He says she'll have a black eye. She went to the petrol garage a wee minute ago for a lift home. She was going to phone somebody from home—Colonel Bowen, is that it?"

"That's it."

"She knows you're in my house. She got in their way when they tried to come after you. That's why they hit her. She saw you. She's a terrier, that one, I'm telling you." She was angry.

"They hit a crippled old woman!" She handed him a box of cartridges from her coat pocket and barred the door. "I shouldn't be doing this," she said. "I'm engaged to a minister's son." The thought seemed to tickle her. "We were both working for the summer last year in a hotel in Portrush."

"Why aren't you married?"

"He's doing his Ph.D. He's a"—she looked doubtful—"botanist. But he drinks." It was a character reference. She hefted the shotgun. "I'm a farmer's daughter. I've shot more wee rabbits with one of these . . ."

"It'll be almost an hour before any help can get here," he said. "They'll start working the houses any time now. They know I've got to be in one of these houses. We have twenty-five bullets for this and twelve cartridges for the shotgun. I've got a proposition to put to you."

She sobered. Men were not like rabbits, her face said.

"I want you to call that one across the street over to the front door." He went over everything carefully. She licked her lips and rubbed her hands together nervously and listened.

Then she began to gather things together: a clothesline and a sharp clasp knife; three milk bottles, with cardboard stoppers and strings of cotton wool; paraffin poured from the reserve lamp beside her bed and from what was left of a can under the kitchen sink. She loaded the shotgun and put it around the corner of the kitchen doorway. Miro went into the bedroom and waited. Mary Robinson went, swallowing hard, to the front door.

"Hey, mister," he heard her call, and after a pause, "There's a queer-looking man in a big baggy suit that doesn't fit him, sitting in my outhouse. Do you think you could come through the house and get him out for me? He has me scared out of my wits."

"Jist a minit, missus."

She came running to the bedroom door. "It's not working," she whispered frantically. "He's gone for help."

"Play it the way I told you," he said. "Go on back. Keep your nerve." He heard the shrill whistling and feet running to the front door. They were inside. Two of them by the sound of it.

"Where's yir own man, missus?"

139

"I'm not married. But I'm engaged," she said defensively.

"Show iss."

He saw them at the back window, examining the outhouse. "Thon one?"

"Yes."

"Fir how long?"

"Maybe fifteen minutes."

"Big boots? No stockins?"

"Long woolen drawers between his trousers and his boots. That's him. D'you think he's daft? If you get him out for me I'll make you a cup of tea."

One of them turned toward the open bedroom door. Miro sank down behind the bed. "Watch for Jack," the man said. "Is that where you sleep, dear?"

"Yes." She was in the kitchen. Miro heard the kettle rattling.

"I'll have my tea in there with you."

"Jack's on the hill," the second man said.

Not two of them. Three. And one of them in the bedroom door. Miro's finger curled around the trigger. "That's a nice-looking bed, dear."

"Come on." Their guns were out. The hand of the man at the back door reached for the latch. His companion was still looking at the bed. *"Come on."*

"We'll rush it and shove it over on him," the man in the bedroom door said, turning away.

Miro said from behind the bed, "Keep very still."

They kept very still, but their feet were shifting gently, sliding. "Look at the kitchen door," Miro said. "That's a twelve-bore sticking out there. Let the guns fall. Don't try to set them down. Drop them."

"Do what the man says," Mary shouted. "If I have to hold this thing any longer I'll use it." It was an appeal, not a threat.

The guns clattered on the floor. Miro went out behind them. "Hands on the door. Up high," he said and slashed twice with his gun. They went down, moaning briefly, bleeding behind the right ears. Their hands were quickly tied behind them, their ankles lashed together. The man on the slope was tight against the side of the outhouse, his gun in his hand. He was looking anxiously at the back door, expecting company that didn't come. He slid down to the grass and lay out of the line of fire of any enemy who might be inside. "Billy," he shouted, watching the door.

Miro pressed against the wall and threw open the back door. Billy and the other man were on the floor, in full view.

"Is yi back, yi dirty peepin bastard?" an angry man shouted a few houses down, and Jack scrambled around the outhouse, out of sight.

Mary was on the floor under the window, peeping from the edge of her curtains. "Two more at the top of the slope," she said. "They've got rifles." The man farther along slammed his back door.

Miro held his arm down towards her. "Light it," he said, and she struck a match and lit the cotton wool in his milk bottle. He lobbed it up over the outhouse. The man behind it screamed in the core of the *woof,* and appeared, rolling down the hill.

"Run! Git up!" Henry yelled.

"Stay down, girl," Miro said and rolled across in front of the open door, kicking it shut. From far back in the room he watched the burning man rise and run up the hill. Henry's rifle cracked and the man jerked and fell, flaming. He burned where he lay.

"He shot him," Miro said. "Keep low, Mary, and roll across the door."

The two men stirred on the floor. They were less than men and more than boys.

"If you could look up the field," Miro said to them, "you would see your comrade Jack, lying on the grass, burning. He may or may not be burning to death. He may be dead. Henry shot him. If he were alive I think you'd hear him."

They looked at him steadily.

"I can't explain to you why Henry did it. I suppose Jack saw him kill Mrs. Strong. I suppose Jack would have been a nuisance to look after if he'd lived after being hit by a petrol bomb. Don't you think so? I suppose Henry has the same high regard for you two."

A bullet smashed the back window and slammed into the front wall.

Miro said, "If Henry starts shooting through the door, you two are in the line of fire. Is your liberating mission worth it?"

He hadn't impressed them. They didn't believe him. "Which of you is Billy?"

One of them stared sullenly. The other smiled. "I'll assume that you're Billy," Miro said to the smiler. "You're a leader type. You called this young lady 'dear,' you proposed to have your tea in her bedroom and her in her bed. You're a cavalier. Did you see Henry kill Mrs. Strong?"

Billy looked away, with youthful disdain.

"You don't believe Henry shot your friend, do you? You occupy some private world because you can't get people to regard you seriously in the real one. You're a kind of bacteria. Well, lad, I doubt if anybody could teach you much, but maybe your friend can learn." He hauled the young man from the floor, pried open his knees and set him on a kitchen chair, facing backwards, imprisoned by his bound legs around the back of the chair. "I'm going to push you over in front of that window where Henry can see you. Maybe he thinks you know too much to go to jail. We'll see."

He pushed the chair in front of the window and said to the other youth, "All you can see is Billy. Watch him. I have some questions for you too."

Henry's bullet hit Billy in the chest and knocked him back. He lay on the floor, his legs around the back of the chair, looking up through the bars. He was still smiling.

"Now you," Miro said. "We have another chair and Henry's a disinterested idealist."

"No, mister, please . . ."

"You saw Henry kill Mrs. Strong?"

"Aye. Under the bridge at Glendun."

"Henry who?"

"I don't know, mister. First names ony."

"Is Henry his real name?"

"I don't know, mister. Honest to God."

"Keep it honest to God. The minute I doubt you, I'll get another chair."

Henry and the man with him were smashing the windows at

the back of the house. There was glass all over the floor, chips of window frame, chips from furniture and the front wall.

"Who is Dew-Boys?"

"The chief."

"Ever seen him?"

"No. Only Henry sees him. Henry says he's a great thinker, mister."

"Where do you hole up?"

"I only know four places. Two flats in Belfast and the Tin Mission in Belfast—that's on the Crumlin Road. The flats is on the Malone Road. An the lodge."

"There are more?"

"Dozens, mister."

"How many of you?"

"Thousands, mister. All over."

"Poor boy. These places cost money. Whose?"

"The banks'. It's nobody's money, yi see. Ony the banks'."

"I see, only the banks. You believe in the revolution?"

"Aye."

The two men in the street were shooting the windows out of the front of the house. Miro and Mary dragged their prisoner under the sink and drainboard in the kitchen. "We can't watch the back from under the sink," Mary said.

"We can shoot them on the way in," Miro said cheerlessly.

"Oh, God." Mary looked as if she wanted to be sick.

The shooting stopped suddenly. They ran from room to room, squinting at an angle, trying to enlarge their vision. Henry and his man were standing on the lip of the slope behind, surveying the country around through field glasses.

The commotion started in the street. The two men in front were driving people from their houses, using them as cover—women and children and four old men. They herded them in a bunch across the street, opposite the house. Each man had a gun in one hand and a bottle in the other. They were against the wall, safe from Miro's gun, bobbing behind the heads of the women.

"They're going to firebomb the house," Miro said. "You made a poor deal when you came back to your house, Mary."

She was crying. "I'm going to vomit," she said.

"I've done it myself," Miro said. He put his face against the wall close to the window and yelled, "There's a girl in here. Will you let her out? I'll let your man come with her."

"Nobody's comin out!"

"Mac! Mac! Let me out," the man on the floor shouted.

"Yir a bloody fool fir goin in." That was all.

"We'll burn to death," Mary Robinson said. She was scarcely audible.

"It'll be half an hour before Bowen gets anybody here," Miro said. "Move to the bedroom and lie down under the back wall."

Mary scrambled and took the shotgun with her.

"What about me?" the man said.

"To hell with you." Miro crawled to the bedroom and upended the bed, springs against the window. He traveled back and forth between the kitchen and the other rooms, carrying buckets of water, throwing it over everything. "It'll give us a few minutes," he told her. She lay chittering along the base of the back wall. "Watch Henry," he said. "Don't just wait for it."

"What're they doing?" Mary asked him.

"I don't know." He went to the kitchen for their prisoner.

The first petrol bomb woofed through the kitchen window as the man's feet reached the middle room. The second one came through the next window into the tub, and sputtered out in a cloud of smoke and acrid smell. The third came right through and hit the back door. It woofed and spilled, pouring flame towards the bedroom door. Miro shut it.

He looked up the field at Henry. The little man was pointing to the southwest, over the top of the houses. He signaled the man with him, and they ran across the top of the slope and around the post office.

Miro took the shotgun from Mary, and with its stock, smashed the jagged glass in the window frame. "Get out," he said.

"They'll shoot us!"

"They've gone. Get out."

"Mister! Mister! Git me out, fir Jasus sake!"

Miro helped Mary through the window. The bedroom door was burning, the heat rising wickedly. He kneeled beside the man and shouted over the roaring fire, "Will you talk to the police? Tell the bloody lot?"

"Yes! Git me out, for Christ's sake."

Miro dragged him through the window and left him on the grass. Mary was crouching down a little way from her burning house, crying. He ran past her, across the wide gaps between the little houses, to their end. Henry was running to his car. Something had to be coming. None of the men down here could know enough to do more than disrupt their arrangements—Henry was the one who knew where the links met, and he would abandon the others to tell the little they knew.

One thing they probably knew: where Henry left his car; they would try to reach it. Miro kneeled down against the gable of the last house and waited. Mary's house was flaming. Miro ought to be dead. Why should the two men down the street hang around to find out?

He heard the screaming women and the yelling men—not fear now, but rage; yelling at the backs of the men who had used them as cover. Then he heard the pounding feet. They came past the last house at a gallop, one a foot ahead of the other. Miro held the gun knee-high and fired. They went down, howling, in a stumbling fall, and when they tried to rise, he was standing over them.

"I still have the other barrel," he said.

"I'm bleedin, mister," one of them pleaded.

"Bleed, you bastard," Miro said and took their guns from the road. He sat down against the gable of the house, the shotgun on them, and listened to their whimpering.

The people blocked the street, staring at the freak with the gun, shouting at the wounded men lying in the road.

"Wis thir somethin ye'd like, mister?" a bold little girl asked Miro.

"Sleep, love," he said.

The postmaster took the gun. "I'll watch them," he said. "What'll I do if they move?"

"Shoot the bastards." Miro went to sleep against the wall, and all the people stood in the road and stared at him. Then somebody laughed at his long drawers between the ends of his shooting knickers and the tops of his field boots. They were all laughing; the danger was over. Things like this only happened in Belfast and Derry. The men on the ground bled and moaned.

But Mary Robinson sat down beside Miro and went on crying.

"They were going to burn me to death," she said, shaking.

"I haven't been dry for twelve hours or asleep for twenty-four," he told Mac Donnell and slept all the way to The Deer's Cry Press. He slept through the delivery of Mary Robinson to her father's farm south of Ballymena, went to sleep in a hot bath, and had to be dragged from it to bed.

"Did they get Henry?" he asked Mac Donnell on the way to the bed.

"No. Over the hills and far away."

"Did you get Dew-Boys?" he asked Bowen.

"Gone with the wind. Didn't even lock his house. There must have been one hell of a fight in his living room. It's a shambles."

"Did he phone Strong last night?"

"He phoned the registrar of births, deaths, and marriages at Coleraine. His name's Gordon."

"You picked up this Gordon?"

"We didn't. The same wind took him . . ."

"God! You're a speedball. My wife?"

"Shamus and Mary Riada are at Summerfield with her. She knows you're all right. We told her you were in hospital taking an enforced rest . . . under sedation . . ."

"Christ . . . It's easy to see you're single, Bowen . . . Send somebody to get my car and clothes from Strong's place."

"We've done it. We've got your clothes from Oliphant's lodge. And we've questioned him and will do so again. What else?"

"I've got to sleep. Wake me at eleven tonight."

They tried to wake him at eleven. "Bugger off," he mumbled. They woke him at twelve. "I said eleven, you bloody clods," he roared at them.

"You're a sweet boy," Bowen said in the first moments of the tenth of July.

Two

A friend loveth at all times and a brother is born for adversity.

The Tenth of July: "We can take my car," Mac Donnell said.

"We'll walk," Miro said and checked his pockets. He had everything he needed. "We'll go over the fields—no roads."

They went over the golf course behind The Deer's Cry Press. The wind came in off the sea. The clouds scudded across the sky. The moon glared through brief gaps and was quickly shuttered. The grass was wet. "Bloody rain," Miro grumbled. "I haven't been warm since we dug up Barney."

"You were a bit out of touch, yesterday," Mac Donnell said. "The shipyard workers told the Catholics at the yards to swim the lough fully dressed or get to hell out of their jobs. Then they marched on the Unionist party headquarters to scream for the Prime Minister's head—and Strong to replace him. The next face you see on an Orange banner will be Mrs. Strong's, a new Protestant martyr."

Miro was absorbed in his thoughts, trying to sit behind the eyes of men he didn't know. Strong, Dew-Boys, Henry. "Out of touch?" he said. "Is that what you'd call it?" and got his mind back on his prey.

"They're putting Corkey on television tomorrow," Mac Donnell said.

"Shut up."

They crossed the little sluice-gate footpath on the boundary of the golf course, climbed the wall that sheltered the Barn Mills Dam, and went on over the fields towards the back of the village of Eden, and Kilroot beyond it. The grass was longer and wetter. They went through dripping hedges, over wet gates and slippery stiles. Miro's mind gnawed at Strong and Dew-Boys and Henry. Their men were very young, from different backgrounds. But *they* were not young. It was a pattern. His mind wandered over all he knew about active destroyers everywhere: they were all children's crusades not led by children; paranoid children led by paranoid adults. Led? Pressed like putty by the fingers of men who had their own ends to serve, their own sickness to feed. Strong, Dew-Boys, and Henry. Nowhere in the world, he thought, could paranoid men find a more deeply paranoid setting than this one to work in. He was groping nervously and uncertainly into Strong when they pushed through the hedge into the field behind Dew-Boys' bungalow.

The bungalow sat in a four-acre field, an acre of which had been ploughed and dressed and refined over many years. It was an immense flower garden behind a tiny bungalow. At each corner of the field were little groves of trees—like corporal's guards in position, marking off a parade ground. The moon glowered down for a moment and was gone. It was as if a dimmer had been turned up and down.

"What did you see?" Miro asked Mac Donnell.

"Somebody went on a rampage through his flowers."

"Let's take a good look."

"Why? I thought it was the bungalow you wanted to search."

"Do you hunt, Mac?"

"No."

"You should. Men and animals are the same in many respects. When you hunt animals you're just as well to know their habits. Especially wounded animals. Some run, some stand and fight, some seem to have a reserve satchel full of cunning and revenge they only draw on when they're hurt."

Somebody had indeed been on a rampage, charging an erratic course through the flowers, falling among them here and there, and through the whole course of his passage, slashing the blooms with a sharp blade, Miro said, probably a bill-hook. He named the flowers for Mac Donnell. "That's Dove's Dung to the Bible. To you it would be Star of Bethlehem . . . That's myrrh. To you it's ladanum . . . They're all Biblical flowers . . . Mustard; saffron, that's a crocus; Rose of the Brook, to you oleander; Rose of Sharon, that's a narcissus. The trees, too. Green bay, mulberry, cedar, sycamore . . . Interesting man, Dew-Boys."

"Queer."

"I knew a man once who paid thieves to steal great paintings. Then one day he slashed them all and shot himself in the mouth. In his house they found a room full of his own paintings. They were very bad. He bought a lot of paintings, too. Patron of the arts. Everybody knew that—then he couldn't take it any more."

"Couldn't take what?"

"That he wasn't good enough at the thing his ego told him to be—a painter. He'd hated good painting all his life because he couldn't do it. I wonder why Dew-Boys hates what he put so many years into?" Miro's foot struck something hard. He groped carefully at his feet and brought up a bill-hook. "He just buried the blade in the ground with a great bloody wallop. That was a great rage, son. I wish I knew why."

They came out of the flowerbeds and stood under a tree. "This is a green bay tree, Mac. The Bible says, 'I have seen the wicked in great power spreading himself like the green bay tree.' If you're interested in commerce you'll want to know that in Old Testament times a fourth part of a cab of Dove's Dung cost five pieces of silver."

"You're sure?"

"It's in the Bible. There's one other thing."

"In the Bible?"

"No, in the house. There's an amateur in there waving his light about like a storm lantern."

Mac Donnell gave his first serious attention to the house. "How long have you known that?"

"About two minutes. We'd better see who it is."

They came carefully up under the sill of the kitchen window. It was Strong, searching pots and pans, cupboards, under the sink, on the shelves. His searching was frantic, unsystematic. He jumped from place to place, stood in the middle of the kitchen wondering where to try next, and having decided, tore at it wildly. They followed him around the house to the living room. It was a shambles. First he righted some furniture that had been thrown over; he was no more successful than he had been in the kitchen.

Miro drew Mac Donnell away from the house.

"Did he drive here?"

"I'd doubt it. He'd be a fool."

"Maybe he is by now. We'll check. He's nearly out of his mind. I don't think he had the patience to walk up here. He waited till the small hours—I'll lay ten to one he couldn't take time to walk—that man's desperate."

They found Mrs. Strong's little car down the road from the bungalow, parked tight against a gate into the next field. Fifty feet down the road and across it, the iron side gates of Dobbs Castle were shut and padlocked.

"I'll bet you carry a notebook, Mac, and a pencil."

Mac Donnell handed them over. "For what?"

"He's scared as hell. So we'll lean on him."

He printed notes on pages of Mac Donnell's notebook.

MRS. STRONG DIED FOR OUR SINS.

the first one said and he put it on the driver's seat.

"How callous can you get?" Mac Donnell asked Miro.

"I could have murdered Mrs. Strong. Would that be callous enough, son?" He printed the next note. It said,

PAPER CHASE. TRY GLOVE COMPARTMENT.

This one he put under the windshield wiper, and in the glove compartment, a hierarchical portrait:

Through the Dark and Hairy Wood

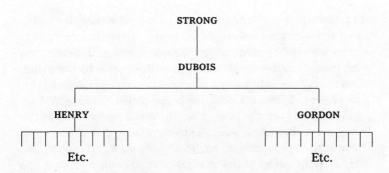

STRONG

|

DUBOIS

|

HENRY   GORDON

Etc.   Etc.

THIS IS WHAT THEY'D LIKE TO KNOW.

LOOK UNDER YOUR SEAT.

Under the driver's seat the note said,

YOU DIDN'T FIND IT.
IT ISN'T THERE.
LOOK BEHIND YOU.

Behind the seat, the note read,

ALWAYS LOOK BEHIND YOU
WHEN YOU'RE PRIME MINISTER.
I'LL BE THERE SOMEWHERE
WITH THE STORY.

"What're you trying to do with that bullshit?" Mac Donnell said.

"I'm not sure. But he's scared, young fellow, and maybe he'll tell us what I'm trying to do with this bullshit, as you call it. A frightened man always looks at what scares him. Get over the iron gate and we'll see how he takes it."

Strong ran from the bungalow to his car. He almost missed the note on his seat. Then he went for them one by one, making angry sounds as he scrambled for the glove compartment, groped under the seat, and leaned behind it, searching the floor.

He folded the notes and put them in his shirt pocket, looking about him like a man afraid of the dark.

"Dew-Boys?" he said softly. "Dew-Boys?" and listened. The wind from the sea pushed the leaves of the trees across the wall. "Dew-Boys?" he said louder.

Over the gate into the field, the hedge yielded nothing. He ran up the field toward the bungalow, and down again as far as the iron gate in the estate wall. "Dew-Boys?" he called. His voice shook with fear or excitement. The wind shook the leaves.

He stared steadily at the iron gates, then pushed through the hedge and crossed the road. His face was against the bars. "Dew-Boys!" Miro could have touched the face with a stick. "Dew-Boys! We can *talk*, can't we? Dew-Boys? I only want to *talk*." He was pleading. "I'm sorry about the fight, Dew-Boys. My arm's all right. Look! I know you're in there. You can see me. *Look!*" He held up his left arm and pulled the sleeve. The arm was bandaged above the wrist. "You did very little damage with the bill-hook, Dew-Boys. It's *past*. Just let's sit down and *talk. Just talk.* I won't harm you, Dew-Boys. Before God I won't. Dew-Boys? I know you're there . . ."

The note was shrill, desperate, hopeless. Strong turned away and walked slowly to his car. He stood by it, listening. Miro stood up behind his sheltering bush and walked deeper into the trees, dragging his feet through the wet leaves of a past autumn.

Strong ran back to the gate, and Miro went down and stayed still. Strong gripped the iron bars and shouted, *"Dew-Boys! Don't do it! Talk to me, for God's sake."*

There were no more steps dragging the dead leaves. The living leaves hissed.

"All right. All right," Strong said. He went to his car and drove down the road.

Miro and Mac Donnell ran back to the bungalow. Miro found a swabbing mop in the kitchen, broke the shaft in half, and blocked up the thick cotton strings with towels and dishcloths till the mop looked like a human head with long, disordered hair. He stuck the broken shaft into a pillow, put one of Dew-Boys' jackets on the pillow and propped the thing on a chair in front of the living-room window. They pulled down the blind, switched on the light, and went to the bedroom to wait.

Strong came back by the field. He walked to within fifteen feet of the living-room window. He drew a revolver from his pocket and took careful aim, his gun arm out, his left hand steadying it. He shot the pillow through the glass and the blind, and watched it slide from the chair. As he turned and went down the concrete path to the gate in the hedge, his stride was strong, military, and confident. He walked down the middle of the road.

"Let him get well away," Miro said. "If that gun was registered, he wouldn't have used it."

"It must have been some fight," Mac Donnell said. "Dew-Boys hit him with a bill-hook."

"Lock the doors and we'll cream this place."

They went over the bungalow inch by inch. It was a professional search that ignored nothing. "It would help," Mac Donnell said, "to know what we're looking for."

"That's a fact." Miro offered no explanations. He had none to offer. "But if you *think* enough about these two birds, you'll see something that fits."

"And what have you *thought?*" Mac Donnell was skeptical.

"Just feelings, sonny. I think the kids call them 'vibes.' Am I right?"

"Right."

"I feel fear and malice and insanity."

"You're just feeling Ulster, Miro."

"That's fair comment. But Mary Robinson is Ulster—Protestant Ulster. That postmaster at Newtown Crommelin is Ulster, and he was a Catholic, wasn't he? Mrs. Ogilvie is Ulster . . . They're not all sick to the same degree, Mac. These two, though, they're . . ." He stopped searching. ". . . Agar is a jelly made from seaweed. If you take ordinary tap water with a little beef extract in it, and seal them in a petri dish of agar for a few days, you'll get growing colonies of bacteria. Did you know that?"

"No. I didn't even want to."

"Well, Ulster is the petri dish; Ulster's kind of religion, its social hatreds, and its envies are the agar, the tap water, and the beef extract. And Dew-Boys and Strong and Henry and the IRA and the Ulster Volunteers are the bacterial colonies. They thrive on a host that gluts them."

"I now know more than I want to know. I'm only interested in evidence."

"You've just demonstrated that you don't know what evidence is. We'll check the bedroom carpet."

It was securely tacked down around the edges. They went around it tack by tack, moving the bed. "This end's a bit chewed up," Mac Donnell said. "Too many tacks too often." They hauled it up. The floor under the edge was raw with tack marks. "Get it off," Miro said.

The trap door was quite close to the edge of the carpet, near the wall against the head of the bed. The trap hole was large and stairs ran down from it into a room that covered an area the size of the kitchen and the bedroom. The printing press was set on a steel plate in the middle of the floor.

"Put the light out and stay up there," Miro told Mac Donnell. "I wouldn't want somebody to trap us down here."

It was a well-lit room with baseboard electric heating, several comfortable chairs, a desk, and wall shelving stacked with box files. It had a ventilation shaft at the kitchen end. He traced the shaft to a vent under the kitchen sink. It had a fan that forced air down the shaft and a reverse switch that sucked it out.

Miro took down some of the box files. The spine of each file had a year marked on it—nothing else. The first year marked was 1934. The file opened with a birth certificate: John Edward Dubois, born to John Dubois, flax-spinner, and his spouse Mary Wilson. Year of birth, 1921. Place of birth, Number 2 Taylor's Row, Carrickfergus. There were letters from cousins and aunts and uncles in the United States, with bitter annotations in the margins, presumably by John Edward Dubois, to whom the letters were addressed. "You must come and visit us," a cousin wrote. "Send the bloody money," the commentator wrote. "We go to Florida next week for Easter," a cousin wrote. "Rich shits" was John's comment.

School reports began in 1934. John was thirteen. The reports were often good, but uneven. "Uneven disposition," some of them said. "Finds the work easy when he is inclined to do it." They were signed that year by William Stephenson, against whose name John had written in a maturer hand, "Fat stupid little shit. Used to feel Maggie Evans' leg."

Miro skipped quickly through the years. Copies of applications for lectureships at Queen's University and kind letters of advice in reply. "Do your postgraduate work and apply again." And John had written, "Where's the money, you stupid whoremaster?"

There was no university appointment. John was conscripted into the army. He came back to schoolteaching. "I'm a country schoolmaster," he wrote. "None of the stupid bastards who got the jobs had fathers in a spinning mill."

"Is that phone still working, Mac?" Miro yelled up the stair. "Yes."

"Call your people and get them to send a van out here to carry back Dew-Boys' life history. And a squad to seal up this house. Tight."

"We'll have to go through all that tomorrow, I suppose?"

"It is tomorrow. It's two-thirty in the morning. We'll get some bodies out of bed and start when we get back. He's a man who keeps records, Mac. Strong didn't know where he kept them."

Miro told them: "I want to know what he hates, who he hates, and why. In one-liners on filing cards. One card to each year. I want to know in what year he grew his hair long, what year he stopped all but necessary speech with adults. Who he knows. Why he knows them. And I want to know before breakfast."

He read the cards over breakfast. They told him that as he grew older Dew-Boys knew very few people and held them all in contempt. He hated publishers. They had "stupidly" rejected his manuscripts, and Dew-Boys filed the manuscripts to witness against him. He hated universities. They were centers of pretense, staffed by men of small talent whose fathers had not been flax-spinners. He hated churches. They nourished the castes in a caste society. He hated priests and ministers; they were parasitic. He hated the rich. They were undeserving and arrogant. He hated the poor. They were ignorant and vulgar. He hated adults. They talked back when he made pronouncements. He hated socialists. They denied superiority its due. He hated capitalists. They made money into power and denied talent its share of power. He hated women. As far back as Maggie Evans, who let Mr. Stephenson feel her leg and Bill Ross take off her knickers, he had no success. Maggie made fun of him and scratched his face. His only triumphs were humiliations—with drunk waitresses who knew somebody was there and had forgotten which man it was. "I hurt the bitches," he recorded.

By 1960 his hatred of the society he lived in singed the pages. He thought of "fire," of "ashes," of "rubble," and wrote more directly of himself. In 1961 he grew his hair long as an additional "wall of separation" between him and Them. "They do not know me. I do not need Them," he wrote. Through his hair, he "spied out on Them," like a "lurking retribution." In 1965 he noticed Strong for the first time, taking his night walks. For six months he observed him, brooding on a man who shared one of his own habits. "Why does this man walk in the night?" Then he waylaid him. "I was surprised when he accepted an invitation to come into the house for a drink. I felt like a weasel, watching him talk. That was the night I thought of it." And a notation: "Record transferred to Strong file."

Now he went away for weekends. Not far. Nowhere is far in Ulster. But he stayed away from his bungalow. *Bushmills* and dates. *Coleraine* and dates. *Belfast* and dates. *Derry* and dates. Then names. Henry. Bill. Matt. Barney. Kane. Mac . . . And when each name and place first appeared, a notation: "Record transferred to Strong file."

There was no Strong file.

Miro slept till noon, and lunched on corned beef and cheese, beets, little onions, crusty bread, and coffee. He wanted to call Eva and was afraid to face her. Later, he told himself, when I think of something reasonable to say.

The Prime Minister, Bowen told him, will be on television at one o'clock with a special statement, "a kind of political first feature," he called it, "trying to talk down the rage that's running loose in the province. And he's agreed we can keep Strong under discreet surveillance. What difference does it make now? There's no time left. Nobody'll believe him anyway. Tomorrow we'll be shooting down Catholics and Protestants to keep them from shooting one another." He shrugged hopelessly. "I suppose there's a difference."

"Where is Strong?" Miro asked him.

"That's another laugh. Nobody knows where he is. The police at the house say he left early. His wife's little car is at Stormont. He isn't."

Miro drove down into the town to watch the Prime Minister in a pub and to watch the people in the pub as they watched their Prime Minister. He went to the Castle Arms in the Scotch Quarter, where the landlord was Catholic and the customers Protestant. And round and round in his head the question went, "Where is Strong?"

The pub had two rooms and was packed. The television was above the bar and could be seen from both drinking areas. Those who were a little out of line at the edges crowded into the middle. Miro stood at the back of the second room, looking over and around moving heads.

The Prime Minister's face was haggard. He had trouble getting started.

"I have co . . ." He swallowed his saliva at the wrong moment and it must have lodged in the wrong place. He coughed, was distressed, and cleared his throat vigorously.

"Givim somethin t'wet his whistle," one of the drinkers shouted.

"Where'll I put it?"

"Up his . . ."

And in chorus they all said, "Ah-h-h-h" and "Ssssssss." Their good humor made an acid sound.

The Prime Minister breathed deeply. His eyes were watering. He touched them in turn with the knuckle of his first finger.

"He's cryin . . ."

"Boo-hoo . . ." they wept in chorus and cut off their own sound when his lips moved.

". . . come before you with the full knowledge that my leadership is under attack . . ."

"Yir bloody right," a man in the middle shouted.

"Shut up!" Miro said.

The man turned in his chair and said, "Was that yous?"

"Shut–up," Miro said again, and hands pulled the man down into his chair.

"I'll see yi whin he's done," the man said, pointing aggressively.

". . . so I am able to speak frankly . . ."

"Yir a bloody liar . . ." the man shouted.

Miro roared, "Listen to him, you mindless ape. If you open your mouth again I'll mash it."

The man leaped from his chair and rammed his way to Miro, who didn't wait. He brought the heels of both hands hard up under the man's nose and his knee into his crotch. Hands hauled him away, yelling his agony.

"Take him out," voices demanded and he was taken out.

". . . I have tried to pursue a course that would prevent needless bloodshed. I am not prepared to change that course and plunge the country into a savage civil war, as some among us are trying to do . . ."

"Tell that to the IRA!" The drinkers cheered.

". . . there are three of them in custody. Several are dead. Here are the three in custody." One by one three pictures appeared, with names. "Not one of these men is a Catholic, not one of them is IRA, yet all of them are to be tried for their complicity in recent crimes of violence.

"This picture (Barney, briefly out of his grave) is of the man whose dead body was snatched from the ambulance. His name is Barney McClure. The police are searching for his brother Matt, who with the help of accomplices snatched him from the ambulance, as part of an organized campaign to make us all believe that the IRA was everywhere and invincible.

"I want to tell you a little of this man's story as the police have learned it from his uncle and aunt, Mr. and Mrs. Barney McClure of Trooperslane. Their nephew Barney contracted consumption and was hidden for years on the uncle's farm until it became evident that he had very little time to live. They say they were ashamed that a member of their family had consumption. So they took him to Whiteabbey Sanatorium and left him at the gate, with a dead man's health card obtained for him by his brother Matt. He was left there to die. The rest of his story and how he actually died and was taken from the ambulance will be told in court at the trials I have already mentioned."

The drinkers had been quiet, listening not to their Prime Minister but to a story—the kind of story some of them had known before, or heard from their fathers and mothers: the shame of consumption, and its concealment.

But the story was over. "The police are searching for this man (Dew-Boys) . . ."

"Holy Jasus, it's the Eden schoolmaster . . ." and the laughter was loud and derisive.

"They will be charged with the kidnapping of Dr. Corkey, who will speak to you in a moment, and little Georgina Cromey, and Mrs. Strong, whose murder will be one of the charges against them, and of the kidnapping of Mr. John Miro . . ." The pictures went up on the screen, one by one—including Miro's.

Heads everywhere in the pub turned to Miro, looked to the screen, turned back . . . there were no more interruptions.

". . . I appeal for calm. I ask that the ban on all parades be observed. The danger is from both sides, not one side. It is therefore a greater danger, with graver consequences, than some of you realize . . . Dr. Corkey . . ."

Dr. Corkey was interviewed in his hospital bed. "IRA? No, they were not. Well, one of them was a Protestant, an evangelical. He was really a bit . . . a bit . . . eccentric . . . the rest . . . No, they weren't Protestants as I understand it . . . They were revolutionaries, really . . ." Dr. Corkey was very tired, fragile, uneasy. "Yes, Mr. Miro . . . A man was killed . . . carried us both, he did, in the rain . . ." The heads turned. ". . . eight or nine of the men I saw at different times . . . As I said, no . . . not Protestants . . . not as I understand Protestant . . ."

The inevitable comments followed.

Shaun Herron

Oliphant of *The Whig.* "I do *not* own the Lodge. I sold it to a professor at Queen's, who says he rented it to an American . . ."

A trade-union leader: "It's hard to believe. If you oppose this government you're guilty of a crime. Dr. Corkey? Well, he's an *old man,* isn't he?"

The Grand Master of the Loyal Orange Lodge. "He said nothing to change our minds. They have made arrests. They haven't got verdicts. Will we walk on The Twelfth? We will."

Captain Strong "asked to be excused in the tragic circumstances."

That was all. They turned to stare at Miro.

"Yir the man?" somebody said.

"Yes. You didn't hear half of what he said. He's telling you the truth."

"Where d'yi live, mister?"

"Donegal."

"In the so-called Republic of Ireland?"

"Yes."

"Ir ye a Fenian?"

"What does that mean?"

"Ir ye a papish?"

"No."

"Ir yi a prod?"

"No."

"Yir *nothin?*"

"That's a very simple thing to say."

"Mister," a new voice said. "There's more'n fifty of us in here. Away on while yir able to walk . . ."

Miro walked through them and out to the sea front. The sea was slate gray. Little pockets of moving air riffled it in patches, like gray-green corrugated paper. He shivered in the heat and got into his car. Men believe what they want to believe and in time they do what they are determined to do. They were singing now in the Castle Arms, tunelessly, like tribesmen tuning their nervous systems for battle . . .

"Slitter, slatter, holy water,
Gimme no more o yir cheese
Fir the last I got it stuck in me throat
An gimme the heart disease . . ."

Last week they may have wanted to avoid the spilling of blood. But that, if it were true, was last week. He drove away from the sounds, with no idea where to go or what to do. Home, he told himself, if he had any sense. He had done all he could for Bowen, and more than he'd promised. He turned up North Road to The Deer's Cry Press. Louis MacNeice, the Irish poet, had lived up this road in his father's rectory. What was it he wrote about leaving here for England? Amelia Jane Strong had quoted it the day he met her. He couldn't remember too exactly, but MacNeice wrote something about being tired of their well-bred hunters, their dolled-up virgins . . . and their ignorant dead. On both sides. Their ignorant dead hung over the ignorant living like a plague. They were tribesmen. Their conflict was tribal. Both sides attacked British soldiers for trying to keep them apart. Their rage was breaking the bounds. Rage, rage, rage . . . Miro could taste it in the air. He turned and drove along the Shore Road, among the middle classes. Orange arches were working-class folk art. There was an Orange arch across the Shore Road, slung from flag poles. Rage. Middle-class rage. He drove back into town and through the Irish quarter. The houses were mean, with half-doors and the smell of fried bread and fish and chips at every hour of the day. There were no arches, no flags, no symbols. But men stood in their half-doors, and their faces and every movement of their bodies announced their reciprocal rage. Why don't they say to one another, he thought, "I know *you* didn't do it." But it wasn't possible, and he knew it. The most innocent of them carried a burden of sympathetic guilt. All of them had thought, "There's something in what they say," and kept silence in face of the excesses of their own; now it had gone too far; they had been silent too often, too long; their collective guilt fed their collective rage. Rage, rage, rage . . . Go home and clean your guns, he said, and wait for Mahood to come burning the foreigners . . .

Colonel Stephen Riada was at The Deer's Cry Press. "They're up in Colonel Bowen's room," the leggy girl at the desk said. "They wanted you."

"I want my car back and my things. I'm going home," Miro said and went to his room to pack. He phoned Eva. "Don't say anything, love," he said. "I'm coming home . . . no, don't say anything. I'll tell you everything when I get home. I'll come leaping upon the mountains . . ."

"Quickly," she said. "Please come quickly."

"Mahood and his people are on the move," Colonel Riada said behind him.

"You said you had them taped," Miro said. "Tell Bowen where and they'll take them."

"I don't know where."

"You had them 'infested,' I think was your word."

"All I know is that they think you've wrecked this Strong gang, so they're going to make sure nothing dies down. The North will be swimming in blood, Miro."

"I'm going home, Steve. To oil my guns. Mahood said they'd be coming to burn out the foreigners. I don't know where to turn here. I'll at least defend my own." Bowen came into the room. Miro said, "Where's my own car, Bowen?"

"In behind the house. I don't blame you, Miro. I'd do the same. I wish I was out of this bloody insane asylum."

"I was in the Castle Arms," Miro told them. "They're slavering for blood. They don't believe your Prime Minister and they think Dr. Corkey's doddering. Good luck, Bowen. You'll need it."

"Thanks for what you did."

They watched Miro pack. He left alone.

The sun went ahead of him into the west, like music calling the cattle and the children home. I forgot to give Bowen his gun, he thought and hurried, like a horse on its own road. He was grateful to be out of it. He would be in Summerfield by nightfall.

A great crowd, the car radio said, was marching on Stormont, the seat of the Northern Parliament, carrying Union Jacks and placards demanding action or the Prime Minister's resignation.

FIGHT OR QUIT

some placards said;

WE HAVE THE GUNS
YOU FIND THE GUTS

others said.

Miro listened, driving through the ancient land of the O'Neills. This was the country known as The Fews, which had been loped off the O'Neill land and granted to the Johnstones, who came from Scotland during the seventeenth century, in the days of the Protestant plantations. He could hear rhyming in his head the couplet the Irish used to say, in fear and irony,

> *"Jesus of Nazareth, King of The Jews,*
> *Protect us from Johnstone, the King of The Fews."*

The Johnstones had hunted them like game, as the white men in Newfoundland had hunted the Indians. The Indians were no problem in Newfoundland, the hunters had exterminated them. The Irish remained a problem. They were still here.

For no reason that he understood, except perhaps the magic of the O'Neill name, Miro turned north for Tullaghoge. He had time to look at the Tullaghoge ring fort he had seen with Eva last summer.

The cool, genderless voice of the BBC announcer went on with its report. In broad daylight, a sniper on a roof in a small Catholic slum enclave off the Newtownards Road—known derisively as Skipton Mansions—had fired into the marching crowd, killing one young marcher. A section of the marchers stormed into the tiny slum of miserable whitewashed houses and battered two men to death. They discovered, too late, that both men were members of the march, both members of Ireland's Heritage Loyal Orange Lodge 1303, which—"ironically," the announcer said—had on its banner a map of all Ireland, with no partition marked, and *Ireland's Heritage* painted on it—in the Irish language.

163

Miro parked his car in a tree-sheltered car park that would hold no more than a dozen cars. His was the only one. He walked up the nettle-and-thistle-overgrown path to the ring fort on top of the hill.

It was a simple circular earthwork. Centuries of green grass had bonded it firmly. In a square around the fort, great trees grew—hazel and oak and maple and chestnut. On the inside slope of this fort a stone chair had once been embedded, and in it O'Neill kings sat to be installed by the house of O'Hagan. Where in the ring the stone chair had been lodged no one now knew. The last O'Neill to sit in it had been Great Hugh O'Neill. In 1602 Lord Mountjoy destroyed the chair. In 1645 the Johnstones came from Scotland. One of them, in the long passage of time, founded the Loyal Orange Order. In time—in the 1960's, which is only a day or two from 1645—an O'Neill again governed Ulster and Johnstone's Orangemen dragged him down.

It was dark and cold under the massive old trees. The air smelled of damp and moss and must, as if the trees themselves felt the length of time and the persistence of enmity. Miro went down the overgrown path to the car park. He needed Eva. He wanted to hurry home.

There was another car in the park, but no one in sight. Nobody had passed him on the path. He looked about: no, there was nobody in sight. He got behind the wheel. No more stops till he reached the Border.

Matt came out from the brush at the base of the trees, with astonishing speed. "Don't start it," he said, his gun at Miro's head.

"No, Matt," Miro said wearily, and took his hand from the key. "I phoned my wife to tell her I was coming home."

"I'll tell her where you went," Matt said. "You made fun of Barney." His voice had a note of incredulous complaint.

"No, Matt. I just tried to save four lives. What happens now?"

"You made fun of Barney. They dug him from his grave. You made fun of the Lord Jesus. *You made fun of me.*" That seemed to matter most. Miro's nerves quivered and a cold shiver ran through him. He blocked off thought.

"So?" He turned his head to look at Matt. Henry was climbing out of the brush. Behind him came Dew-Boys. His hair was pushed up under a blue beret. He was wearing a dark gray lounge suit, and looked quite unlike himself. His long face was heavily bruised. He beckoned and two more men came out of the bushes on the other side. "We have a use for you," he said to Miro and got in behind him. Matt followed him. Henry took the wheel of the other car. "Just follow Henry," Dew-Boys said, "or I'll blow a hole through the middle of your back. And turn on your radio." He reached into Miro's pocket and removed his gun. "You don't seem able to hang on to this."

Henry led them up the west shore of Lough Neagh and across its north shore, by a maze of narrow roads, at a leisured pace. There were no risks to be taken, no attention to be drawn. They passed very slowly through villages. In one of them an old crone sat on her doorstep, smoking a pipe. Her face was seamed with the dirt of the ages.

"Interpret her for me," Dew-Boys said grandly to Miro.

"I leave that sort of thing to superior intellects. Cows are my business."

"You should have stayed at home with your cows."

They left the shore but not the winding little roads, always moving east. Henry appeared to know every narrow road in the North and every village without a police barracks.

"There is great irony in our situation," Dew-Boys said pompously.

Miro kept quiet and wished he could see the irony. He felt sick. The sight of Dew-Boys' discolored and excited face in the rear-view mirror made him feel worse.

"If I had to find the Ulster equivalent of Britain's Britannia, I would use that old crone back there. Would you agree, sir?"

"You're the thinker."

"All right. I'd call her ignorance. She's as good as any primitive on the African veldt. She pees where she stands, no knickers. Just sets her feet wide and lets go. She washes when she falls in a dung heap, and then only if her hands go in. I'm exaggerating."

"You have the habit. It's in your box files."

"You got them, did you?"

"We did."

"Then you read my treatise on *The Comedy of Ulster's Tragedy*."

"I glanced at it."

"You should have read it. It explained how for generations Ulster's generals and colonels and majors and captains—never any lieutenants; isn't that a nice note?—cultivated that old crone's ignorance and fear like twin plants. That's how they kept their place. If the old girl's a Catholic she thinks the smoke from her Sacred Heart lamp can cure her arthritis and she's afraid of Protestants. If she's a Protestant she thinks if she sits on a Bible it'll cure her piles . . ."

"You're still exaggerating, of course?"

"Of course. I have a point to make . . . and she's afraid of Catholics. Now *there's* a garden for any green thumb to work in, don't you think?"

"You're the thinker."

"If the captains find out too late that the seventeenth century is over, yes. And they did. They had one sort of emotional serf and they needed a new sort. So they told their serfs what to do next: They said 'change.' But not enough of them could. It was too sudden, too late. And now what the captains created is a monster"—he gurrred in illustration—"and it's going to eat them up . . . It's saying to the captains, 'You're the traitors, you're betraying our ignorance, give us back our ignorance . . .'" He leaned close to Miro's ear and snarled like a cougar. "Their loyalty to their warm old ignorance is greater than their loyalty to their fickle captains. Ignorance is reassuring . . . Fear is exciting to the ignorant. It's their *theater*. Rob them of both and you leave them naked, and in this climate nakedness is *cold*. Do you follow me?"

"Clearly."

"So we put a little pepper on their ignorance and a little vinegar on their fear—and they're turning both on the captains. The monster the captains made is about to gobble them up and turn this place into ashes and rubble. You follow me?"

"You put it very simply."

"That's the comedy of the Ulster tragedy."

"You want this place to be ashes and rubble?"

"I do. I do indeed." A helicopter crossed their sky about a thousand feet above them. It lifted and crawled sideways and away, like an airborne crab. "Noisy bloody things," Dew-Boys said and squinted up at it as it passed. "Noisy."

They were going north now, traveling faster. The land was thinning and rising. The villages were merely inhabited places, three or four houses at crossroads. The hills were rough—sheep land.

"You sound quite rational," Miro said.

"I am. One of the few in this poisonous province."

"I once knew a man who believed he was Napoleon. He even had a birth certificate. He didn't know he forged it himself. But he knew he was two people—Napoleon and the Duke of Wellington. It was Wellington who forged the birth certificate. Napoleon told me so himself. You remind me of him."

"Blow your horn," Dew-Boys said sharply.

Miro sounded the horn.

"Now slow down."

Henry got the message. He pulled in to the side of the road and came back.

"Get him out, Henry. Out, Matt. Hold him."

This was sheep land. There were low hills and rising moors around them. The road was barely wide enough to allow two small cars to pass. To their left, Miro recognized a hill he had climbed with Eva last summer—The Pap of Slemish, rising like a young girl's breast. As a slave St. Patrick herded swine on and around that pap. Now the swine are back, and they have me, Miro thought. They took him off the road into a little copse around an abandoned farmyard.

"We're nearly there, Dew-Boys," Henry said. "Wait till we get there."

Now, Dew-Boys said. "Bring the cars in here." Two of the men brought them to the cover of the farm buildings.

They took Miro to an immense oak tree, the branches of which overhung a duck pond. There were ducks on the pond from some other farm. "Hold him," Dew-Boys said. Four of them held him, his arms out wide. Miro looked at the door of the farmhouse across the yard. It was red, in a dull gray cement-wash wall. At some time a man labored here. He had a wife, raised a family, sent them to school somewhere on this high ground, had hopes for them in this place . . . Dew-Boys was in the corner of his eye. He saw the arm draw back and tightened his stomach. His legs buckled. The bunched knuckles seemed to drive into his backbone. All the disappointments of Dew-Boys' life were in Miro's stomach and all the hatred his flaws projected were in his knuckles. Dew-Boys was finding release. Miro gathered his legs and braced himself again . . . eight times, nine, ten . . . His legs gave, his vision was going . . . They had to hold him up . . . The man who laughed the first time was still laughing . . . They lowered him down against the tree . . .

The red door floated, keeled, came and went like an image beyond a wall of frosted glass. Dew-Boys stood somewhere in front, bent back like a bow and twenty feet tall. His head was in the lower branches of the oak tree, its leaves in his hair; all the movements of his arms were slow and immense and extravagant. Someone was laughing like a corn-crake and the ducks quacked in the pond in long stringy quacks that snaked up and down like a rope shaken from one end across the ground.

"Tell him about the coming of the Lord Jesus, Matt," Dew-Boys said. That was strange too. Dew-Boys' face contorted and the words came out long and lopsided. Matt twined in beside him, broad as a barn door and as twisted as a thick thorn stick.

"Jesus is coming tomorrow," Matt said out of the oak leaves. "Jesus is coming tomorrow and on Monday the dead will rise . . . the whore of Babylon, the mother of harlots, will be cast down, the woman drunken on the blood of saints will drown in her own blood . . ."

"Pick him up," Dew-Boys said in a wavy voice and started again. Over the heart; flat on the nose, blood spurting like wine; in the stomach.

"Tell him about ashes and rubble, Henry."

He couldn't sit up. His head was on the edge of the pond. The ducks dipped and flapped, but he didn't feel the water splashing his face. He could see the ducks as big as fat battleships in a fog . . .

". . . at Bushmills Presbyterian whin the Orangemen are in it

the morrow . . . through ivery window and the front door . . .
when they find youse and Strong . . . wi hand grenades in yir
dead hans . . . then they'll rage an there'll be nothin but rubble
. . . right, Dew-Boys . . . ?" "Right, Henry . . ." Henry's voice
sounded far and loud, like a foghorn. It was hurting Miro's ears.
In his mind he felt a distant thought creeping around looking for
a place to rest . . . His car radio was on, and the music blurred
the thought . . . It was . . . then it was gone . . . and vaguely
back . . . Rage, rage, rage, something to do with the rage of the
corrupted, the rage of the entrenched . . . the rage of the insane
. . . Ulster rage . . . Nothing more of the thought would come
. . . It was something about people, being gobbled up by deformed images . . . The pain closed down against it . . . The
ducks and the red door and the oak leaves and Henry and Matt
and Dew-Boys all dissolved, slowly, and Miro began to float
away, and sink away. Everything sank away . . .

A light plane came around Slemish and circled. "Noisy bloody
things," Dew-Boys said, lordly. "Counting sheep."

But Miro knew nothing about light planes, or sheep or anything else, lying in the back of his own car, half on the seat, half
on the floor. He did not hear Dew-Boys' laughter. He did not
hear him say, "Tomorrow, my ashes and rubble, Matthew, and
on Monday, your millennium! In my plans there is something for
everybody . . ." He did not hear the laughter like the retching
of men who have drunk more than they can hold.

He heard the music. Thin transistor music. His eyes opened
slowly. The gums were inches from his face, in a gaping mouth.
They were pale gums and between them a lolling, white-coated
tongue. Miro raised his eyes. God, how lowly were the great,
parted from their public and their teeth. It was Strong, without
his dentures. Mrs. Strong had known how to diminish the man:
Dew-Boys had his own way.

Miro hurt everywhere. His belly and chest ached. His head
ached. His face ached. He allowed his eyes alone to move.
Down. He was sharing a bed of potato sacks with Strong. His
wrists were tied. So were Strong's. What did Henry tell him—
yesterday, was it . . . today? About a church and Orangemen

Shaun Herron

and grenades in dead hands? His hands and Strong's. He wasn't
sure. He was on a dirt floor. He was sure about that.

Where was the music? He tried squinting up beyond Strong's
head. All he saw was an old plough, the curve of its blade
against Strong's head. He arched his back, but not far. Potatoes.
Sacks of potatoes against his back. They were in somebody's
barn. He turned his head slowly.

Matt. Sitting on the sacks of potatoes, an automatic rifle
across his lap, a big transistor radio beside him. They were always listening, as if messages came to them by radio. He was
watching Miro. Miro lowered his head to the sacks again and
moved his feet. They parted, but there was pressure around his
ankles. He kept moving them apart, eighteen inches, two feet?
The pressure jarred him. He was hobbled. Like a donkey. He
tightened and loosened his muscles, in his arms and legs. In his
stomach. His arms and legs were good. His stomach—God, how
it hurt. He closed his eyes, shifted like a man going back to
sleep, and presently he snored.

Matt climbed down from the potatoes and stretched. He went
to the barn door and shot the bar. Miro could see the back wall
of the whitewashed farmhouse, thirty feet from the barn door.
Matt breathed, stretched and closed the door again. He leaned
against it, watching his charges in the poor light. He was bored.
The light came in under the barn door on Matt's boots. They
were big boots.

Jesus was coming soon, with Barney for Matt. Every hurt
spirit has its own utopia or its own cynicism. Matt had the millennium. The thousand years of the Jesus Reich? Miro wondered. He lay watching the big black boots, thinking about
Matt's religion. Jesus was coming. Matt loved Jesus. Jesus loved
Matt. Awhile ago Matt was one of the four men who held him
while Dew-Boys beat him savagely in the guts. Matt loved Jesus.
It didn't seem to make any difference. Matt needed to love Jesus
for some reason that had nothing to do with Jesus. Matt needed
to believe Jesus loved him for some reason that had to do only
with Matt. At Ardoe Abbey, Miro remembered seeing a devout
Catholic family prying out of a dead old tree the pennies pil-
grims had been driving into it for centuries. The devout parents

170

pried out the tokens of piety other devout persons had hammered there—and gave them to their children. The mind was a system of sealed compartments. Matt needed to destroy something. He would do it for Jesus' sake. That was a fine reason.

Miro barked like a dog.

Matt sprang to attention. Miro worked himself to his hands and knees and sniffed Strong. In an insane asylum only the insane are real. He crawled around Strong to the old plough and sniffed it. He sniffed the sacks of potatoes, the heap of cut turf across the barn. He lay down like a dog and scratched. He barked. He got back on all fours and went again to his potato-sack bed. "Even so, Lord Jesus, come quickly," he said and lay down.

Matt climbed slowly on top of the sacks of potatoes and sat down, watching Miro with caution and alarm on his big peasant face. Miro got back on his hands and knees and sniffed Matt's boots. He whimpered like a dog smelling its master. The barn was heavy with the stale smell of sacking, of wet earth, of turf. Matt's boots smelled of farm dung. Miro barked again. He put up his head and bayed.

"Stop that," Matt said nervously.

"Even so, Lord Jesus, come quickly," Miro said, and swiveled his rump and lay down on his sacks. Strong was awake, his face bathed in alarm, his eyes staring. Miro barked at him and closed his eyes.

"*Stop that!*" Matt said sharply.

Miro whimpered happily. Matt gripped his gun, kept it on Miro, and the alarm on his face deepened.

"What are you trying to do?" Strong whispered and his toothless gums made a watery sound.

Miro was up again on his bound hands and both knees. He whimpered joyfully over Strong and was hastily pushed back. He pounced on the captain, pinning his hands, pressing on him with one heavy leg, snarling and barking.

"Stop it!" Matt shouted and jumped off the potatoes. "Get apart." He prodded Miro's back with the gun.

Miro turned to Matt again, crying like a faithful hound. "Even so, Lord Jesus, come quickly," he said and lay down, his head close to Strong's. He wanted to wink. But he wanted to bring down the heels of his bound hands on Strong's face. He wanted that much more. He didn't wink. "O, Lord, support us all the day long of this troublous life," he said and heaved again to his knees and held his paws before his face, "until the shadows lengthen and the evening comes"—he barked in supplication and whimpered sadly—"and the busy world is hushed . . . Don't blame Matt for Barney's death, O Lord. Barney was full of consumption, rotten with the plague . . . Now he'll rise, made new, whole, clean, without disease, without sin, on Monday, The Twelfth of July . . ." He barked and bayed. It sounded almost like singing. "Even so, Lord Jesus, come quickly." He lay down and closed his eyes. "That's why Matt did it," he said. "He wanted Jesus to take away Barney's consumption."

"*Stop it!*" Matt shouted.

Somebody was coming across the yard, kicking the door. Matt jumped down and backed to it. A man came in carrying a pan of soup, two spoons, and a crusty loaf. He put the pan down on the floor and threw the spoons and the loaf to the sacking.

"That one's out of his head, Gordon," Matt said. "Dew-Boys hit him too much."

So that was Gordon, registrar of births and deaths and marriages and the source of this lot's resurrection power.

"What's the odds?" Gordon said.

Miro said, with his eyes closed, not stirring, "Do not take a bath in Jordan, Gordon, on the holy sabbath; on the peaceful day . . ."

"He's out of his head," Matt said again.

"That's a lot of balls," Gordon said. "Go on over to the house an eat. Yir on again at twelve the night. Get yir sleep. Then wir goin. You'll be here wi them."

He took the gun, barred the door behind Matt and climbed onto the potatoes. "None of that balls," he said to Miro, who sat up to take his share of the soup. He smiled at Gordon now and then, but said nothing. When the bread and soup were gone, he lay down and appeared to go to sleep.

Matt came back at midnight. There was quiet talk and much

walking in the yard. There was no moon. The night in and out of
the barn was black. They were loading a car. Miro could hear
bottles clanging together. He could smell petrol. "Mind thon
pair, Matt," Henry said.

They drove out of the yard, in two cars, without lights. Matt lit
a lantern and built a wall of full sacks around it, to kill its little
glow. He took up his place on the pile. The lantern at his feet
sent a funnel of yellow light into his face. It was a big, simple
face in which all complexities had been resolved. There were no
more questions in it, only answers. Miro turned on his other side
to watch the face; the face watched him. It didn't matter. He
thought he knew what went on in the big head.

He began his puppy whimpering again, and pushed saliva out
of his mouth. The small eyes, like holes in a mask, grew smaller,
then larger. Matt swung his gun to cover Miro and pushed his
back against the end wall of the barn. His mouth drooped.

Miro wailed and howled. He tried to make tears and couldn't.

"*Stop it!*" Matt shouted at him and waved the gun with
strange irresolution.

"Therefore I will wail and howl, I will go stripped and naked: I
will make a wailing like the wolves and mourning as the
owls . . ." Miro scrambled to his hands and knees and bayed.
"Even so, Lord Jesus, come quickly."

He crawled across the barn floor and sniffed the turf pile.

"He beat you too much," Matt said. "Lie down, for the love of
God."

Miro struggled to open his fly and relieved himself on the
turfs. He barked happily and crawled again, the big face all yellow and black, always in the corner of his sight. Somewhere in
that big head was a street map of heaven. There was a simple
constitution for the millennium: Jesus would solve and settle all
questions before they arose; there was to be no pain, no sorrow,
no humiliation, no strain, no struggle, *no effort.* They would
bask all day in a celestial sun—those who deserved it, that is.
Once a man said to Miro in a Belfast pub, "Is yi sayin yi know
better'n the Bible?" He bayed pitifully and lamented, "They return at evening; they make noise like a dog and go round about
the city." It was from some psalm, if he could only remember

clearly. He made noise like a dog. The Bible was full of dogs. Eating the remains of men, drinking the blood of men: "For without are dogs, and sorcerers and whoremongers and murderers and idolaters . . ." Men like Matt had a great horror of the fine rolling obscenities of the Bible . . . dogs, sorcerers, whoremongers, murderers, idolaters . . . "Even so, Lord Jesus, come quickly," Miro said pleadingly to Matt's big boots. He whimpered and rubbed his head against the boots, braced for a kick. There was no kick. Matt was frozen in Biblical horror. Miro whimpered up into his big superstitious face, "Come quickly, Lord Jesus . . . even so come quickly . . . Lord Jesus, Lord Jesus . . ." He raised his paws to his chest, dug his toes between two sacks of potatoes, drew back his head, and howled. The muscles of his legs were set . . .

"What the hell's up in there, Matt?" Dew-Boys was kicking the barn door.

"Get down," Matt said to Miro. "Go on, get down."

Miro didn't know whether the big man believed he was talking to a dog, or simply didn't know what to say. He crawled back to his sacking and lay down.

"You could have got us killed," Strong whispered angrily.

"Shut up."

"I'm coming," Matt shouted and backed to the door. "It was him," he said to Dew-Boys. "He's off his head. You beat him too hard."

"What's wrong with him?"

"He thinks he's a dog."

"My arse." Dew-Boys stamped across the barn and stood over Miro.

Miro watched his boots, set firm on the earthen floor a foot from his face.

"I was having a sleep," Dew-Boys said. "Your bloody caper wakened me." His right foot went back and lashed at Miro's head. The head rolled and Miro's hands came up behind the heel. He swung himself away, pushing hard with his legs, and Dew-Boys went down, one leg in the air. His back hit the floor. Miro threw up his feet and dug them viciously down into Dew-Boys' stomach. He dug again, rolled over and up onto his knees, half-

174

leaped on his knees onto Dew-Boys' chest and swung his locked hands across the man's jaw. It began as a desperate act of self-defense. It ended as a savage attack made in a savage rage. Matt's gun went off beside his ear. He stopped his pounding and said, "The next time, put the muzzle in my ear, for I'm not through with that black bastard."

When the other men came back, they carried Dew-Boys to bed and left Miro and Strong on the farm kitchen floor, with two men to watch them.

Miro went to sleep in a draught that blew a gale under the kitchen door.

Three

That ye may eat the flesh of Kings and the flesh of Captains and
the flesh of mighty men . . . and the flesh of all men free and
bond, both small and great.

The Eleventh of July: The mood was carnival.

They shaved all over the farm kitchen, at steel field mirrors
propped on anything that would support them. They were all in
their undervests, and blue serge trousers and braces. They were
all in black shoes, brilliantly polished. They were all in high spirits.

They listened to the news and laughed at it. The Prime Minister reiterated his warning that all parades were banned, and this
included the annual church parades of the Orange Lodges.

But, said a commentator, in spite of the Prime Minister's
warning that dire consequences would follow if the parades
took place, thousands had marched on Stormont yesterday and
the only dire consequence had been three deaths, one by sniper
fire from a roof at Skipton Mansions and the other two "by inad-
vertence," when the marchers killed two of their own. These
two deaths were laid at the door of the miserable people living in
Skipton Mansions, who harbored and helped to escape an assassin with a gun.

There were statements and counter-statements on the air. The voices were measured, responsible, dignified—the voices of men of affairs, molding events.

The Grand Master said quietly: "We shall be in church today. And tomorrow, The Twelfth, we shall walk." He was restrained; responsible. "Even if we have to carry guns," he said.

Miro listened to the news from his chair against the kitchen wall and felt like a man within a real nightmare staring out into a world of unreal men playing unreal games. The reality was here. The kings and captains danced a stately pavane in the public eye. In the asylum, the other lunatics prepared the day.

They prepared Miro and Strong. They were shaved, their clothes taken from them, sponged and pressed under an old newspaper with an old flatiron. ("Whin a man goes t'church he puts on his good clos," Henry explained to them.) Their shoes were polished, their hair parted and combed. They were fed and taken to the outhouse ("Gentlemen don't pee in church," Henry explained. "Yi can't put yir hand up and tell the minister yi have t'leave the room"). Their spirits were high. Hysterically high. To act is easier than to wait.

The high moment in their preparations was the cutting of Dew-Boys' hair. They were like a football team watching a playful castration. They glued a mustache to his upper lip, put on their shirts and ties and blue serge jackets. Dew-Boys brought out a cardboard sheet on which had been drawn a plan of the area surrounding Bushmills' Presbyterian Church.

"This is the church. This is the graveyard. This is the hedge around the lot. This is the road in front of it. This is the manse across the road. Gordon and Matt will go up to the manse and keep the minister's wife away from the phone.

"Now here"—he indicated crosses along the hedge—"on the north, south, and east hedges, the stuff is lying, well covered. The hand grenades and firebombs are together . . . here. The guns and ammunition are here . . . here and here. They're in waterproof bags. They've only been in place since last night and it hasn't rained since they were planted.

"The police are armed. Revolvers only. They're Henry's business. He has a silencer. When they're dead, he'll kill these two with a police revolver, put hand grenades in their hands, and we'll cover the sound with the grenades in the windows. Grenades first, then the firebombs—in the windows, the front door, and the side door at the rear, on the south side.

"Now, about approaches. Here, number two and number three cars in this lane, one field away from the back of the church. Number one car will meet the parade here at the distillery and fall in behind it. We'll show Captain Strong off to them. They'll be pleased to see him." This little touch delighted them. There were no questions. "We'll park on the road in front of the church. When we leave, number two heads for Ballycastle, number three for Ballymoney, number one comes back here.

"If they don't fight after this, they're not going to. We'll scatter for two months.

"One more thing. No guns when we travel. The guns we need are already in place. We'll keep these two in order with these." He took two switchblades from the drawer in the kitchen table. "I'll have one. Matt will have the other. And if they make a move they'll get these in the guts or the kidneys. But no guns when we travel. If we're stopped, we're clean."

He was happy. "There's just one other thing," he said, smiling. "We can't show the captain to his faithful without his teeth." Everybody enjoyed that. He took Captain Strong's teeth from his jacket pocket. They were spattered with biscuit crumbs. "Open your mouth, Captain."

"Wash them," Strong said.

"Open your mouth!"

The captain set his gums together and drew his lips tight. He looked unlike a leader.

"Open his mouth," Dew-Boys said, and they clawed at Strong's face till his jaws parted. Dew-Boys rammed his teeth into place, cutting Strong's gums. Blood seeped from the corners of his mouth.

"And what can I give *you?*" Dew-Boys said to Miro and planted himself before him.

Miro drew his feet back slowly. He knew what was in store for him. In a couple of hours he would be shot. There wasn't much point in being more careful now than he had been last night. He waited for Dew-Boys to move. The kitchen window was directly behind him. Miro measured the distance and wondered whether he could drive him that far with the hobbles on his ankles.

There was a madness in him and he let it run. Why not? There was nothing to be won, but when everything else is lost, do all the damage you can. "I'm going to kill you, Dew-Boys," he said. "You haven't told these poor dupes that when you recruited them it was to make Strong Prime Minister . . ."

The hand swept his face.

"He wrote it all down. The army has all his files . . ."

The hand came back across his face.

"You didn't tell Matt you were using Barney as a cheap gimmick . . ."

Dew-Boys slashed him twice, viciously. Miro's mouth was bleeding inside.

"All your names, everything about you is in his files. The army has them . . ."

This time it was Dew-Boys' fist. The chair keeled and settled. Miro's head was fuzzy. "He has a lot in his files about you and Barney, making fun of you, Matt." His head dropped as Dew-Boys' fist swept round again. His toes were hard on the floor deep under the chair. He lunged his head into Dew-Boys' stomach, whipped his bound hands into his crotch, and charged.

They were all frozen in place, too astonished to act. Miro rammed Dew-Boys against the kitchen window. His back was arched. It went through the window. But the window was small. Its panes were small and their binding frames strong. Dew-Boys' head slammed violently against the upper window frame, and he slumped down heavily on Miro's shoulders. His weight bore them both to the floor. He was unconscious, with a bleeding cut across the back of his head.

Miro was dragged back to his chair. Blood ran from his mouth.

"He's telling you the truth," Strong said suddenly. "Dew-Boys was my second-in-command."

Only Matt heard him. The others were ministering to Dew-Boys. Matt stood back before the open fire, staring questioningly at Miro. "He wrote things about Barney?" he said.

"I read it, Matt," Miro said. "He wrote that he got you to put

Barney on the roof and make the snatch from the ambulance as
a gimmick. He made fun of you and Barney and what you believe. He said you were an ignorant, superstitious, big lout . . .
He . . ." But he decided to leave it there. His invention was failing. Matt did not speak. He stood looking at Dew-Boys.

"I'll kill that bastard myself," Dew-Boys said when they left.
"It's too late to make changes," Henry protested. "Leave it the
way we planned it."
"*I'll do it,*" Dew-Boys yelled, and Henry went to his car.
Strong's hands were free, his feet were still in a two-foot hobble. "Drive," Dew-Boys told him and got in beside him, his blade
against the captain's lower back. He had a long plaster across
the back of his head and his hat was on his knees.
Miro sat behind Strong, still bound hand and foot; Matt was
with him, his knife in Miro's side. There was no third car. They
met it at a crossroads a few miles on and took different roads to
their objective.
The day was sweet. The sky was blue, the clouds high and
white. In ten minutes or an hour or in three hours it might rain.
Sometime today it would almost certainly rain; for a minute, ten
minutes, an hour, or the rest of the day. It did, almost every day.
Miro could smell the grass. He could smell turf burning. He
loved the smells of the Irish land. They were native to no other
place. He glanced at Matt and found him staring at him, watch-
fully, curiously. There was no talk in the front seat.
"Keep it slow, Captain," Dew-Boys said.
Miro's mind turned, probed, puzzled. But there was no way.
That long blade was a fearful thing to die by. He would rather be
shot. He would be shot. There was no way. Eva wouldn't be
poor. That was small consolation for the loss of their short summer.
They met little traffic on the quiet roads. There was a great
stillness on the land. Once through Broughshane they turned
north, always following Dew-Boys' directions, finding the back
roads; to Clogh Mills, still going north. East of here were the
high hills and moorland above Newtown Crommelin. They kept
well east of Ballymoney, went through Stranocum and Moss-

side, where cattle trapped them on the road for almost a mile. They stopped in a farm road south of Bushmills.

"Watch them, Matt," Dew-Boys said and got out. He opened the driver's door. "Lie down," he ordered Strong. He cut his hobble. "Pull your socks over what's round your ankles," he said. "Untie that bastard, Matt."

Matt was clumsy. Miro pulled his feet up and Matt worked laboriously with his big, blunt fingers. He drew his left hand up, fumbling at the knots with his right.

"Cut the goddamned thing," Dew-Boys yelled at him.

Miro felt the fumbling at his jacket pocket. He couldn't reach it. Matt cut his hobble, then untied his wrists with surprising ease. Miro rubbed his wrists and felt his jacket pocket. There was a gun in it. He moved his hand to take it and Matt laid the point of his blade on the hand. "No," he said quietly.

"No what?" Dew-Boys snapped.

"I was warning him," Matt said.

"Keep him still."

They went on and parked again at the broad intersection before the Bushmills Distillery. The marchers were on time.

"I should explain," Dew-Boys said, smiling, "that the order not to carry a gun did not apply to me. If either of you makes a mistake, you'll be gut-shot." He showed them his gun. "I'm sure you'd prefer it through the head."

"Did you, Dew-Boys?" Matt said oddly.

"Did I *what?*"

"Write things about Barney and me?"

"He's a liar."

"He's not," Strong said quietly.

They could hear the flute band, playing a hymn to march to. There were no policemen.

> *"Forward! be our watchword,*
> *Steps and voices joined;*
> *Seek the things before us,*
> *Not a look behind;*
> *Burns the fiery pillar*
> *At our army's head;*

> Who shall dream of shrinking
> By our captain led?"

"Do you know the words, Captain?" Dew-Boys said.

"Certainly." Strong was composed.

" 'Who shall dream of shrinking, by our captain led?' " Dew-Boys laughed.

"Did you, Dew-Boys?" Matt said. The flute band was just around the corner.

"Will you for Christ's sake drop it, Matt? We'll talk about it later."

"Now, Dew-Boys."

"Not now." He was yelling again.

"He wrote it, Matt," Miro said.

"In your bloody guts, you interfering bastard," Dew-Boys yelled.

It was a good flute band. It came round the corner, proclaiming . . .

> "Forward through the desert,
> Through the toil and fight;
> Jordan flows before us,
> Zion beams with light."

"It wasn't worth it, Strong," Miro said.

"No. It's over. It's a miserable way to end it."

"It was squalid, beginning, middle, and end."

"Was it?"

"Jane was a . . ."

"I've got myself braced for it, Miro. Don't break me."

"Matt," Miro said. "Captain Strong was the boss. He's the one who told Dew-Boys to kidnap his wife."

"Did he, Dew-Boys?" The big man's face was blank with bewilderment.

"I'll shoot the next one that opens his bloody mouth."

The lodges were marching past in columns of four. They were a peasant-faced party; there was little intelligence in their features; red-necked, red-faced, brick-faced, grim-faced, they were conscious of defiance. Onward Christian soldiers, their faces said, marching as to war. In a gloomy, intense way they seemed to be enjoying a defiance to which they had expected no challenge and to which there had been no challenge from the government. They made Miro think of small boys marching into a sand-fort they know to be unoccupied. There was a childish and triumphant belligerence in their bearing. They looked neither to the right nor to the left.

"Fall in behind them, Captain," Dew-Boys said.

The men at the tail of the column looked around nervously. "Captain," one of them shouted, and told his comrades. They looked around and waved. One of them came back.

"Get rid of him or I'll shoot him too," Dew-Boys snapped.

"Captain!"

"Don't spoil the column, Watson. I'll see you after the service," Strong said.

They followed the marchers through the town. The flute band was playing "Fight the Good Fight" with all its might. But there were no watchers lining the streets. The people were leaving the lodges to their own defiance. They passed the RUC barracks. There were no policemen in sight. The front door was closed. Around the corner into the square at Catholic Henry Martin's grocer's shop; Henry and his wife were at their upstairs window, watching. The Miros bought their groceries from Henry last summer and his wife called Eva sweetheart. She called everybody sweetheart. She did not look happy now.

Left, out of the square, and left again across the bridge, and up the hill to the edge of the town. The band was playing,

> "Our fathers were high-minded men,
> Who firmly kept the faith;
> To freedom and to conscience true,
> To danger and to death;
> Great names had they but greater souls,
> True heroes of their age,
> Who like a rock in stormy seas,
> Defied opposing rage."

Rage, rage, rage.

Two policemen barred the way, standing in the middle of the road just below the church. They were wearing black leather holsters. The flaps were buttoned. They held up arresting hands. The band faltered in its defiance of opposing rage. The column halted.

"Git t'hell outa the bloody road," somebody shouted.

"I have t'tell yi that this is an unlawful assembly," one of the policemen shouted.

"Unlawful my arse, Sam. Get off the road."

"I've warned yis," the constable said. They withdrew to the side of the road. The column advanced. The band did not take up its music. They reached the church in silence and marched through the gates. Slowly they passed into the church.

"Park the car by the wall, on the left," Dew-Boys said.

"Dew-Boys," Matt said and laid the sharp point of his blade on the nerve center at the top of his spine. "Did you?"

"Take that bloody thing away, Matt."

"Did you?"

"I'll shoot you if . . ."

"Move and I'll shove, Dew-Boys. Did you?"

"No."

Matt pressed a little and reached his immense hand into the front seat. "I'll take that." He took Dew-Boys' gun. "Do you want this, Captain?" he said.

"No! I'll take it, Matt."

Matt handed it to Miro. "You wrote bad things about Barney, Dew-Boys. I love Barney," he said pathetically.

"Hold him till I get out, Matt. Give him your knife, man." Dew-Boys handed over his knife and got out.

Strong got out. "What now?" he said.

Miro pushed them inside the church gate. "Go on over to the manse, Matt, and make sure Gordon doesn't hurt the minister's wife. While you're at it you might tie him up and leave him there. The minister probably has a clothesline at the back." Miro was searching the hedge for the men in position. They were coming out of the field. He looked for Henry and saw him down the road, talking to the two policemen. They turned and walked towards the gate. Henry walked behind them. There was nothing to be done for them. Their widows would get small pensions. Miro's rage festered. His hands were in his jacket pockets. The two policemen fell in the gateway. Henry dragged them inside and came forward, smiling, one of their guns in his hand. He waved it and the men inside the hedges lobbed their grenades. Miro shot Henry as he walked forward. He fired through his pocket.

The grenades roared in the windows and doors. He could hear the screams of frightened or wounded men in the church. Shouting men were opening the front doors. A grenade exploded against the doors and the petrol bombs began their woofing. They exploded on the roof, in the windows, against the front and side doors.

Matt came charging across the road from the manse. His great driving strides burned the distance. He was screaming, "Barney! Barney! I'm coming, Barney!" He charged the jammed front door and hauled on it with all his frantic strength. An automatic rifle chattered and Matt lurched against the door, fell back almost doubled over, and lay still.

"Get back to the car," Miro told Strong and Dew-Boys, "and you drive, you bastard." One gun was out. He struck Dew-Boys in the face with it. The screaming from the church was tearing his head. *"Get back to Slemish,"* he screamed. *"I want to kill you, I want to kill you."*

"Faster!" he yelled. "Faster!"

He watched the petrol gauge. The tank was almost empty. The car pulled into the farmyard sputtering. "Tie him up," he told Strong and kept a gun on Dew-Boys till it was done. "Now help me take this place apart. If you find his file on you, you can keep it."

They went from room to room, ripping furniture, mattresses, emptying drawers, throwing china from cupboards, clothes from wardrobes. They found nothing. They speared the thatch with hay forks and found nothing. They heaved aside the sacked potatoes and the peat in the barn. There was nothing. They went through the hay in the byre feed-racks, turned over the milk containers . . . and it fell out onto the byre floor. Strong picked it up and ran to the kitchen. He stirred the fire and threw on some kindling.

He felt Miro's gun in his back. The file was lifted from his hands. "You said I could keep it," he said, disconsolate.

"I didn't say for how long," Miro said grimly. "Lie down over the table. What made you believe I'd let you walk away? Can you hear the men in that church? What makes you think you didn't help to put them there? *For what,* Captain? Lie over the table."

He tied his hands behind his back and hobbled him. He did the same with Dew-Boys, found Matt's rifle, filled his pockets with shells for it, brought the transistor from the bedroom where the big man had left it, threw cheese and bread and the box file into a knapsack and said, "Where's the nearest phone, Dew-Boys?"

"Find it."

There was nothing in the house that gave him any help—no maps, no school atlas. He had driven about in this country last summer, but he didn't know it. Nor did he know whether Dew-Boys' bombers had seen how they left or how Henry died, and he was afraid of what he didn't know. They could come after him. Or they might be busy saving their own necks. Or they might not. He went into the barn and hooked down the leather reins from a peg, looped them over Dew-Boys' shoulder, pointed south, and said, "Walk."

"What do you want the reins for? You're not going to ride on my back, I'm bloody sure." Dew-Boys was mocking.

"Walk." His goal was south. He would move them south. Sooner or later you came to something, in this country.

They started south, over the rising and falling ground. He had never regretted that in Ireland the phone is not ubiquitous. It had been a sweet relief. Now it was a curse. He had to reach Bowen or The Deer's Cry Press. He had to reach *somebody.* He had to reach a phone that didn't need money. He had none.

"Have you any money?" he asked them.

None. He wondered how often men go out without money and in their own places found it no inconvenience? They knew the storekeeper, the man at the bank. He was on a moor . . . He switched on the big transistor and noticed the police circuit on it. The music annoyed him and he switched it off. The thing was heavy. He thought of dropping it and didn't. He switched it on again. He had brought it to keep in touch, to hear news. So keep in touch. He kept about ten feet behind them.

They walked, one leg long, one leg short, up and over the east slope of Slemish. Strong was silent and sullen, striding steadily, his head up. Dew-Boys smiled, looking back often at Miro. He stopped them on the crest of the slope. Before him, if he had known it, was the wide expanse of what was called Back Park, a moorland valley whose width he couldn't estimate and which rose again to a hill immensely broader and as high as Slemish. It stretched to the east for miles; it might be a narrow ridge, it might be a tableland. He didn't know. There wasn't a house in sight. A few sheep seemed lost in the valley. Here and there, there were drystone sheep pens. He wondered about his decision to go south. But Dew-Boys was watching him, grinning.

"Lonely," he said.

"I've seen lonelier. Go ahead alone, Dew-Boys, for fifty paces, then drop your hat. About a foot from your feet."

"Why?"

"Ask me one more question and I'll beat you to a pulp. Stay where you are, Strong."

Dew-Boys paced it off as well as his two-foot hobble would let him and dropped his hat. Miro shot a hole through it and brought Strong up beside the schoolmaster. "I don't like you," he said to Dew-Boys. "Give me an excuse and I'll put holes through your thighs and leave you to be collected later. Walk."

The music on the transistor stopped. "Here is a news bulletin," the announcer said. Miro let them gain on him and turned the volume down.

In view of the massive defiance of the government's ban on parades, the announcer said—a defiance that had gone on all day in morning and afternoon marches—the government and the security forces agreed that a state of emergency existed. The defiance of the Orange Order had led to a number of shooting incidents in which two people had died in Londonderry, three in

Belfast, one in Armagh, and fighting was taking place in Enniskillen. In the last hour word had been received of a disaster at Bushmills.

A state of martial law had been declared at two o'clock; the Royal Ulster Constabulary had been fully armed; and since eleven o'clock this morning the gun clubs made up of former units of the B Specials had been recalled to service as a reserve police force. Belfast and Derry had been sealed off by the army. Certain areas, including Mid-Antrim, had been assigned to B Special Forces and the Royal Ulster Constabulary; the Border had been closed. Hundreds of arrests had been made. The streets and roads and fields of Northern Ireland were to be cleared by six o'clock this evening. Asked if this meant that anyone outside after six o'clock would be arrested, a police spokesman said, "No, it means that after six we shoot at anything that moves. This thing will be stopped and stopped now." He sounded as if he meant it.

Miro switched to the police circuit and moved them faster. He wondered how long Matt had been running the batteries of his transistor. He prayed about that, in a desperate sort of way.

There was a lot of static on the police circuit and occasional voices that came and went . . .

"FUZ . . ." he heard, ". . . FUZ 451. It's a Free State number . . . all right, the Republic. We found it at . . . farm . . . out of petrol . . . they're walkin . . . aye, armed . . . no sign anywhere north . . . No, not west . . . B Specials comin in . . . I said from Ballymena, Kells, Broughshane and . . . and from . . . along the Ballymena–Larne Road . . . aye . . . in from the Coast Road . . . Not too particular, to tell yi the God's honest truth. Not too close . . . can't hang the bastards now . . . cheaper . . . how much dis the guverment pay fir three bullets? . . . who'd blame yi? It's a long walk . . . Transport to . . . then the oul leather . . . aye . . ."

Miro called Strong back. "You want to live, Captain?"

Strong appeared to think about it seriously. "I was asking myself," he said.

"Any answers?"

"I don't think so."

"No answers or you don't think you want to live?"

"That file of his will get me what?"

"I don't know."

"In my shoes would you want to live? In jail? With scum?"

"You're better than that?"

"All right. I'm not of their circle. I'd prefer not to spend twenty years in their company. I'd prefer not to face people after this kind of failure."

"You'd rather die?"

"I think so."

"Where is Ballymena from here? Kells? Broughshane? The Ballymena–Larne Road?"

Strong pointed their direction one after the other. The only way out was to pass through them. The Coast Road was due east. "Go on up with your friend," Miro said to him, "and start running across this valley."

"We can't run with hobbles."

"I'd advise you to try."

"Why? What did you hear on the radio?"

"Martial law."

Strong seemed to draw comfort from it. "Well. I can at least surrender to an officer."

"You're unbelievable, Captain. You'll more likely be shot by a B Special. They're moving in here from the west, east, south and north. They think we attacked the church. They think trial and incarceration would be too expensive now that there's no hanging. Try running."

They tried running. They settled for hard jogging. Miro drove them towards the height across the valley, looking for cover of any kind. They labored up the slope with hobbled, mincing steps, their hands tied behind their backs. Winded, they were not allowed to pause. They stumbled and fell and protested the agony of getting to their feet on trembling legs, without their hands to help them.

"I'm thinking of your victims," Miro said. "Get up and get going."

When Dew-Boys went down, halfway up the slope, and declared that he couldn't move, Miro said, "Neither can Mrs.

Strong," and slapped him with the rifle. Like a sheepdog he herded them, snapping, barking, prodding, and fighting for breath himself, but moving up relentlessly. Their ankles and wrists were bleeding from the chafing of the ropes against their straining limbs. *"High! Up high, you bastards!"* he yelled at them and brought them to the summit and the drystone wall of a sheep pen. They lay on their faces, choking and coughing. He sat down with his back to the wall and watched them with hostile satisfaction.

"The B Specials want you," he said. "I could leave you here to wait for them."

The coughing and soughing stopped.

"B Specials?" Dew-Boys said and struggled to his knees.

"You didn't tell him, Strong?"

"I did not," Strong said with as much condescension as a voice filtered through sheep droppings made possible.

"Tell me what?"

"The B Specials are out. They're looking for us. They're coming this way. The police found my car in the farmyard. It has an Irish Republic license plate. They think we're IRA. Isn't that funny, Dew-Boys? You've been issuing IRA communiqués for months. Now the Specials are after the author."

Dew-Boys got to his feet. "Do you know anything about the Specials?" he asked intensely.

"Very little."

"Well I'll tell you, then. Their uniforms are green. They don't fit them. Most of them are small. Their guns look too big for them. You'd think when they have rifles they were having trouble carrying them." He shook his head as if his long hair was still on it. "They love their work," he said. "There's not a more vicious crew of little bastards from here to China."

Miro smiled and did not feel like it. "They've been told we're not worth the cost of arrest and imprisonment. They'll not come close enough to check our Protestant credentials."

"And you're sitting there on your arse?"

"You need a rest."

"Take the bloody ropes off us."

"Sit down and shut up." Miro went through the gap in the

wall and looked over the country. Behind the south side of the
wall a deep gully dropped down to a depth of about sixty feet.
The lip of its far wall was seven or eight feet lower than the side
on which Miro was standing. The walls were jagged all the way
down, and at its base the gully narrowed to about two feet. It
began a few feet west of the sheep pen. It ran east through the
downward slope of the hill, growing shallower as it went. About
four hundred yards to the east it had been filled in to carry a
track that was invisible from lower down the hill to the north.
Through the fill, a culvert had been let in to take the runoff of
snow or rain. Miro estimated that the depth of the gully beyond
the track and the culvert was less than six feet. He stood thinking about it for a long time.

The opening in the pen was on the east side of the circular
wall. Miro went back into its shelter and untied his prisoners'
arms. "Limber up," he said, "and get busy. I want a hole in the
south wall right over that gully. I want the stones from it used to
fill up the entry. Get at it."

He watched them, and the valley to the north, and the rising
and falling ground to the west and south of them. He saw nothing but high moorland, and more sheep. The clouds were no
longer white. They were multiplying, moving across the sky
from the northwest. They were bringing rain.

"They'll shoot everything that moves outside after six
o'clock," he shouted.

"Why the hell don't we move now?" Dew-Boys yelled back.

"When it's dark."

When the entry was filled he ordered them to make peepholes
in the wall all the way around. "Every six feet all the way
round," he said and abused them when they slowed. When they
had finished, he made them remove their white shirts. They
were the only whiteness for miles. He tied rocks in them and
dropped them down the gully. Through all their labor, Dew-Boys
cursed him and hefted rocks, but thought better of letting them
go against the steady muzzle of the gun. Strong did not speak.
When their work was finished, Miro tied their hands again, in
front this time.

"Now watch for them," he said, "through the holes."

But the rain came first—hesitantly, then steadily. They huddled under the north wall, out of its way. It got to them anyway; it spattered them, dampened them, soaked them, left them sodden. Miro willed the heavy clouds down to the hills. They stayed high. The wind gathered. It hissed at them through the loose-laid wall. It was cold. They were chilled to the backbone.

"When it's dark," he said, "we'll go down into that gully, through the culvert, and try to pass through them going east."

"I can't climb," Dew-Boys chittered.

Miro touched the leather reins looped over his shoulder. "I brought this in case I had trouble with you," he said. "I was going to tie it round your necks and drive you like mules. Now you can tie it round your middles."

"With our hands tied?"

"With your wrists tied. You can hold it."

"We'll get killed if we do."

"You'll be killed if you don't. Or you can walk out to meet them now."

"We won't get through them," Strong said.

"Likely not. But if I can get you to the army, I will."

"Then I could give myself up to an officer," Strong said, "not to one of those guttersnipes."

"There ought to be a graveyard for gentlemen only," Dew-Boys said.

"Both of you shut up."

He didn't expect to get through them. He supposed they'd be caught down near the culvert and shot like curs. The B Specials wouldn't leave that hole open. They were a paramilitary force. They knew the three of them were somewhere in this bleak landscape and they wouldn't come close to ask questions. They didn't want to. He didn't think he'd want to either, in a place where the children played at barricades and bombs, at "Catholics and Protestants," and lobbed bottles of Heinz tomato ketchup at one another and developed twitches and couldn't sleep at night. What the hell was he doing here? It was none of his business.

Yes, it was his business. Mahood was his business; Strong was his business; two-year-old Michael was his business. The people who didn't come out to line the streets and encourage the defiant Orangemen were his business. And Mary Robinson, and the postmaster of Newtown Crommelin, and Mrs. Ogilvie . . . they were strong, but society was fragile and men like Mahood and Strong and Dew-Boys knew it, and knew how to shatter it.

Strong's hands were resting on his drawn-up knees. He folded the fingers of his left hand over the knuckles of his right and swung them viciously into Dew-Boys' face. They rolled on the stony ground, in the sheep droppings, clawing, swinging two-handed, trying to kick one another. Strong was silent; Dew-Boys cursed and howled and made choking throat noises. Miro let them fight. He didn't care. Strong was getting in good two-handed wallops and suddenly he was kneeling on Dew-Boys, a rock in his hands. Miro swung him off and threw Dew-Boys back against the north wall. "Over there, Strong," he said, "sit over there in the rain." The captain went to the south wall and sat against it. The rain drove into him, ran through his hair, down his face. He licked it from his mouth and said nothing. He set his sight to Dew-Boys' face and kept it there.

"You should've seen her, Captain," Dew-Boys said. "She had her skirt up round her waist, lying against the big rock at the mouth of the Kilroot River with her legs open and this man in front of her with nothing on but his shorts. I told them to go home and do it in your bed . . ."

Miro hit him, and he fell sideways and stayed down. "He's a liar," he said.

"I know."

"Why in God's name did you start this lunatic business, Strong?"

"Sores."

"What does that mean?"

"Sores," he said and rammed his thumbs against his breast and his head. "Sores in here. Little humiliations. Like that scum's, but higher on the chart. Big humiliations. The magic circle shut me out."

"So you're here, in a sheep pen in the rain. Any regrets?"

"I failed. I regret that."

"And your wife?"

"I regret that. I didn't intend what that scum did."

"You 'regret' it? That's penitence of a high order."

"I'll kill him. You'll not stop me."

"That'll put everything right. Get up and watch." He stirred Dew-Boys with his foot. "Shake it," he said. "You've played that game long enough."

They saw the Specials first in the west. They came in a long line across the moor, driving sheep before them. They must have been gathering sheep all the way across the hills, he thought.

They came down from and around Slemish in a long line. There were fewer sheep, but what there were they were bringing. They came from the south without sheep.

"What's the sheep for?" Dew-Boys demanded nervously. "What're they doing?"

"Cover," Miro said. "To check the sheep pens. They'll send men up here among the sheep, on their hands and knees."

"There's nobody east of us. We could go that way."

"They're coming that way. We'll stay."

"You've got two revolvers and a rifle. Give me a gun."

"I wouldn't give you a foot rule. Stay down."

"There's one with a wireless. I can see his aerial. That's the one to kill."

"I'm not killing anybody. For you two? Try the police circuit on that radio. They'll have their own, but try it anyway."

They didn't have their own. They were on the RUC circuit. "You were wrong," Dew-Boys said. "What else are you going to be wrong about?"

There were other walkie-talkies in the lines. Somewhere there had to be a transceiver, but what did they carry it in? They had to have some sort of transport for it and its generator.

He heard the truck engine. That was what he had been wrong about. He hadn't expected it. Across the pen he saw it stop above the culvert and disgorge its Specials. They spread. "Watch them, Strong," he said. A whip aerial bent above the truck, through the canvas. He could hear the generator. "Tune that transistor. They're sending."

"Are we going to get through them?" Dew-Boys was afraid.

"It's unlikely. Work on the radio, damn you."

"Why wouldn't you kill some of them if it does any good?"

It was the sheep Miro found puzzling. They were bunched in a flock in the center of the west line. How they kept them tight he couldn't understand. "They're not going to wait till dark," he said. "They're going to check this pen as soon as they can reach it."

"Charley, Charley, Charley . . ." the radio said.

"Am wi yi, Jack . . ." It was an informal force. Like-minded men; comradely men. They were small, for the most part. Their uniforms were green. They did not seem to fit them well. Their rifles looked enormous, slung on their shoulders.

"Vicious wee bastards," Dew-Boys said. "Oh, Holy Jesus."

Miro saw the dog, a black-and-white collie. It came out from behind the flock to nip a straggler back into line.

"Charley, there's an old sheep pen up Douglas Top. Hold yir lines and we'll check it. Sandy, hold yir line till we see what's on the Top. Where are yi, Bob?"

"In place, Jack—I'm sittin in the truck on top of the culvert . . ."

They knew the ground. He didn't. There was no chance of getting through them in daylight or dark. If he could stop them until it was dark. He watched the dog. What little he might do, he had to try to do.

"Strong." Strong crossed the pen. "What sort of men are these? What do they work at?"

"Anything. Factories. Farms. Tradesmen. Working men. Their officers are bank clerks, prosperous farmers, insurance agents . . ."

"They have wives and children?"

"Most."

"Go on back."

They couldn't go through a concrete culvert quietly enough. They probably couldn't go down a rocky gully quietly enough. He watched the dog.

They had wives and children. What do men with wives and children worry about? Their own lives.

He sighted on the working dog. It was darting and wheeling now as the flock took the rising ground. The sheep wanted to climb the easy way—not straight up as men do. The sheep had time and grass.

"Have you any money in the bank, Dew-Boys?" he said to keep his spirit steady.

"Why?"

"The government will probably take it out of your estate to pay some farmer for his sheep."

He smelled the wind, held a blade of grass against it, calculated the drop of the slope and sighted again, leading the dog as it moved around the side of the flock. It darted suddenly. "God damn you," he mumbled. It had to be one shot. The range was about four hundred yards. They had to know with one shot what kind of rifleman was in the sheep pen. They had wives and children. They wouldn't take risks, but a wild shot would give them comfort. It had to be one shot. He sighted again. His hands were wet and cold.

"What're you going to shoot at?" Dew-Boys said.

"If you speak again, I'll crush your bloody skull." Miro tried to compose himself again, breathing deeply.

He sighted on the white on the dog's shoulder, then led it by inches. It was walking. "Stay that way," he whispered and breathed in. Slowly he let his breath out, slowly he squeezed. The dog dropped. The lines dropped. Around the slopes four straight lines of little green men lay flat on the soaked ground. He sighted again on the ram walking solidly at the point and squeezed. The ram went down on its knees, stayed on them for seconds, and fell over, its horned head twisted at an angle.

"Charley, Charley, Charley . . . did yi see that, for Jasus sake . . . that was four hunder yards . . ."

"Near five . . . that was a dear bloody dog too, Jack . . ."

"I'm not gettin anybody kilt fir them cunts, Charley, this isn't the second front . . ."

"I'm fir waiting till the dark . . ."

"We'll hold till the dark . . . Jasus . . . I'm soakin wet . . ."

The sheep strayed stupidly, cropping.

"They're moving back down the south slope," Strong called.

"Could they see the upper lip of the gully?"

"Not if they go another fifty yards down."

Miro crossed the pen. "We'll encourage them." He picked a rock on the south slope and bounced a bullet off it. It whined away into the far distance. The men below backed down the hill on their bellies.

"Charley, Sandy, Bob . . ." the radio crackled. "Keep thim jumpy. Don't lit on wir not comin. Where yi see daylight in that bloody wall, send a few shots at thim . . ."

Miro turned off the transistor. "You heard them," he said. "Pick your own wall." He lay down at the base of the north wall. "They'll wait till it's black. We'll go before it's black."

They broke the cheese and the bread and ate. The bread was wet. It helped to ease their thirst. Strong and Dew-Boys looked covetously at the knapsack with the box file in it.

"Why you want it I can't imagine," Miro said. "Your chances of leaving here are a thousand to one against."

They waited for the dark. Bullets pinged off the wall and sang away. If they wound or kill one of their own men with a ricochet, we'll pay for it, Miro thought. Twice, lucky shots found daylight in the wall and left Dew-Boys cowering with his face to the ground.

"Dew-Boys," Miro said, "why do you grow those Biblical plants?"

"My mother. She used to grow them."

"You were fond of her?"

"I hated the bitch. She was a flax-spinner's genteel wife. She thought the only way to live was to lick the arses of your betters."

"Then why the flowers?"

"Every time I cut one I was cutting the old bitch's throat."

"You're a lovable bastard. You deserve the Specials."

The sheep settled and cropped where they bedded down. The men below lay in the rain or fell back to walk about, beating their arms, wringing the water from their tunics and trouser legs, letting off a round or two to keep their quarry nervous, and calling to one another, cursing the weather, cursing the enemy, promising a short end to a long day.

"I'm perishing to the marrow," Dew-Boys whimpered. "My hands are no use."

"You can always wait for them here."

Strong sat silent, staring at Dew-Boys. He stared as the light died. He stared when he could scarcely see across the pen.

Miro unlooped the reins from his shoulder and gave Strong an end. "Tie your own knot. It's your own neck," he said.

The light was almost gone. The sheep were stirring down the slopes. There was no more calling. It was dark, but not black. The bleating animals were moving. The small men in green were moving, shortening distances, preparing for blackness.

Miro thought of Eva, warm in bed, and shut his teeth tight and rubbed his hands together hard. "Go," he said to Strong. "Lay on these reins and do it straight or I'll *throw* you down, Dew-Boys."

Strong held the leather in his bound hands. It was wet and slippery. He said nothing. Miro and Dew-Boys sat down and dug their heels in and lowered him down. His hands must have burned. He bounced expertly down the wall and signaled on the reins. Miro pulled them up. "You now."

Dew-Boys tied the knot. His hands fumbled from cold and fear. The sheep were crying, high on the slope.

"Get a bloody move on," Miro snapped. "They're coming."

"I can't."

Miro took a turn of the reins around his back and kicked Dew-Boys off the wall. His weight fell dead on the leather and almost jerked Miro over. The man let out a long, terrified scream. It was answered and misread down the hill. From all sides on the slopes of Douglas Top men *yeuched* to one another in the dark, coming higher. The sound was barbarous. It ringed the hill. *Yeuch, yeuch, yeuch,* they yelped in a closing circle. Miro thought of jackals, and the sound grew more jubilant. *Yeuch, yeuch, yeuch,* they answered one another, and the jubilation grew with their *yeuching.*

He lowered Dew-Boys by brute strength. His arms stretched, his elbow and shoulder sockets creaked, his feet slid and the body on the line bumped on the wall and swung. The line ran out and the weight was still there. He let go.

There was no sound of falling. He heard the reins fall. He heard a long sound, an *a-a-h-h-h-h*, and nothing below and the rain above, and the wind across the Top was lifting and tossing *yeuch, yeuch, yeuch* about the hill, and the guns were going. They were firing to keep heads down, to keep the enemy from reaching to the top of the wall, from using the blackness as cover to run. Where? Into the guns?

He had picked his route down and had tried to memorize it. He swung over the lip on his belly. The rock was wet. His shoes were wet. His hands were stiff and cold and sore from the leather. He moved down. The knapsack hindered him. The rifle hindered him. The men on the south slope were firing from just below the lip. Their bullets were slapping the higher wall above his head, scattering stone chips in his face. He couldn't hurry. His holds were too uncertain. His hands groped, his feet groped, slid smoothly, recovered, and groped again. He reached a ledge he had seen earlier and pried his shoes off. They bounced off the wall. He would never find them, he thought sickly, and sicklier still that it wouldn't matter. He would be caught on the wall and shot in the back from the south lip. He moved down again. It was easier and very painful in his wet socks.

The Specials came over the wall, *yeuching* and screaming like savages. Miro was ten feet from the floor of the gully. He dug his toes against a thin edge and held himself against the wall. He could *feel* his feet bleeding. The blood from his fingers streamed down his palms and along the inside of the wrists. The Specials were on the south lip, shouting across the gully at the men in the empty pen, who were screaming their rage and bewilderment.

"Thir in the seam—thir's no place else!"

"Quiet!" A whistle blew and they were silent.

The rock ledge was butchering Miro's tender insteps. Water ran down the wall. His fingers were weak and raw. The effort wasn't worth it. They would shoot him anyway; there'd be no listening. He thought of shouting, "I'm a Protestant!" and the thought seemed grotesque. And futile. They'd say, "Recite the Lord's prayer," and listen for the little difference. It had been done. Where did Catholics stop when they said it? Did they say "Who art" or "Which art in heaven?" Men had died on both sides for not knowing.

He wouldn't die that way, by God. If he was about to die, he'd face the bastards in silence. His right foot groped and found a flat hold. He went down again, and again, and again. Hands took his ankles. "Slowly," Strong whispered and swayed as he lowered him to the floor. "I have your shoes." He moved a stone. It rolled, collided, made a deadly racket.

"Thir in the seam." It was a scream.

"Down a few yards," Strong whispered and took Miro's arm. They groped down the gully, from rock to rock. "Down," Strong said and pushed Miro's head down. He guided him under a projecting shelf of rock. "Your shoes."

Miro sat down and put them on. The soles of his socks were gone. His feet were in anguish. "Where's Dew-Boys?" he said.

"I got him with a rock."

"God."

"Give me one of those guns, Miro. I'm not going out like a lamb."

"No."

"We can't get out of here."

"I know that."

"You'll just sit there?"

"Yes."

"I'll not."

"As you please. But I'll not help you kill one of them. After all, you created this situation. Live in it. You're about to die in it." He took a revolver from his pocket and pressed it into Strong's side. "On the other hand, I *might* kill *you* unless you leave it to me."

He heard the engines down the gully. Not truck engines this time, but powerful purring engines. The Specials hadn't been idle in the rain. They'd called up help of some sort.

"Throw a wheen in there," a voice ordered above them and the frustrated Specials poured in rifle fire without purpose or direction. Bullets shuttled between the walls, slammed down on their sheltering shelf. A ricochet chipped the wall behind them.

"We'll give yi three minutes t'get out to the culvert," a voice from above yelled. "Did yis hear that?"

Miro kept quiet and pushed hard in Strong's side.

"How about a hand grenade?" the voice shouted. "We'll give

yi an IRA funeral." There was laughter along both rims of the gully.

"Drop it."

The explosion was somewhere up near the head of the gully. It cracked down the funnel between the walls, blowing blast and chips under their cover. They were both on their faces on the ground.

The engines down by the culvert roared. A loud-hailer boomed along the gully. "Hold your fire and your positions," and after this formal order, the precise English voice said, "Don't bloody-well move."

"Thir ours! *Pour thim in!*" the voice from the rim yelled, and three more grenades dropped into the funnel.

A heavy machine gun chattered up the gully between the rims, and the space above was suddenly light. "Look around you and have some bloody sense," the loud-hailer said. *"We want them alive."*

Miro pushed the gun hard into Strong's side. "Let me have your teeth, Captain."

"My teeth? Why? No, I won't."

"Have them in my hand before I count three."

They clacked into his hand. Miro tossed them among the rocks and heard them smash.

"Why?"

"You in there," the loud-hailer called. "I'm sending a man in to talk to you. I want to hear your guns land on the rocks far down the seam from your position. Understood?"

"Send him in," Miro shouted.

"If you make any move against him, we'll leave you to the Specials. Understood?"

"Send him in." Miro threw the rifle along the gully, the two revolvers after it.

They heard the man coming up among the rocks, a light at his feet.

"You did me in," Strong said gloomily.

"You'll have time on your hands to wonder about that," Miro said.

The man shone his light under their shelf. "Mr. Miro, sir?" He was a soldier. A sergeant, Miro thought and couldn't quite make out.

"I'm afraid so."

"This is for you, sir. Want to use my light?"

Miro took the paper and the light. He read it and handed the light back. "Help me down and then maybe you'd look for a dead man farther up the seam? Sergeant, isn't it?"

"Yes, sir."

He made his painful way among the rocks, supported by the sergeant. Hands heaved and hauled him to the road. He leaned weakly against the plating of an armored car. Two more armored cars were on the lips of the gully, their guns and lights on the Specials. There were soldiers on the track. "Can you make it to the colonel's car, sir?"

It was just behind the armored car. He could see the driver at the wheel. "I can try," he said, and made it. They put him in behind the driver and Strong beside him.

"How are you, Miro?" the driver said.

"Thank you, Bowen," Miro said. "I enjoyed your message."

"It's the thought that counts, old boy." Bowen turned his clerical collar and his melancholy eyes to be seen. "The Reverend John Bowen. Your servant, Captain," he said.

Miro would have liked to smile, but his feet and hands were not smiling matters.

"I have been hoping to meet you for quite some time, Captain," Bowen said. "May I say that you nearly pulled it off? What I can't understand is why you gummed it up in the last days by trying to fool with an old sweat like Miro and why you complicated things by having your wife done . . ."

"I didn't!"

"You didn't what?"

"I had nothing to do with my wife's death."

"You didn't tell Dew-Boys to take her?"

"I didn't tell him to murder her! The man was crazy. He turned on me. He said he had me where he wanted me with all his records, and he'd wipe me out with the rest of them. I killed him up that seam—they should decorate me for that. Do I have to be tied like a goat?"

"Quite," Bowen said.

"My war service . . ." Strong began. "My years of public service . . . they'll count for something . . . ?"

"Five soldiers land-mined. Three young soldiers murdered off duty. Tomalty. Eleven men at Larne. Your wife. Banks, churches . . . Do I have to name them all? What do you think, Captain? And of course, you knew your D-Day was near—you intended to murder Dew-Boys yourself. He was the only one who could name you if we caught him. That's why he turned on you, isn't it?"

"No! It is not! He told me I was one of Them and he had no further use for me. *The dirty guttersnipe . . .*"

"May I say, Captain, that without your dentures you lack the charisma of a great leader of men?"

The captain looked surprised. "I thought I was among friends," he said.

Mac Donnell got in beside Bowen. "All clear," he said. Miro passed him the box file.

"Who is this man?" Strong demanded.

"Let's call him the arresting officer."

Strong said, "What are you?"

"I'm in disguise," Bowen said, grinning. "I wear a lot of disguises. I like dressing up. It's childish, but it's not as dangerous as your little tricks, Captain."

"Shit!"

"Show the captain my message, Miro."

Miro handed it over and Bowen put on the roof light. The page was a sheet from a Deer's Cry Press gospel songbook. It said,

> *What a friend we have in Jesus*
> *All our griefs and pains to bear;*
> *What a privilege to carry*
> *Everything to God in prayer.*

"I heard your prayers, Miro, old boy," Bowen said. "Rather, I heard the number of the car they found in that farmyard, and when they said FUZ 451 I said, 'Padre, shift your arse or the old red fox will be a dead duck . . .'"

"Thank you, Bowen. Get me home, old friend. I want to go home."

Strong made a sudden wailing noise and pressed his face against his bound hands. "I have no home," he said and cried. "I haven't a bloody thing to show for anything. God damn you."

Bowen turned to speak, changed his mind, switched off the roof light, and turned the key. Nobody spoke. Nobody looked at Strong. They went down the track over the moor.

Four

The voice of my beloved! Behold, he cometh leaping upon the mountains, skipping upon the hills.

The Twelfth: There was no rain. There were no clouds. A day without clouds was rare. They came in from the ocean, over the mountains, like the promise of fertility. The sky was blue today. The sun was warm. There were no drums, no guns, no banners, sashes or aprons; no bands. The land had a great stillness to it.

Colonel Bowen did the driving. Miro sat behind, his bandaged feet up, his bandaged hands folded across his stomach.

Bowen said enthusiastically, "We cleaned the lot, Miro. Did you hear the Prime Minister this morning? He was impressive. They believed him this time."

"Gentle country," Miro said.

"Most of the people are gentle," Bowen said. "And prejudiced. Silent prejudice is the seedbed of violent bigotry. How diyi like that one? I must use it in our next package of sermon notes for ministers."

"Have you ever seen so many shades of green, Bowen?" It was country for nature poets and landscape painters and tranquil farmers intoning *The Lord's my shepherd* on Sunday mornings.

"Put your foot down, Bowen. I promised Eva I'd come leaping upon the mountains . . ."

205

The army car in front hurried them through the roadblocks. The army car behind was an act of qualified faith.

Mr. Logan was in his place at the customs post. "Did yi get yir bulls, sur?"

"Half of them, Mr. Logan."

"Poor bloody cows," Mr. Logan said sadly. "They're like the women of Ireland. Half of them'll have to wait for it. Always waitin." He went into the back room.

Colonel Stephen Riada met them and took over the driving across the Border.

"We cleaned the lot, Miro," he said.

"For how long, Stephen?"

"For a while. Till they hear more voices."

They climbed up the valley road and onto the mountain. His pastures stretched below, and the Finn, and the cows and the fish. The Lake of Finna glittered in the day's light. Summerfield shone in the distance.

"Put your foot down, Stephen," Miro said and got his crutches ready. "She'll be waiting. She'll be cross with me in a back-handed sort of way."

Eva met them in the drive, running, with Michael in her arms. She put the boy down and kissed his father and said, "Look, Michael, Daddy's come home."

She walked beside him as he struggled awkwardly on the sticks, up the steps to the front door. He turned towards the lake, filled his lungs, and let out a great yell.

"*Yah-huuu!*" he yelled, and his voice rolled and echoed up the Lake.

At the bar in the village pub a man arrested his bending elbow and said, "Himself's back."

"Did you hear that, Michael?" Eva said. "The voice of my beloved! Behold, he cometh leaping upon the mountains, skipping upon the hills."

She laid hold of one of Miro's crutches as he groped with it at the doorstep.

"Can I help you take a little leap and a little skip at this one, love?" she said. "Or can you always look after yourself?"

About the Author

SHAUN HERRON was born in Ireland and educated in schools and universities in Ireland, Scotland and the United States. He lives now, mentally, spiritually and physically, in North America and Ireland and finds them fundamentally different and mutually irresistible. His wife is North American, and their children—by accident of birth and inclination—European or North American.